Praise for the novels of John Ramsey Miller

Inside Out

"John Ramsey Miller's *Inside Out* needs to come with a warning label. To start the story is to put the rest of your life on hold as you obsessively turn one page after the other. With a story this taut, and characters this vivid, there's no putting the book down before you've consumed the final word. A thrilling read."
—John Gilstrap

"*Inside Out* is a great read! . . . As many twists and turns as running serpentine through a field of fire and keeps us turning pages as fast as a Blackhawk helicopter's rotors! Set aside an uninterrupted day for this one; you won't want to put it down."
—Jeffery Deaver

"[Full of] complications and surprises . . . Miller gifts [his characters] with an illuminating idiosyncrasy. This gives us great hope for future books as well as delight in this one." —*Drood Review of Mystery*

"Twists and turns on every page keep you in phenomenal suspense until the last page. Superb novel." —*Rendezvous*

The Last Family

side by side

a Winter Massey suspense novel

John Ramsey Miller

A Dell Book

SIDE BY SIDE
A Dell Book / September 2005

Published by
Bantam Dell
A Division of Random House, Inc.
New York, New York

This is a work of fiction. Names, characters, places, and incidents
either are the product of the author's imagination or are used
fictitiously. Any resemblance to actual persons, living or dead,
events, or locales is entirely coincidental.

ISBN 0-553-58343-3

Printed in the United States of America
Published simultaneously in Canada

www.bantamdell.com

OPM 10 9 8 7 6 5 4 3 2 1

For Susan

Acknowledgments

This book is also dedicated to all of the brave men and women of the United States Armed Forces who, working as a unit, make freedom for us all a reality.

Thanks to the usual suspects; my friends and family inclusive.

My editor, Kate Miciak; my agent, Anne Hawkins; and my readers and friends (some of whom are in picture form on my website).

Just before I started this book, my wife Susan was diagnosed with breast cancer. A year after the initial diagnosis, she had undergone two surgeries, twenty-four weeks of chemotherapy and intensive radiation therapy, as well as reconstruction surgery. She never doubted she would get to the other side of it, thanks to the professionals we drew. I wasn't much help, though I offered what moral support I could. On chemo days I would set up my laptop on a rolling tray and hack at the weeds while Susie absorbed whatever cocktail they had prepared. Thanks to the efforts of a lot of people, Susan is now cancer-free.

So I want to express my heartfelt thanks to all of the doctors and the staff at Northeast Medical Center's George A. Batte Cancer Center in Concord, N.C., who saved my dear Susan. Thank you, surgeon Richard Ozment, oncologist Thomas A. Steffens, reconstructive surgeon David Klein, and the ever-smiling oncology study nurse Rebecca Lyon Witkowski, who acted as our interpreter throughout.

Also thanks to the dear Dr. Wanda Crowley, our glorious cheerleader GP.

Also to Jill and all of the wonderful friends Susan works with at Wachovia, who made sure she didn't stay at work when she felt bad, and to our friends and neighbors who sewed by hand (and secret) a friendship quilt for Susan.

1

Fast-moving clouds were mirrored in the puddles of standing water left by a late afternoon rainstorm. Halogen fixtures set on tall poles spaced fifty feet apart painted the landscape an unholy orange-blue.

A solitary figure dressed entirely in black slipped through a vertical slit in the tall hurricane fencing topped with loops of concertina wire. The fence surrounded a forty-acre lot beside a train yard where several hundred steel containers had been stacked and ordered with Mondrian-like precision. Here and there the painted steel skins of some of the boxes showed brown fingers of rust from years of exposure to the weather.

The man dressed in black, a thirty-year-old whose name was Patrick Taylor, slipped a hand-drawn diagram from inside his jacket and checked the inventory numbers on the closest container, then moved swiftly to the next one. Hours earlier, he had copied the coordinates from a scrap of paper he'd found secreted in Colonel Bryce's safe. Opening his cell phone, he dialed a number he called only when he was alone and in a secure location. As he waited for the number to be answered he inspected the padlock using a small Mag-Lite. The lock was substantial; it would take some coaxing to defeat.

When his handler didn't answer, Taylor assumed he must be on another call, and allowed himself to be routed to a voice mailbox. At the request to leave a message, he said, "This is Dog. I'm hooking up the thumper now. Just going to take a peek to make sure it's all in this box, then I'm leaving it up to you guys." He closed the phone and pocketed it.

He attached the GPS tracker to the steel foundation by means of a magnet. The tracker would allow the special task force to follow the shipment to its destination. Maybe that team would grab the receiving parties when they took possession, or perhaps they'd follow the cargo to the end users—terrorists all over the world and home-grown militias with the resources to buy the latest devices of death and destruction. Taylor's sole responsibility was to stay close to the colonel, to collect the names of people the man met with, then report to his handler. Locating the first shipment of high-tech weaponry was a godsend—icing on the cake.

Taylor had been undercover for eight long years, most of those spent building a faultless background and credentials for an operation like this. Eight years of being someone he wasn't just so he could be of use to his government. He had spent the last three of those eight years getting close to one man and gaining his trust. Three years to find out Colonel Hunter Bryce, a decorated hero, could actually betray his country for money.

Flashlight between his teeth so he could see, Taylor used his lock picks to open the padlock. As soon as he opened the door, he saw that the container was empty. Well, empty except for a sheet of plastic, which had been laid out like carpeting over the rough plywood floor.

The sound of breathing alerted Taylor to the fact that

someone was standing just off his left shoulder, at his seven o'clock.

"Lieutenant Taylor?" a familiar voice asked. "What are you doing here?"

Ice filled Taylor's stomach. He turned, already deciding what his next words were going to be. He had not expected to run into Colonel Bryce, but nobody could think faster on his feet than Patrick Taylor. The colonel's face was lit with ambient light from the halogen fixtures, so Taylor could see the quizzical smile the colonel was wearing. Taylor put on a confident smile and started. "Colonel Bryce, I know you're—"

The razor-sharp blade of the survival knife Colonel Bryce had carried during his years in the field severed Taylor's windpipe, his jugular vein and carotid artery. Taylor crumpled, landing hard on the floor of the empty container, the thud of his body echoing within the space.

Colonel Hunter Bryce used his gloved left hand to wipe the fine droplets of blood from his face. He cleaned his blade on Taylor's pant leg before he replaced the weapon in its nylon scabbard.

The colonel retrieved the GPS tracker that Taylor had placed and put it in his victim's open mouth. Then he grabbed Taylor's collar and dragged him deeper into the steel container.

Before Bryce left, he stopped and spit on Taylor's face. Every man the colonel killed won his mark of disdain. Then he walked off into the shadows, whistling softly.

Two hours later, the ATF and FBI agents followed the GPS signal to the locked container. They noticed the fresh blood leaking from the closed door, pooling on the ground, so they opened it.

The night watchman told the agents he'd heard someone whistling in the darkness out beyond the fence.

"I think it was what the seven dwarfs in *Snow White* sang," he told them. "'Whistle While You Work.'"

2 | Charlotte, North Carolina
Eleven months later

Twelve across.
  Five-letter word for good-bye.
  ADIEU

Lucy Dockery put the paper and pencil down on the bedside table. She liked solving crossword puzzles, but filling in words from clues was too easy. She loved better to build them from scratch, putting her thoughts and feelings into short clues. After she constructed a puzzle, she would file it away in her cabinet, unsolved. The inch-deep stack of pages was a journal of Lucy's life for the past year.

From her earliest memories, her parents always seemed to be working the crossword puzzles in *The New York Times,* other newspapers and magazines. Much to their delight, Lucy had begun crafting her own puzzles at an early age to entertain them. Their praise helped her build her self-confidence to bridge a painful shyness.

Later she made crosswords for Walter. She designed them so that he had to first solve the puzzle and then play with the order of the words until they made up a coherent message. She remembered the one that worked out to say, *Congratulations sir after many fun years of playing around with that wand comma a baby is growing inside Lucy*. Eight down was _____ *in the sky with diamonds*. Although Walter loved a challenge, Lucy felt no need to make them complicated or too difficult.

She still wrote puzzle-grams to Walter, but he was no longer able to solve them.

As a child, she'd been told that any time you say good-bye to somebody it could be the last good-bye. She had never really believed that something that happened in a fraction of a second could change everything in her life forever. You automatically tell a loved one to "be careful" until it becomes as meaningless as "see you later." Walter would often reply with, "But dear, I was looking forward to being reckless."

Lucy was bone-weary. Looking back, it seemed to her that her energy and enthusiasm for life had been boundless before the accident. And while Walter was beside her, she had felt invincible and filled to the brim with anticipation of a future—an ideal family nestled in a perfect world.

She knew other mothers of small children complained of tiredness due to washing, cooking, cleaning, and all the million things you had to do daily, but the weakness Lucy felt was different. Lucy didn't have to cook, or clean, or even watch her own child if she didn't feel like it. And when did she feel like it? How many times had she—while propped up in her bed, or lying on the couch—watched like a member of an audience while her son interacted with one of his sitters, her father, or the maid?

Lucy and her father shared the services of a woman who cleaned their houses three times a week. She had a list of competent babysitters to choose from. She subscribed to a gourmet service and once a week a chef prepared all of Lucy's and her father's main meals and put them into the refrigerator or the freezer, labeled.

Lucy had a very nice house, five thousand square feet of modern appliances and every convenience. She had a BMW X5 and a Lexus sedan in the garage. There was more than enough room in the place for her and Elijah, and everything was paid for, thanks to Walter's obsessive desire to take care of his family. Her husband had carried a disability policy as well as one that paid all of his debts upon his death. He had a third insurance policy for two million dollars that carried an accidental-death clause that doubled that amount. Thanks to Walter, Lucy had plenty of everything except what she needed most—Walter.

She'd been an odd-looking youngster, with big aqua eyes, a high forehead, and a narrow chin. The boys in the first grade called her "alien." As she grew older that oddness evolved into "exotic." Even when teenage boys suddenly found her attractive, she had still felt like an odd duck. She had dated several boys in high school, gone steady twice, but she had never fallen in love but once.

She knew that there was only one Walter Dockery, and anyone coming into her life after him would be less.

For three months after the accident, Lucy had lain in bed in the darkened bedroom she had once shared with Walter, crying and taking pills to make her sleep. For the year since, Lucy's depression had taken the form of apathy, chronic fatigue, and difficulty making decisions. Her doctor said her depression would run its course as her grief lessened. He even had a list of the steps she could expect to pass through, like it was a disease with a progression of symptoms and even medicines to make it bearable.

Modern people took a pill to combat grief. Indians suffering the same pain took off a finger. Lucy didn't take mood-altering pills because Elijah was her most effective medication.

Since he had been an infant when Walter died, Elijah wouldn't remember anything about his father except what he was told.

At seventeen months her baby was walking and talking a blue streak. He used recognizable words, but mostly they came out embedded in a string of nonsense, which Lucy knew was his attempt to mimic conversation.

Elijah was a beautiful child, curious, affable, even-tempered, and, it seemed to Lucy, better coordinated than most of the children his age. He loved being read to, which Lucy did when she felt up to it. He watched more TV than he should—something Lucy had always sworn that her children would never do. But it was just easier to let the TV babysit. Some days, after Walter died, even little Elijah seemed too heavy a weight for her to lift.

Lucy rubbed her eyes and considered watching a late-night talk show.

Night, after Eli was asleep, was when she missed Walter the most. Sleeping alone was a problem because she had grown accustomed to having his warm, familiar body beside her. She missed having him to hold on to as the darkness closed in—to press her back against, or to spoon with, or to nudge when his snoring awakened her. She missed playing with him before they went to sleep and waking up to his fingertips tracing the line of her leg, stomach, and her breasts. Familiar lips nibbling on her shoulder, kissing her neck, her nose . . .

Lucy wasn't suicidal, but she fantasized often about waking up in paradise wrapped in Walter's embrace. Together for eternity . . . But that would mean that Elijah would be an orphan, a young man raised by his grandfather. Sometimes Lucy thought that might be best for him.

If a sitter was spending the night, Lucy could take a tablet to put her to sleep. Otherwise she lay in bed all night thinking, berating herself, longing for something she'd never have again. What if she took a pill to sleep and Elijah woke up and she didn't hear him cry out for her?

Life was fragile.

People could die.

It happened all the time.

Throwing back the covers, Lucy left her bed to look in on her son, to reassure herself that he was breathing. Since Walter's passing, she'd had a terror that she might go into the boy's room to find his little body wrapped in cold blue death.

The carpeting silenced Lucy's approach as she opened his door wider and slipped inside. At the side of the crib she reached down and rested the backs of her fingers on his forehead. The night-light allowed her to study his chubby pink cheeks, his perfect lips, and the chin with the beginnings of Walter's cleft. His little fingers were curled tightly into his palms. His chest rose and sank slowly with the precision of a Swiss watch. Eli's fat little feet would grow narrower as they lengthened. His squat frame would stretch to six feet or better. His curly locks would straighten. Imagining him as an adult was easy since she was familiar with the genetic models he was constructed from.

She leaned over and kissed him gently, whereupon he shifted his legs and opened and closed his hands. She was tempted to pick him up and carry him to her bed, but she resisted, remembering Walter's admonition that such an action was to be avoided for the child's sake. It had something to do with building a healthy self-image, a solid foundation for later independence. Walter had been raised in a large family of fierce competitors. Her husband had been the youngest of seven overachievers. Walter was the best of the brood, and he'd achieved without seeming to try very hard, or allowing a drive to succeed to consume him in the way it had his siblings and parents.

Lucy went to her bathroom to wash her face and brush her teeth. When she turned off the water, she heard the sound of a floorboard or a ceiling beam creaking. The house, built in 1880, made plenty of odd noises as it settled, or from changes in the weather. She heard

Elijah fussing, and wondered if she had wakened him after all. She would have to stand beside the crib and rub his back to get him back to sleep.

She left the bathroom and went through her bedroom into the hallway. The night-light seemed to have burned out again. She walked into Elijah's bedroom and looked down into the crib. To her shock, his crumpled blanket was there, but he wasn't. She heard him say "Momou" behind her and was wondering how he had climbed out of his bed, when she turned to see that her son was in the arms of a giant of a man who stood there in the doorway.

Lucy cried out in horror.

The huge man rushed from the room and Lucy raced after him.

"No!" she yelled out. "Stop! Give him back!"

She ran through the doorway. The man carrying her son was thundering down the stairs.

As Lucy passed the guest room there was a bang of the door hitting the wall as it was flung open, and a powerful arm grabbed her around the chest and constricted her lungs. She was aware of Elijah screaming downstairs and the fetid breath of her captor on her neck. She screamed, clawed, and writhed until a powerful hand holding a cold cloth covered her mouth and nose.

Chloroform!

Within seconds, Lucy Dockery fell into a silent darkness.

3

Across the expanse of bright green meadow, two men in a Ford 250 pickup watched three riders on horseback. The passenger, Hank Trammel, took off his Lyndon Johnson–style Stetson, set it on his lap, and ran his hand over the stubble that covered his head like the bristles of a hog's-hair brush. Taking a handkerchief from his jacket pocket, he removed his wire-rimmed glasses and, after fogging the round lenses with his breath, cleaned them. Once he put the glasses back on, he twisted the ends of his gray handlebar mustache.

The Rhodesian Ridgeback in the center of the rear bench stared out through the windshield, intently watching the riders. Seated beside the dog, an infant dressed in a one-piece pajama suit waved her chubby little arms in the air.

"Red Man's a nice piece of horseflesh," Hank Trammel observed. "Faith Ann's done a hell of a job with him. She's a Porter all right."

Winter Massey, the driver, lifted a pair of Steiner field glasses and focused them to better see the horse and rider in the trio's center, noting the smile on the blond boy's face. His son, Rush, had never looked happier. Shifting the glasses slightly, Winter watched his wife, Sean, who rode alongside her fourteen-year-old stepson. The rider on Rush Massey's left side was Hank's fourteen-year-old niece, Faith Ann Porter. All three were smiling. Faith Ann's red-blond hair was growing back from the trim she had given herself a year earlier to make herself look like a boy—an intelligent, lifesaving measure.

"Now that's a sight I'd never get tired of," Hank said.

"Agreed. Getting hungry yet?" Winter asked.

"Anytime you see me, I'm ready to eat," Hank replied.

"Well, let's get this party started." Winter flipped the truck's headlights on and off several times and stuck his arm out of the window to signal.

Sean waved to acknowledge that she saw him, pointing at the grove of twelve pecan trees growing on a gentle rise ahead.

Winter slipped the truck into gear and aimed it toward the grove, leaving parallel depressions in the pasture grass.

Sean had purchased the three-hundred-acre parcel as a long-term investment, but one that she knew they would all enjoy. There was no question that the land would increase in value, because the area, just twenty miles from Charlotte, had been growing for years, and large tracts of land like this one were increasingly rare and expensive.

The farmland was surrounded by a whitewashed rail fence on the front and an electric fence on the other three sides. The one-hundred-year-old main house, where Winter, Sean, Rush, and their new daughter spent weekends, contained two thousand square feet of hardwood floors, tall ceilings, and pine board paneling. They could have lived there full-time, but Winter couldn't bring himself to vacate the house he and his first wife had lovingly renovated before she was killed in the flying accident that had blinded their son. Eleanor had crashed in the craft she had learned in as a child, on a clear day when she was giving her son Rush lessons in touch-and-goes. A descending Beechcraft Baron had swatted her Cessna from the sky.

Rush didn't remember the accident, but there wasn't a day that passed, no matter how wonderful and full it was, that Winter didn't see Eleanor still and motionless in a hospital bed in the hours before they pulled the plug on the battered and broken shell of his perfect wife. He mourned her daily.

For the past six months, Hank Trammel and his niece Faith Ann had lived in the farm manager's house on the property. Hank, newly widowed, had sold his home outside Charlotte and, with his newly orphaned niece and his horses, moved to the Massey farm. Hank had been Winter's superior officer when they had been U.S. marshals, but the two men were as close as a father and son, and Faith Ann Porter had quickly become family to Winter and Sean. So far, the livestock included six horses, an unknown number of feral cats, and one Seeing-Eye dog, the Rhodesian Ridgeback that Rush had named Nemo.

After the truck came to a stop, Winter turned and looked back at the infant seat. Olivia Moment, Sean's and his three-month-old daughter, was sound asleep.

Winter let the dog out, unclipped the baby seat, and set it on the warm hood. That done, he grabbed Hank's crutches from the truck's bed and handed them to him.

When the three riders entered the grove, Nemo barked ecstatically.

"Sit and stay, Nemo," Winter commanded.

Nemo whined impatiently, eager to join his young master, but because he was trained to obey, he remained seated on the ground beside Winter.

Charger was Rush's eight-year-old mare. They had bought the animal after looking at a dozen horses in three states. A blind child who is going to ride a horse needs a special one. Ideally, they had wanted an animal that would sense it was serving as his rider's eyes and at least be intelligent about its own safety. They had to find a horse that had a gentle disposition and that responded to its rider's commands, as well as having a noncompetitive nature that would allow it to ride alongside or behind other horses without feeling insulted. Charger met their criteria and now, although Rush never rode without companions, he was always in the saddle alone.

Winter's instincts were to be overprotective, to build a wall around his impaired son to keep him safe. Sean and Faith Ann refused to allow that, and as a result his son was doing things—like riding a horse and climbing trees with Faith Ann—that Winter would otherwise never have permitted.

Faith Ann reached over and took hold of Charger's bridle, while Sean slipped from her horse, a chestnut gelding named Rattler, tied his reins to a tree limb, secured Charger's reins to a fallen limb, and helped her stepson down from the saddle. After Rush was aground, Faith Ann slipped off Red Man and hitched him to another branch.

As the riders walked away from them, the horses lowered their heads to the lush grass.

"Where's my little angel?" Sean demanded as she came over to the truck. "Hello, Miss Olivia," she crooned, as her daughter opened her eyes and smiled up from the infant seat. "I hope these rough old men didn't teach my sweet-cheeks any naughty words."

"You know better than that," Winter said.

"Won't require lessons," Hank added. "If she never hears a single one uttered, Olivia will still be able to cuss a purple streak. That's because Winter's from Mississippi . . ." He winked. "So cussin's in her DNA."

Sean laughed, unhooked the belts, and lifted the child into her arms.

"Does Olivia need changing?" she asked. "Is that why you flagged me down?"

"I smell fried chicken," Rush said. He reached down and rubbed Nemo's head, which was pressing against his leg.

"Me too," Faith Ann said.

Winter said, "I thought we'd eat a picnic lunch under the trees." He reached into the truck's bed and lifted out a basket and a pair of blankets. "Time to eat."

"A picnic!" Faith Ann exclaimed. "I'm practically starving to death."

"I don't know why you don't outweigh your horse," Hank teased the girl. "You eat twice as much as Red Man does. Maybe I better get you checked for tapeworms."

"She might have one," Rush said, laughing.

"I don't think so," Faith Ann said, frowning. "Tapeworms

get transmitted by fleas who eat the eggs, and you have to ingest a flea to get them."

"You'd get them if cooties ate flea eggs," Rush shot back, giggling.

Faith Ann leaned over and mussed Rush's blond hair, which erased the smile from his face. He used his fingers as a comb to repair the damage.

Winter and Faith Ann unfolded two blankets on the grass so they overlapped and formed a large rectangle. He opened the basket and took out a bucket of chicken.

"Winter, you went to so much trouble," Sean joked. "Hours in the kitchen slaving over a stove."

"If you're pleased, the intense manual labor was worth it." He dropped ice from a small cooler into two plastic cups, opened a large cola, and poured them full. "For Faith Ann and Rush—the brown stuff." Using the corkscrew on his Swiss Army knife, he uncorked a bottle of chardonnay and poured some in three plastic glasses.

"And you even packed the good china." Hank handed around paper plates from the basket. Winter saw his friend wince in pain from the movement, but said nothing.

Sean lifted a shawl, placed it over both her shoulder and the baby, then opened her blouse and positioned the baby to suckle. Winter smiled when her eyes met his.

"Girl's gotta eat," Sean said.

"That poor child is going to be a teenager and every time she gets hungry she'll start hunting for something to cover her head with and not have the slightest idea why," Hank said.

Sean laughed. "I seriously doubt that, Hank."

"That's silly, Uncle Hank," Faith Ann said.

"They did a hundred-thousand-dollar study all over the world. Harvard sociologists found out that seventy-nine percent of women who were breast-fed as babies while under a blanket become nuns."

"What?" Faith Ann said.

"It's so they can wear those head rigs—veils."

Faith Ann laughed louder than anybody else at her uncle's stupid jokes.

"Winter, we could go to Charlotte tonight," Sean suggested. "There's a play you wanted to see."

"What play?" Winter said.

"The one about the poets."

"Three acts of four actors playing e. e. cummings, Allen Ginsberg, Ezra Pound, and Robert Frost playing poker and discussing the modern world? Sean, I was being sarcastic when I said I wanted to see it," Winter said, frowning.

"I was pulling your chain," she replied, mimicking his scowl. "You are far too young to be such a curmudgeon."

"Dad's a cur-munchkin," Rush crowed. "That's like a small mongrel."

"A car monkey," Faith Ann added. "A vehicular simian."

"There's still a lot of work for Winter to do on the barn before cold weather sets in," Hank said. "This warm spell won't hold long."

"Work for *Winter* to do? You can help me, Hank," Winter told him.

"I reckon if sitting in a rocker, sipping liquor, and

pointing out the shortcomings in your carpentry work product is any help, I'll be a world-class assistant."

"Well, I can help. I know how to use a saw and a hammer," Faith Ann told Winter. Winter and Faith Ann Porter shared a special bond. Winter had saved her life, had been there when it counted, and she would never forget it.

"I'll hammer," Rush volunteered. "You can hold the nails for me."

"I got a *big* picture of that!" Laughing, Faith Ann reached over to muss Rush's hair again, but he caught her wrist before she had done any real harm.

The sight of a silver sedan barreling up the driveway ended their banter. The vehicle continued to the farmhouse, parked, and a woman wearing a business suit stepped out and strode rapidly to the porch. She carried a leather shoulder bag.

"Salesman?" Hank wondered out loud.

"Salesperson," Faith Ann corrected.

"Sign at the front gate says No Soliciting," Hank said.

"Maybe she's selling eyeglasses," Faith Ann said.

Winter rose and got his field glasses from the truck. "It's Alexa."

"Who is Alexa?" Faith Ann asked.

"She's an old friend of Winter's," Sean told her.

"Alexa's cool. She always sends me a check for twenty bucks on my birthday and something neat for Christmas. Not just some dumb sweater either. She and my daddy have been friends forever, since they were in high school," Rush said.

"Did you know she was in town?" Sean asked Winter.

"No," he said.

"Go down and get her," Sean told him.

"Whistle at her, Daddy," Rush said.

"Everybody cover your ears," Faith Ann said.

Winter put his fingers to the corners of his mouth and emitted an ear-piercing whistle. All three horses stopped eating and, ears erect, looked over at Winter.

The woman in the business suit turned at the sound and waved.

"So, I'm finally going to meet Special Agent Alexa Keen," Sean said. "And here I sit dressed like a man who smells like a horse."

Alexa started toward them. Winter didn't get in the truck to go get her; he just stood with his hands on his hips with a look of worry on his face, watching his dear friend stride purposefully up the long green slope.

4

"Hello, Massey!" Alexa Keen called as she approached him.

He opened his arms to her and they hugged warmly. The crown of her head came to Winter's chin.

Sean was surprised. Based on Winter's stories about Alexa, Sean had imagined she would be a tall tomboy—not nearly as attractive as this woman was. Winter had told her that Alexa's anonymous father was white, her mother black. He hadn't mentioned that her honey-colored hair was soft and straight, her eyes as green as emeralds.

Sean and Rush were standing, smiling. Faith Ann remained on one knee, unsure. Sean had stopped feeding Olivia and had buttoned her blouse.

"Don't I get a hug?" Rush said, opening his arms.

"Who are you?" Alexa asked. "Who is this tall, handsome young man who sort of resembles a beautiful woman name of Eleanor Massey?"

Sean swallowed and tried to hold her smile in place.

"Who do you think I am?" Rush demanded.

"'Fore God, as I live and breathe! This Greek god can't be little ole Rush Massey!"

"You think I'm bigger?"

"Enormongus. And stunningly handsome."

Alexa hugged Rush, then leaned back and held his face between her hands and kissed his forehead. "You're going to break a bushel of hearts, you are. If I was twenty years younger..."

Rush's face turned red. "Thanks. I guess."

"Hello, Sean," Alexa said, turning to her and opening her arms. The two women hugged gently and briefly. "And, oh my, this must be Olivia." Alexa knelt beside the infant. "Where did that name come from?"

"My mother was named Olivia," Sean told her.

"I'm sorry we haven't met before now," Alexa murmured, eyes on the baby. "The wedding pictures Lydia e-mailed me didn't do you justice. I'm so sorry I missed your wedding."

"You were probably working on a kidnapping," Rush said.

"Something like that," Alexa said. "Actually, I was in Peru looking for a missing executive."

"Did you find him?"

"Her. Yes we did." Alexa turned and smiled. "Hi ya, Hank."

"Excuse me for not standing," he told her. "I'll take a hug if you've got another one."

Alexa hugged him. "I was so sorry to hear about Millie. She was a wonderful woman."

"She was that," Hank agreed. "Want you to meet my niece, Faith Ann."

"Goodness, I thought Rush was dating fashion models."

"Heck no," Rush said. "Faith Ann's going to be a lawyer. She's way too smart to be a model."

"Pleased to meet you," Alexa said, shaking Faith Ann's hand. "I've heard a lot about you, Faith Ann. But I didn't know how pretty you were."

"I hope you haven't eaten. There's plenty of chicken," Sean said.

Sean noticed that Alexa's only jewelry was an inexpensive wristwatch. The sensible gray wool suit—jacket and slacks—was good quality, but had probably come off the rack in a chain department store. The loafers had thick rubber soles for comfort and sure-footedness. The handbag was machine-stitched with nylon thread. The smooth brown leather purse was large enough to carry all of a woman's necessary equipment like makeup, cell phone, address book, tissues, and a wallet. There was also room for a handgun, extra magazines, a badge case, and a pair of handcuffs. Everything Alexa had on was practical and functional. She dressed like an FBI agent.

"Thank you, Sean. I'm ravenous. I went to your house in town and your next-door neighbor told me how to get here. Beautiful land. How's Lydia?"

"Mama loves Florida," Winter answered. "She's dating a retired physician. Nice fellow . . . she says."

"She's living in sin," Rush snickered. "With an old doctor."

Winter watched how effortlessly Alexa folded herself into the picnic. She'd always been like that—instantly at home wherever she found herself, and she had a way of putting people at ease, making them like her. It was why she was so good at her job. Sean seemed to like her, but he was getting odd vibes from Alexa. Women had their own way of seeing things. Winter had talked to Sean about Alexa—but hadn't really gone into their relationship in any depth. He hadn't seen the point. It had been a long time ago.

Winter had known Alexa for twenty years. They had met under an odd set of circumstances and had almost instantly become friends. Their interracial friendship had raised a few eyebrows in the Mississippi Delta, and a lot of people assumed their friendship was more than platonic, but they were wrong.

After high school, Winter went to college in Mississippi and Alexa had selected Berkeley. They had remained in touch by mail and telephone, but the young woman who had been his closest companion for the last two years of high school had become merely a dear friend fondly remembered.

In the days before the avenues of intelligence had been ruthlessly widened by the air attacks on September 11, 2001, Alexa had sometimes given Winter an unofficial hand with a case. In return, she had used him as a sounding board when she didn't trust the advice of her contemporaries.

The FBI and the United States Marshals Service maintained an outwardly cordial association out of procedural necessity. However, since every federal agency's territory is about power as defined by budgets and manpower, their turfs had to be guarded by the agents on both sides, which made them natural competitors. It was no secret that the Bureau, especially under Hoover, had wanted to absorb the duties of the USMS. The FBI would have been happiest if it owned the good-guy monopoly.

In the two years since Winter had last seen her, Alexa had grown thinner and the lines in her face had deepened. For the first time since he'd met her, there were dark circles under her eyes.

Alexa took a seat between Rush and Winter on the blanket.

"What brings you to Charlotte, Alexa?" Hank asked.

"Business," she said.

"What kind of business?" Faith Ann asked.

Alexa smiled sadly. "The big bad kind," she said.

5

Lying perfectly still, Lucy Dockery fought off the dizzying effects of the knockout drug she'd been given several times since she had been abducted. She shivered at the thought of the horrid man who had administered it. He drugged her the last time only after assaulting her skin with hands so rough that they had snagged the surface of her gown and abraded her skin. He had cupped her breasts, squeezing her nipples, had run his hands over her stomach and up and down her legs. His labored breathing made him sound like an asthmatic. When he decided he was finished with his exploration, he had put the chemical-soaked cloth to her face. She'd held her breath as long as she could, then drifted off.

When conscious, Lucy listened for the sounds Elijah made. Lying in the dark, she had heard at least three different adult male voices and one that sounded female. The woman sounded like a braying mule when she laughed. Lucy took the fact that there was a woman involved as a hopeful sign.

After a long time, Lucy was able to sit up in bed—a lumpy foam mattress covered by an incredibly gritty sheet. She wore only the nightgown and panties she'd been wearing when he took her from the house. In front of the bed a thin line illuminated the base of a narrow door, but did nothing to light the room's interior. She wasn't tied up or otherwise secured.

Whatever these cretins wanted of her, no matter how painful or debasing, she'd have no choice but to go along.

She couldn't imagine why they had abducted her and Elijah. Were they burglars drawn to her house in its wealthy neighborhood? Had they impulsively decided during a robbery to take her and Eli? Or did they know she had money they would force her to withdraw, or that her father had a substantial trust? In both cases, the assets were not liquid. Lucy doubted she had the sort of sex appeal that warranted being kidnapped for someone's prurient pleasure. Even if she was attractive to them, why take Elijah? She was terrified that maybe they intended to sell him on the black market to some desperate couple. Maybe the woman in the next room had wanted a baby and Eli somehow caught her eye. Maybe the men had agreed to grab the baby if they could have a sex slave in the bargain. Her imagination was running wild.

Her deceased husband had prosecuted all sorts of criminals, and her father had sentenced hundreds of people to federal prisons. Some of those people were dangerous and powerful. Maybe Walter or her father had convicted one of their abductors, or had sentenced a relative. If revenge was behind this, their chances of surviving were not good. So far, their abductors hadn't physically harmed her son or her. All Lucy could do was pray and wait and see what they had in mind. The possibilities racing through her brain tormented her.

Hearing Elijah jabbering beyond the door was both

sweet and painful. He didn't sound afraid or uncomfortable, but that didn't mean he was safe.

The woman had been talking to Elijah using the sort of adult baby talk that someone might use to communicate with a spoiled Pomeranian held in the crook of her arm as a fashion accessory.

"Hello?" Lucy called out. "Hello?"

The approaching footsteps made the floor tremble. When the narrow door slid open, an enormous woman, illuminated from behind, filled the doorway. Her teased hair radiated out from her melon-shaped head like pulled fiberglass. Her shoulders were broad and it looked like her neck was several inches too short. In fact, she looked more like a man than a woman.

"What you want?" the woman demanded. Her deeply Southern accent was accentuated by the distinctive clicking of ceramic dentures.

"I was wondering . . . if Elijah was all right?"

"Why the hell wouldn't he be? Do I look to you like somebody who would hurt a little baby?"

"No, I suppose not." *I pray not.*

The woman was silent for five seconds before saying, "Don't you dare take a uppity tone with me."

"Sorry. I didn't mean to. It's just that . . . I'd like to see him."

"I'd like a lot of things myself. But you best get in your head right from the get-go that I'm not your maid. No sir-ee, missy."

"Of course not," Lucy soothed hastily. "Can you tell me where we are?"

"Well, I'm in a single-wide. I expect you and your kid

are too, unless I'm dreaming you both up. And I don't see how it matters, anyhow, unless you've got some place you need to go like a country club tea party. If that's the case, I'll go call you a limousine."

"Can we leave?"

"Y'all *could* if I wasn't told to keep you where you are. You think I wouldn't be a hell of a lot happier somewhere else, you're dumber than you look."

"I'm sorry. It's just that—"

"Let's you and me not blab any more than we have to, because this isn't no social occasion. You just stay your skinny ass in here and be quiet as you can and don't yell at me to come back like I was your maid. You need to pee, or whatever, there's a bucket there by the bed. I'll bring you food and water when I get around to it. In the meantime, keep your yippy-yap shut or I'll dope you up like Buck did. We straight?"

"I'm sorry," Lucy said, contritely. When the woman turned, Lucy caught sight of Eli in a playpen just beyond the open kitchen. He looked to be playing with some toys. This creature wasn't going to tell her why she and Eli were there.

"You don't spank him, do you?" the big woman demanded.

"Sorry?" Lucy said. Despite the dentures, Lucy realized, the woman was probably close to her own age.

"Your diaper slayer, little Lord Fart-not. Elijah."

"No, we don't believe in corporal punishment."

"You people," the woman said sourly. "It's no wonder the whole world's gone to hell. I had a cousin named Elijah."

"It's a nice name," Lucy said, hoping to endear her son to the woman so she would do him no harm.

"Cousin Elijah was a bratty little creep. His daddy ran him over while he was backing out their driveway. We was all playing in their yard. His head looked like a dang pizza. We all—"

"Please, could I—?"

The woman flew into the room and, before Lucy could raise her arm to shield her face, the woman slapped her so hard her ears rang and she fell back onto the mattress.

"Could you what!? Could you what!?" the woman snarled. "I was talking about something important! But only what you say is important!"

Lucy saw that her captor's T-shirt read, HELL IS HOT FOREVER.

The woman stormed out and slammed the door shut with a resounding bang, plunging the room back into a musty darkness.

Lucy's face went from being numbed by the blow to stinging dully as she lay there stunned by the sudden burst of unprovoked violence. The woman was obviously mentally unstable and probably dangerous. She mustn't do anything else to provoke her. There was no telling what she and the others were capable of doing if they got mad.

Surely her father had called the police.

The police would surely come.

They just had to come.

Lucy wished Walter was there.

Walter would know what to do.

All she could do was wait and see.

Lucy squeezed her eyes shut and lay still. She couldn't afford to make these people angry.

6

After the picnic ended, the group made their way back down to the house. Faith Ann and Rush led the horses to the barn to put the animals away.

While Sean put Olivia down for her nap, Winter and Alexa took cups of the coffee and went into the small den they called the office because there was a desk in it when they bought the place.

"Fallen Angel Farm is an interesting name," Alexa said, raising a brow. "Some sort of a statement?"

Winter shook his head. "There's an old graveyard that dates from 1806 just on the other side of that hill where we had lunch. Family members and workers who died here were buried there—slaves in a nearby plot. Most of the headstones are still there. There was a hand-carved stone angel there. During the Civil War the wrought-iron fence around it was melted down for ammo. Late in the war a company of Union cavalry used the angel for target practice. After they got bored with chipping hunks off her, they knocked her over on her back. She's still lying where she fell, looking up at the sky."

"Sometimes I wish all I had to do was to be lying out in the grass, looking up and watching the clouds drift by," Alexa said. "I guess I was always too ambitious to relax. Or remember how to, if I ever knew." She sipped coffee. "I was thinking the other day about prom night."

Winter nodded. He remembered the night as clearly as if it had been weeks before instead of almost two decades back. How many times had he relived it?

"Why didn't you call to let me know you were coming?" he asked Alexa.

"You start hunting again?" she asked. She was frowning up at a deer head mounted on the wall.

"While back. Rush, Lydia, and I like venison and Lydia said I needed to get off and clear my mind. I have Daddy's old rifle and I enjoy the woods, the company of friends. Mama bought a cookbook with like nine hundred venison recipes in it. We were working our way through it one season at a time. Sean isn't as fond of venison as the rest of us are. I missed the last two years and looks like I won't make it this year. My friends may stop asking me to come if I don't go soon."

"You're good about remembering your friends. I'm sort of counting on that being the case with you and me."

"You need something, Lex, just ask."

"I figured maybe you left the service because you wanted to get away from the . . . excitement." She smiled crookedly.

"I was a little tired of seeing the darker side of people. Last year Faith Ann's mother was murdered for no more reason than being in the wrong place at the wrong time.

When Millie was killed, Faith Ann saw the car run her and Hank over. And I was forced to kill someone."

"I know the killing weighs heavily on your soul, Winter. Eleanor used to tell me about what the Tampa thing did to you."

He shrugged. "You can get a bloody mouth before you know it."

"Bloody mouth?"

"A perfectly good farm dog kills a chicken and he gets a taste for the blood. There's nothing to do about him because it's something that becomes part of his nature." Winter tried to smile, but failed. "The weight a kill puts on your soul is a good thing because it means you're human. What made the difference—why I really retired—was that last time I killed I didn't mind it—I didn't even feel remorse. It's not that I liked it, but I didn't feel any more than if that person had been a deer."

He smiled, because just saying it had lifted a burden. He smiled, too, because after twenty years of not doing so, he was telling Alexa things he couldn't bring himself to tell Sean or Hank or anybody else. She seemed to sense that and she smiled, too, and put her hand on his wrist. Time melted away and the Alexa he was looking at was again the skinny sixteen-year-old castoff he had loved with all his heart.

"Luckily, I've never taken my weapon out of the holster except on the range," she told him. "Winter, I came to ask you for something that you might not be able to say yes to. If you can't, I'll understand."

"Tell me what's wrong, Lex."

"I need your help for a few days."

Winter nodded, still waiting for the request.

"It's a job."

He was silent.

"Yeah," Alexa said. "See, I'm trying to save the lives of a woman and her infant son. In the process there could be the kind of trouble you have dealt with in the past. I need your instincts, your . . ." She faltered.

"My gun?" Winter felt a hollow burning in his stomach. His ability with a weapon was a natural talent; it was also a curse.

"Yes, that, but also your instincts, your man-hunting skills. I need what makes you exceptional at this sort of thing."

"Alexa, the Bureau has plenty of people who can do what I used to do far better than I can."

"Nobody in the Bureau can touch you, Massey. We both know exactly how good you are. I don't deserve your famous modesty crap. Save it for somebody who doesn't know you."

Winter felt himself bristling at her accuracy. He had been very good at being a deputy U.S. marshal, and circumstances had demanded that he go far beyond the parameters of that job in handling some very sticky situations. His skills had kept him alive, but he'd also been extremely lucky, which wasn't a skill anybody could call on. "Lex, your Immediate Response Team can handle anything you face."

"Damn it, Massey! If I could call in the IRT, I wouldn't have come here to beg you to help me with this. Do you think I would pull you into a dangerous situation if I had any other choice?"

"Lex, last time out, I could feel the odds shifting, and a professional who should know warned me that I was operating out of my depth in a world of monsters like him. And I knew he was right about part of it, and wrong, too. I am fully capable of operating in his world, but I had to decide whether I would let go and join his world—with the monsters—or stay in this one. I know how good at this crap I am, Lex. But I owe it to Sean, Rush, and Olivia to stay alive."

"You're right, Winter." Alexa smiled weakly as she searched his eyes with hers. "You have too much here to chance sacrificing it for two strangers. But I had to ask. It all seemed so perfect in my mind. The two of us side by side again. The only person I know I can totally trust with my life. Someone who will stay on goal and succeed no matter what other people throw at him."

"Why didn't you tell me you were coming?" he asked again.

"Wasn't something I could discuss over the telephone. And because I guess I thought you couldn't refuse me if I was sitting with you when I asked."

"Alexa, I'm a civilian now. No badge. Even if I wanted to help you, I couldn't do it legally. Why can't you involve the Bureau? Locals?"

"We go back too far for me to deceive you, Massey. I thought I couldn't do this alone. I thought I had to have you to succeed. But I really don't. You were my first choice, but I can go with a second or third."

Her smile didn't play. Winter saw the disappointment in her eyes.

"Tell me what the problem is," he said.

"You know Judge Hailey Fondren?"

"I've been in his courtroom a few times on marshal business. Spoken a few times."

"Night before last, somebody kidnapped his daughter, Lucy Dockery, and her son, Elijah, from their home in Charlotte."

"So, you are here with the Immediate Response Team."

Alexa shook her head. "The judge didn't call the FBI," she said. "He couldn't without risking their lives, so he called me for help...as a friend. I've known Hailey for years through the job. I knew Walter Dockery, his son-in-law, who was an assistant federal attorney."

"Fondren going to pay a ransom?"

"This is not about money."

"Revenge?"

Again, Alexa shook her head. "How much do you know about Hunter Bryce?"

"Ex–Army colonel. Charged with killing an undercover ATF agent. Something about a weapons deal." Winter remembered something. "Hailey Fondren's been trying Bryce on the murder charge."

"Bryce was a Special Forces honcho, connected at the hip to Military Intelligence. He has powerful friends in the intelligence community, and he knows secrets about powerful people who don't want him talking about them. His military records are mostly officially authored lies. He ended his career as a field functionary for M.I. in Afghanistan. Something happened there that should have ended in a court-martial and a life term for him and a couple of his men. Instead, Bryce was allowed to retire honorably."

"I'm not a big fan of shadowy men with powerful friends. I've never found it smart to trust any intelligence agency, and that's based on near-death experience."

"Judge Fondren knows enough about Bryce to understand that his intelligence friendships extend into the Bureau, so he can't risk any official FBI involvement in the kidnappings. Patrick Taylor, the ATF agent that Colonel Bryce killed, was a deep undercover agent who was known only to ATF personnel with top-level security clearances. Somehow Bryce found out about him."

Winter had seen the headlines about the high-profile trial. He despised the political nature of the intelligence organizations and the fact that their concern for people's lives and safety often ran second to what was best for the advancement of an individual agent's career. And he knew far too much about the human vipers that thrived in the intelligence community den.

"Winter, the physical evidence against Bryce is overwhelming. His saliva was on Taylor's face, his knife had Taylor's blood under the handle, his boot prints were at the murder scene. Bryce declined any deals and waived a jury trial," Alexa said. "I think he knew with one man to make the call, instead of twelve, exerting influence on that man was possible. So happens, he drew a judge whose soft underbelly is his family. Judge Fondren lost his wife and son-in-law in a car wreck a year back. Two days ago he got a call in the middle of the night telling him that his daughter and grandson had been taken. The caller told him that, unless he finds Bryce not guilty, Lucy and Elijah will be killed."

"If it was my family, I'd cut Bryce loose."

"If I can't find them before Monday morning, he'll set Bryce free. But..."

"But what?"

"They'll kill them anyway," she told him.

"How do you figure that?"

"The people who did this for Bryce have nothing to gain by setting them free, and everything to lose. Hailey changes his mind, or Lucy Dockery says she and her son were kidnapped to make sure Bryce got a walk, and the decision to release him gets reversed. If the people who took the Dockerys have kept them alive, they'll only keep them that way until Bryce is free on Monday. They might keep *her* alive in case they need to get her to speak to the judge before he goes into that courtroom."

"The judge will raise hell when he doesn't get his family back," Winter said. "So either way, the kidnappers lose."

"These people aren't amateurs. They'll make sure Judge Fondren never gets a chance to do anything."

"They'll kill him, too?"

"I'm certain of it. And the world is left with a mystery surrounding a disappeared daughter of a dead judge and her missing child."

"But they'll keep them alive until after court Monday." Winter was thinking aloud.

"Odds fifty-fifty. They may keep the child alive to control Lucy. A mother will do anything to save her child. Lucy's smart, but she's been diagnosed as chronically depressed since her husband's death, and she's in the hands of violent people. She isn't going to know how to outrun this kind of situation."   •

"Sounds like you have it figured. Who's your second choice for a partner?"

She shrugged. "I lied, Massey. There is nobody else. I can't turn to anyone in the Bureau. This one is strictly off the books. The judge says he'll make anything I have to do kosher after the fact."

"You know I want to help you."

"I know what I'm asking," she said. "This is life-or-death, or I wouldn't be here."

"I have to think about my family."

"Will you at least talk it over with Sean?"

"Talk what over with me?" Sean said. She had come into the room soundlessly, holding the pot of coffee.

"Alexa wants me to help her find a woman and a baby who've been kidnapped."

Sean said nothing. She waited for one of them to go on.

"They'll be killed unless I can locate them," Alexa said.

"Lex is off the books," Winter told his wife.

"Off what books?"

"Means no official involvement or support," Winter explained.

"I can't do it alone," Alexa said. "If I could, I wouldn't be here."

"Will it be dangerous?" Sean asked. Her eyes were on Winter.

"We're dealing with people who wouldn't hesitate to

kill us if we get close," Alexa answered. "People who know how and don't mind doing it."

Winter said, "Alexa is sure they'll kill the family if she doesn't find them."

"Damn it," Sean said. She shook her head slowly. "Alexa asked you to help her, Winter?"

"I hated to ask, Sean," Alexa interposed. "But I had to try."

"Isn't there *anyone* else you can ask?"

"There's nobody like Winter, Sean. And there isn't time to look for anybody else."

Sean's features were like stone. Then she leaned down and kissed her husband on the cheek. "Well, if that's the case, you two guys better get moving."

7

Ferny Ernest Smoot, who was supposed to keep tabs on the old judge's comings and goings, hated his name, so he answered only to "Click." Click had followed Judge Fondren from his big house in Meyers Park to the Westin Hotel in downtown Charlotte. There the judge met a light-skin black woman and the pair sat down at a table in the hotel restaurant. Click took a seat at a table across the room.

Click's father, Peanut Smoot, would want to know if

the lady was a cop, but since she wasn't in uniform, that wouldn't be easy to figure out unless Click was to ask her, which of course he couldn't. She could have been a businesswoman, a lawyer, another judge, the judge's secretary, or even a mistress. She was old, but not half as old as the judge was. She was pretty good looking, but she didn't have breasts that amounted to much, and she was more short than tall.

Click knew the woman was staying at the hotel because she signed the bill that the waitress put on the table. What was odd was, after she signed the ticket, she leaned over close and said something to the judge, who turned to glance at a bearded man seated by himself across the restaurant. The woman leaned back and also looked over at the man. The bearded man they looked at didn't notice them looking at him. So Click studied them all without acting like he was doing anything but eating—somebody who didn't have any reason not to be minding his own business.

The bearded man was narrow-shouldered, pudgy, and looked to Click like a college professor whose mother still dressed him. He seemed to be reading a newspaper, but his eyes didn't shift around on the page. He was either the world's slowest reader, or he wasn't reading at all. Then Click saw that the man was actually looking at the window beside him, using its reflection like a mirror to keep an eye on the woman and the judge.

Click wondered if the man had noticed him, too.

The judge got up all the sudden, said his good-bye to the pretty woman, and walked out of the restaurant. Click was only half done eating his nine-dollar hamburger—for which he didn't even have a bill yet—couldn't very well get up and take off after the old man without attracting attention. What he did was sit tight, eat the rest of his meal, and watch the woman, who waited a few minutes before she too walked out. That happened just as Click was forking up the last of his french fries.

As soon as she left, the bearded man set his newspaper aside and left the dining room. Click noticed that the man had signed a ticket too before he got up. So that meant they were both staying at the hotel.

Click set fifteen dollars on the table by the bill and walked out chewing. He would rather have used a stolen credit card, but that would take too long. As it was, by the time Click made the turns that put him in a position to see the end of the lobby, the woman and the bearded man were getting into separate elevators even though the man clearly had time to get in hers with her. They didn't look at each other, but the woman did glance at Click. Click was sure they were together when the cabs both stopped at the fourth floor.

Even though his daddy would be pissed that Click lost track of the judge, the news about the meeting with the stranger should make up for it. His daddy couldn't get too mad seeing how Click had warned him earlier that very morning that they needed more people to follow the judge right. Peanut had said, "No need to leash a bitch when you have her puppies in a box."

Click went outside in the courtyard to use his cell phone. He was right about both things—Peanut was mad that the judge got away, but real interested in the woman and the bearded man.

"I shoulda known better than to send a child to do a man's job," Peanut told Click several times to let him know he meant it. And don't think Click didn't know better than to mention the fact that he had told his daddy following somebody wasn't a one-man job.

Peanut agreed that, since the bearded man and the pretty woman were both staying at the same hotel on the same floor, but acting like they didn't know each other, they were up to something. He said they needed watching more than the judge.

"It's the damned FBI," Peanut said.

"You sure?" Click said. "The man with the beard was goofy looking. He looked like he was supposed to be a college prof in some low-budget porn video."

"Feds," his father told him. "Sure as caged chimps sling balls of monkey dung. All the agents aren't in slick suits. I need to think on it some."

Click knew that the judge had screwed up by defying his father's orders not to bring in the cops. Watching the judge was pointless now because the jurist was going to be punished exactly as he had been warned. Blood would have to flow or Peanut's threats would be seen as less than certain.

Click was ready to leave the hotel. What more could he do? He wanted to go by Best Buy and pick out a few CDs, get some more memory for his Dell laptop because it hung up on his favorite interactive game, Urban Plague, and that lag had gotten him killed the night before. His heart sank when he found out that wasn't going to happen today.

"Stick around there and keep your eyes open," Peanut told him. "Call me if anything happens."

"What kind of anything?" Click asked.

"You'll know when you see it. Like more cop-looking people coming from and going to her floor."

"Daddy, I can't very well park out on College Street and watch."

"Stay inside then. Blend in and keep a sharp eye out."

"What the hell do I do to blend in—get a job here?"

Click snapped the phone shut before his daddy could ream him out and frowned. He looked at the tree growing in a giant pot and at the plants that took up a whole corner of the hotel lobby and imagined himself squatting in the prissy foliage wearing camouflage overalls. Of all the members of the Smoot clan, only Click didn't hunt. He didn't like being in the woods, especially after he'd gotten chiggers so bad he'd gone to the emergency room about it. He'd known the nurse was trying hard not to laugh because his privates were swollen up and itched so bad he was crying. He also didn't like sitting still all day with frozen toes, and once he killed a deer, he had to get really nasty field-dressing it. And his siblings always smeared his face with deer blood even though it was only done when you killed the first buck of your whole life. Peanut, Click's brothers Buck, Curt, and Burt, and his sister Dixie could have the damned woods all to themselves, as far as Click was concerned.

Looking around at the ocean of open space punctuated with modern furniture, the polished marble and glass, he tried to figure out just how the hell he was going to manage an act of camouflage.

8

With his perfect white hair, bushy brows, his neatly trimmed mustache and perfect nails, attorney Ross Laughlin looked like an actor playing a distinguished senator. He wore a three-thousand-dollar Brioni suit, a three-hundred-dollar custom-made silk dress shirt, an Armani tie and thousand-dollar British shoes sewn especially for his feet. A massive gold signet ring bearing his family crest encircled his ring finger, and a platinum Rolex President wrapped his wrist. The attorney sat on the chilled steel chair and placed his briefcase to his right side on the tabletop, which was marred with graffiti. Popping open the briefcase, he removed the crocodile-skin notebook and opened it. Taking his Faber-Castell ink pen from his inside coat pocket, he uncapped it and started scribbling on the thick paper.

When Colonel Hunter Bryce was led into the room by two jail guards, Laughlin was busily making notes. Only when the guards exited the room did Laughlin look up at the middle-aged man built like a gladiator in his prime.

"Colonel," he said.

"Ross," Bryce said, running a hand over the gray stubble on his head.

Laughlin turned his eyes to look out through the security glass panel, and saw that the guards out in the hallway were not paying any particular attention to the prisoner and his attorney. The room had no audio or video surveillance because it was strictly for client-attorney conferences, which made it every bit as secure as the confessional.

"Sarnov is in town," Laughlin told Bryce. "I am meeting with him this afternoon. Max is keeping him company." Max Randall was Bryce's right-hand man and his official representative until he was free. Max got Bryce's orders through Laughlin.

"Sarnov should be in a good mood," Bryce observed. "He's two days away from taking delivery on his merchandise."

"I doubt his mood could be described as good. His employers don't like being held over a barrel, and after blaming you, I am sure they hold Serge somewhat responsible for the deal."

Bryce shrugged. "If they weren't over that barrel, I would be facing a life sentence, and they would not have a steady supply of the merchandise in the years to come." As he spoke, Bryce cracked the knuckles on his powerful hands one by one.

Laughlin kept his expression flat as he scribbled gibberish on the lined paper with his ludicrously expensive pen. "Over a barrel" was a euphemism for the fact that Colonel Bryce had taken a three-million-dollar advance from a consortium of predominantly Russian criminal organizations on a nine-million-dollar total payment for a container of military weaponry. Bryce's inconvenient arrest for stabbing an undercover agent to death had put the deal in limbo because Colonel Bryce had refused to divulge the location of the weapons to the Russians until he was free of the murder charge. It was a dangerous gambit, but Bryce had always juggled deadly situations like a clown kept tennis balls aloft. The man had nerves of tempered steel.

"It is a dangerous game you've been playing, Hunter," Laughlin reminded him. "For me, if not for you."

"*Was* playing," Bryce corrected. "After Monday all will be forgiven and we'll be slamming back vodkas with them. You'll forgive me, won't you, Ross?"

"Your holding out on Intermat has put me in a very precarious position with good and valued clients," Laughlin said. "You put me between them and the potential loss of their money, and that is a very dangerous place."

"Your past business with them is nothing compared to the deals we will do in the future," Colonel Bryce said smugly. His eyes radiated total confidence.

Laughlin had done ten million the past year with Intermat in hijacked cigarettes, more than that in pure grain alcohol furnished by a distillery, and they were expanding into new avenues of revenue. Eventually the Russians would take the whole operation, but by then Laughlin would be ready to retire.

"I'm just a middleman in your dealing with the Russians," Laughlin reminded the colonel. "I am getting too small a cut for the degree of danger."

"Being a middleman has its rewards. And its risks," Bryce said, smiling. "They may not like being over this barrel, but they see into the future and the barrels of gold that await."

"They are like Colombian drug lords without the reputation for the drug lords' compassion."

"So, what about the pair?" Bryce asked.

"Locked away," the lawyer answered.

"You trust them to *properly* handle the disposal?" Bryce asked. "Them" referred to the Smoots. "Randall should be doing it."

"They are highly proficient at making things disappear," Laughlin said. "I suspect they enjoy it. And Randall can be connected to you. The Smoots, with one exception, are expendable and totally ignorant of my involvement."

An image of Peanut Smoot's children formed in Ross Laughlin's mind. It was a chilling portrait. The attorney couldn't imagine what it would be like to be at their mercy.

If it weren't for the enormous stakes, Ross Laughlin would certainly have felt very sorry for Lucy Dockery and her child.

9

Winter Massey let the hot water drum on the top of his head. He heard the bathroom door opening and, seconds later, a naked Sean pulled the curtain back and stepped into the tub, closing the curtain behind her.

"You need your back scrubbed?" she asked, putting her hands on his shoulders and squeezing.

Winter wiped the water out of his eyes, and when he turned to her, she pressed herself against him and touched her lips gently to his.

"You know," he said, smiling, "I don't have time for this."

She said, "It's been my experience that you don't take all that long."

Winter hugged her to him and laughed.

Afterwards they dried off and dressed. Sean had already packed his clothes in an overnighter that waited by the door. She sat on the edge of the bed, legs crossed at the knees, and he felt her golden-brown eyes on his back as he stood at the open gun safe peering into the drawers at his handguns.

Winter took out his SIG Sauer 226 and hefted it. The 9mm had been his first service piece, but he had set it aside for one in .40 caliber—a trade-off of fewer rounds per magazine and a bit less penetration, for the extra knockdown it offered. He had a third SIG chambered in

.45 automatic, which he considered because of its superior stopping power. The forty was a compromise.

Sean seemed to be reading his mind. "Massey, just take the forty."

He lifted the .40 caliber from the felt-lined drawer along with a pair of extra magazines and set them on the top of the safe. He took his shoulder holster from another drawer, and a couple of boxes of ammunition from another.

"All you can do is the best you can do, Massey."

Winter opened another drawer in the safe and took out an envelope that contained two thousand dollars in hundreds, fifties, and a few twenties. Having cash on your person and using it for your expenses was important. Most people with information to sell didn't take promises or plastic. And he wouldn't be turning in an expense report.

Winter clipped his cell phone onto his belt, put an extra charged battery into his pocket, and ran through his mental checklist. He decided he had everything he needed, and picked up his lightweight leather jacket by the collar.

"Call me when you can," Sean said, standing. They embraced and kissed tenderly. Reaching behind him, she gave his buttocks a squeeze.

"Call you what?" he said, kissing her forehead.

"Call me in love, Winter James Massey," she whispered into his ear.

"Some guys have it all," he said.

"So do some gals."

She accompanied him to the front porch. Rush and

Faith Ann were seated in the porch swing. Between them, Olivia slept in her car seat. Winter kissed each of them and promised he'd see them on Monday.

"Keep on the sunny side, Win," Hank said, from the rocker.

"Always," Winter said. "Keep everybody in line, Hank." He patted his friend on his shoulder before taking Sean's hand and walking with her to his truck.

Sean held the door open and, after Winter climbed in, she kissed him again and squeezed his forearm.

"Hey, Massey," she said. "Promise me one thing?"

"Anything."

"Just this once, try not to get all busted up."

10

The warehouse was filled with the sounds of men at work. Stanley "Peanut" Smoot finished talking on the phone with his youngest son, Click, and slipped the disposable cell phone into his pocket. He focused his attention on the men who were loading boxes into a step van. Picking one of the cartons at random, he flicked open his knife, cut the paper tape, and opened the flaps. He pulled out a T-shirt, inspected the artwork, and admired the NASCAR authenticity tags complete with the holograms. Some people tried to sell counterfeit shirts and caps from

China, but that was dumb. The company that screen-printed shirts and caps under official licenses ran off a few thousand extra pieces and claimed those were defective. The plant sent the actual rejects along with the good ones to a company that shredded and recycled the rejected piece goods to recycle. Peanut owned the shredding company, and the rejected NASCAR merchandise was recycled onto racks in stores all over the country to be sold to race fans. Initially the owners of the silkscreen printing company had not wanted to cooperate, but they'd come around. Most people did if you used the right persuasion.

The distinctive modified-hourglass shape of Stanley's head had been passed down through the generations—in the way of long, narrow feet or crooked teeth. The fact was that the Sear County Smoots all had high foreheads and lantern jaws. It was not unusual in some communities—and not just the mountains—that one family might have a physical trait they shared down the line.

Peanut's small ears lay flat like they'd been thumb-tacked to his skull, which further accentuated the shape of his head. His hair, which he kept short and oiled, was the color of a molding strawberry and so thin you could see skin through it like bare ground beneath poorly scattered pine straw. His skin looked freshly sunburned, and flaked if he didn't keep it moisturized.

Peanut dropped the shirt back into the box and went back into his office to get the valise that contained the week's cash take from his various enterprises. He threw it onto the passenger's-side floorboard of his shiny black, Hemi-powered Dodge Ram pickup and drove out of the warehouse. He drove downtown and pulled into the building owned by his partner. Every Saturday he parked in the same "client" spot and took the elevator up to drop off the week's cash. As he waited for the cab to arrive, he shifted the heavy, short-barreled revolver from the side pocket of his limited-edition NASCAR jacket to the small of his back where it would be out of sight. The Smith & Wesson .44 special, five-shot revolver was Peanut's favorite handgun. If anybody tried to rob him, they'd be very sorry.

Most people called Stanley Smoot "Peanut." His father, a car salesman by title, had told him that going by a nickname made people feel like they'd known you a long time, and more likely to trust you right off the bat. Peanut had listened to his old man because anybody that put "Pooter" Smoot on his business cards, and sold used automobiles to coloreds and other credit-risky types and collected several times the blue-book retail, had a good handle on human nature. "Pay Pooter Pennies and Drive a Quality Car" was still talked about in regional business circles as being the model for the "buy here, pay here" scam, which was hardly more than legal loan-sharking. And those who didn't pay Pooter always wished they had. Peanut had cut his business teeth on visiting deadbeats in the middle of the night and convincing them to get current on payments to Pooter's.

Smoots had always known who and what they were, and they were taught that getting what their family needed was what life was about. Take care of your own, and they'll take care of you. The Smoots had instilled that philosophy in their offspring for the past two hundred years. That mind-set and physical toughness meant that no man pushed you aside or broke apart what you were—always loyal to your blood. Getting what you needed didn't have anything to do with good looks, but doing whatever was called for. And whatever it took was exactly what a Smoot did.

In the lobby Mr. Laughlin's personal secretary, Rudy Spence, who was filling the receptionist's chair, was looking down at a magazine at some pouty young man in a lime green shirt open to his belly button and a suit that looked like he had slept in it. What the boy in the ad was irked about wasn't apparent, but Peanut thought maybe he'd gotten hold of some bad meth.

Rudy said, "Mr. Laughlin is waiting for you in his office."

Rudy had a fancy college education and acted like he was a member of the royal family. He was a reed-thin boy-man who wore expensive clothes and slipper-looking shoes with soles hardly thicker than dog skin.

Peanut strode down the wide hall whose walls were paneled in rosewood and decorated with ornately carved frames holding oil paintings of farmland, mountains, rivers, shiny-coated horses, and one of hunting dogs.

Mr. Laughlin's door was cracked open and Peanut saw the attorney sitting behind his desk shuffling papers. Peanut tapped on the door and Mr. Laughlin smiled and came around the desk to shake hands with him. Laughlin wore what appeared to be expensive golfing attire—a powder-blue shirt and yellow linen slacks with a crease you could peel an apple with. His white hair was combed straight back on the sides. He had bushy brows, which contrasted with the tidy mustache. The first time Peanut had met him, twenty years before, he'd told the lawyer that he looked just like the little rich guy on the Monopoly board game.

Mr. Laughlin didn't even glance at the valise in Peanut's hand. The attorney always acted like the money was the last thing he cared about, and maybe it was.

"Sit down," Mr. Laughlin said. "I wanted to go over the latest figures with you before Sarnov and Randall get here." He went around the desk and turned a computer printout around so Peanut could see the figures. Peanut was always amazed at how Mr. Laughlin changed their illegal profits into legitimate money with the swipe of his pen. That was a trick not every lawyer could perform. Mr. Laughlin was a legal magician.

11

Winter Massey headed for I-85, and during the twenty-five-minute drive to Charlotte, he had time to reflect on Alexa Keen and their once-in-a-lifetime relationship, which had seemed until that morning like something that had happened in another lifetime altogether.

At one point, around his third year in high school, Winter had desired Alexa Keen in the way only a young male with turbo-driven hormones can, but that had been

the smallest part of his attraction to her. It was a fluke
that he had gotten to know Alexa at all, much less that he
had offered up to her his deepest secrets. Now he found
himself wondering if he had ever been as emotionally
honest about himself with anyone before or since.

It all began with a twenty-nine-cent spiral notebook.
Late for class, Winter had been hurrying down the empty
hallway when he spotted the manila cardboard backing
covered with dusty footprints near the row of lockers outside his biology classroom. He stooped and scooped it up
and carried it in with him. The cover was red, and there
was no name on the outside. He slipped it into his pack
intending to drop it into the lost-and-found box when he
passed the office. But he forgot.

That night he went into the backpack and found the
notebook. Out of curiosity he opened it. The handwriting
was perfect and clean and easy to read. So he read a few
lines and discovered that it was a journal. Since he didn't
know whose it was, he didn't feel the least guilty about
reading it. And an hour later, he was closing it, stunned
by what he had read, and hungry for more.

The journal covered a few months of a young girl's life,
and it was written in third person.

She was alone in a skin she didn't fit into, but couldn't
get out of. She never asked the others circling around
her about their lives, but she picked up bits here and
there by listening to them. How could she learn about
the others if she couldn't gather the nerve to speak to
them, without the fear of letting them see her clearly?
She studied the ones around her over the weeks, and

she wondered what sorts of thoughts were contained in their heads, what kind of world each saw through their eyes. She resorted to clues like the way hair was kept, the styles and amount of wear of clothes, the way fingernails were kept, and from that she imagined their lives. Most of them looked like they came from places that had always been soft, and made warm by those who had borne them.

When one of them looked at her, she closed herself up in a coil, and usually their eyes kept moving because there was nothing here to waste time on. She was always angry with herself for being different, an alien walking among them, a creature of the shadows. She knew that not one of them could ever imagine what her life was like, how empty it was, how deeply she wanted just a little of what those around her experienced. . . .

How many of them had slept with one eye open, worried if someone would come to the bed uninvited, bringing with him the scent of whiskey and an appetite she couldn't understand and was defenseless against? She was a child who wanted only to be loved and cherished and have value, and even a loathsome creature's prodding her and dampening her skin with his sweat was somehow preferable to being ignored—being branded as a being without worth. . . .

Winter's heart felt squeezed by the anguish, which wasn't merely insecurity, the adolescent angst he and his pals suffered. Each paragraph was a spotlight illuminating another chasm of alienation, some emptiness greater than a teenager is supposed to feel. Who was this girl? How would he find her without knowing her name? The journal had no signature, just a star applied with a permanent marker. He had never met anyone in school who talked the way this girl wrote. Such a lonely soul, such a hunger reflected in those lines. He had to find her. Nothing else mattered.

The next day, Winter had taken the notebook out of his backpack when he arrived at school, and he carried it in his hand all morning, like a fisherman trolling for the author. He knew the diary was too precious for anyone to let go of; surely no one would want someone else to have access to their innermost feelings. He met the eyes of everyone he caught looking at him, but nothing. He studied the crowds like a predator.

He went home carrying the journal. In the silence of his room he read it again, and it filled him with emotion, with a longing to know this girl, maybe to put his hands on her cheeks and share her pain. *I feel this! I know your pain of aloneness. The riotous world is revolving around your utter stillness.* He understood it, felt something of it himself. He too was an emotional outcast, a stranger in a strange land, a peg that had no proper hole. He had suffered to a lesser degree. He had never been physically abused, was never without someone who loved and protected him.

It was after five and his mother wasn't yet home. When there was a knock on the door, he figured Lydia had arms loaded with groceries, so he opened the back door to a stranger. He knew her—sort of. The skinny girl in a baggy sweater and loose-fitting jeans who stood there on the other side of the screen door, scowling, with her fists clenched, was in his school, had been in classes with him. Her eyes were on fire, and they burned into him. *Angela, or Amelia or something,* he thought. She was biracial, and, at first look, she wasn't a beautiful girl, because she worked as hard to camouflage her physical attractiveness as other girls her age labored to enhance theirs. This girl wore outdated clothes to hide her shape. She kept her hair as short as possible and she avoided makeup like it was poison. If that weren't enough to discourage approaches, she was aggressively unpleasant, sullen, and acid tongued.

"You read it?" she demanded.

"What?" Winter had said.

"What the hell you think?" she replied, her bottom lip quivering. He suddenly realized that she was not as furious as frightened. "Mine is what. Give it back."

"No," he was surprised to hear himself say.

"It's mine," she insisted, tears starting to stream down her dusky cheeks. "Please, it's personal. You have no right."

He stepped back and opened the door wide. "Come in," he said. "Please?"

She opened the screen door and entered, her eyes casting about the kitchen as though she expected that she was entering a trap.

He went into his room and got the journal. He held it out, and she snatched it out of his hands and clutched it to her chest. "You . . . you . . . you stole . . ."

"No," Winter protested. "I didn't. I found it in the hall. There was no name on it."

"You . . . you read it."

"Yes, I read it."

"I can't believe you'd read a diary! Don't you know that's a sin against privacy?"

"I couldn't help it. It's unbelievable."

"You crazy?" She looked up into his eyes. "Isn't any of it true. I made it all up. It's fiction."

"If it's fiction, it's better than anything I've ever read."

"You tell anybody?" she asked. "Let anybody else read it?"

"Of course not."

"Good. You better not. I got brothers. They'll kick your ass."

"No you don't," Winter said. "And you don't have any friends either."

"How do you know?" she shot back.

"Look, cross my heart, I won't ever tell a soul one word that is in your journal."

"You'd better not," she threatened, and turned on her heel to leave.

"Angela?"

"Alexa. It's Alexa Keen."

"I'd like . . . I mean . . . I want to be your friend."

"I don't need anybody feeling sorry for me, Massey. And I don't need any sneaky-ass diary-reading friends."

"A diary is true," he said. "It can't be fictional if it's true. Even if it's based on—"

"Screw you," she snarled, stomping out. She slammed the screen door.

"*I do*," he called. "I need a friend like you, Alexa Keen."

She stopped in her tracks and turned to look at him, her eyes narrowed. "What? Why?"

"Because you're special. Because you can write what you feel. I feel some of what you feel, but I could never write it like you do. When you write, I can feel it, see it, and taste it. I want to learn to express myself the way you do."

"You don't know me."

"My father was an alcoholic. One day a couple of years ago he ran off. He never told us where he went or why. But he was gone a long time before he left. He made me feel empty and worthless and helpless. He didn't hit me, but what he did was worse than any beating."

Her eyes reflected deep suspicion. "What's in it for you?"

"I don't have anybody I can talk to, tell my thoughts and feelings to. I need someone I can trust. I know you feel the same way. If I could trust you, you could trust me. I give you my word of honor."

She smirked and shook her head slowly. "Sex. You think because I've done some things, that I'll—"

"Never," he blurted. "Alexa, that's not why at all."

"Never, ever try it! You do, we're all done. You do that and I'll hate you."

"I swear that I will never betray you."

"Cross your heart? Swear to God?"

"I swear it."

He had honored his word. But it hadn't been easy. She

grew more attractive as they grew closer, able to tell each other their deepest thoughts, their insecurities and secrets. Some things he couldn't tell her, like how sorry he was that he couldn't explore the deeply sexual feelings he had for her, that he often suspected she had for him. Naturally he had always wondered how things might have been if he hadn't stuck to his pledge—a pledge that was the very foundation of their friendship.

Winter had mixed feelings about working with Alexa. He also had no choice.

12

Buck Smoot showed his brothers, twins Burt and Curt, where he wanted them to dig, watched them get started on it, and then rode his four-wheeler off to the far end of the property, where he let himself out through a seldom-used gate. The trees beside the gate bristled with yellow No Trespassing signs, a formality that was wholly unnecessary. Buck didn't snap the padlock back in place, but closed the gate and looped the heavy chain around the aging posts so it would be easy to get back in after he took care of his business three miles down the road.

He stopped a quarter mile short of the house so the sound of his four-wheeler wouldn't announce him. He took the three-foot-long section of lead pipe out of the rear utility cage. Tapping the piece of pipe against his leg as he went, Buck strode through the woods toward the Grissoms' isolated wood-frame house, smiling to himself as he saw the man of the house leaning over the lawn mower with his narrow back to the trees.

What kind of fool doesn't get himself some kind of a dog to warn him if trouble's coming? Buck wondered. He had killed the man's dogs last time he dropped by, but a man living in the country is a fool not to get replacements right away.

The man working on his mower straightened abruptly when he heard footsteps behind him, but the sudden movement threw Buck's aim off only a little. The pipe came crashing down on the man's shoulder instead of the back of his head, sending him to the ground in a fetal heap, howling in pain.

Buck waited until Grissom looked up from the ground to speak. "Had to go to the sheriff, did you? What good did you think that'd do you, Grissom? You imagine my buddy was going to do something to me about your lie?"

"Buck, I . . ."

Buck tapped his big open palm with the end of the pipe, delighted that this bastard was trembling from fear and pain.

"Shut up and listen," Buck said. "Soon's I finish with you, I'm going to go in your house and see how Miss Molly Grissom is doing. I intend to find out why she lied on me. I bet it was your idea."

"You . . . you . . ."

"I what?" Buck snarled, raising the pipe over his head and shaking it menacingly.

"Why'd you want to go and rape my Molly? She never harmed you. You hurt her bad, Buck. Wasn't no call to do that to her."

"Rape? Is that what she said? How can you rape one that's been sprawled out under every man in the whole damn county?" Buck said, bringing the pipe down on the man's left knee with a sickening crack of bone and tissue.

"She said she wanted me to pour it to her. We all know that's on account you can't keep her itches scratched. I didn't hurt her. She likes it rough-and-tumble. She squealed with pleasure the whole time I was putting it to her."

"Please . . ." Grissom held up both of his hands to prevent a blow to his head. "I won't say anything. I was mad is all. I'll forget all about it. Ever bit of it was my fault."

"I'll give you something to be mad at, Grissom." Buck duplicated his blow to the first knee on the other one. Aiming his next few blows, he shattered both of Grissom's outstretched hands, then broke both of his arms below the shoulders for good measure. "Who you gone run tell now?" he said. "Go call the sheriff now if you think you can dial a telephone."

Buck thought about crushing the man's skull, but he held back. He didn't want to kill him quickly.

"Please, Buck . . . don't hit me no more. I won't tell nobody."

"I ain't gonna hit you no more, Grissom. I'm gone help you feel better."

Buck set down the pipe and jerked the man up, tossed him over his massive shoulders, and carried him over to the old well, where he tore the old boards off the circular stone structure.

"Please, Buck..."

"I do what I want around here, Grissom," Buck said as he dropped the skinny man into the hole.

There was a muted splash twenty feet below followed by thrashing, which made Buck laugh.

"You tell lies on a Smoot just one time!" he hollered down the well, warmed by the booming echo of his own voice. He couldn't see as far down as the water, but it sounded like it was plenty deep. After a few seconds, Buck turned and went toward the house, slowing long enough to pick up the pipe as he passed by the broken-down lawn mower.

He opened the kitchen door to the loud sounds of country music coming from a radio. A pot of greens simmering on the stove caught his attention. Changing the pipe to his left hand, Buck picked up a spoon and scooped out a bunch of steaming greens. After blowing on them, he ate them.

"Damn, that gal can cook. Ass-kicking sure gives a fellow an appetite," he mused.

As he chewed, he heard water running into the bathtub. He figured he had plenty of time, so he stood over the stove to get his fill of the greens, wishing Molly had already baked corn bread.

Buck didn't see any point in interrupting a lady who was taking her last bath.

13

Rudy Spence showed the two men into Mr. Laughlin's sleekly modern office, where Peanut had just finished going over the financial sheets Mr. Laughlin had given him to look at. After reading them over, Peanut had shredded them as he always did in order to keep them from falling into the wrong hands. According to the figures, Peanut Smoot was a legitimate, taxpaying multimillionaire because he was a full partner in several of Ross Laughlin's business corporations.

Mr. Laughlin invested money in art, which Peanut didn't take part in. The lawyer had explained the art to Peanut, but Peanut liked art that you could see a picture in. Aside from the big Mark Rothko painting behind the desk that looked to Peanut like finger painting, a small Klee that also looked like a little kid did it about spacemen, a Matisse that was just shapes of people cut out of colored paper, and a Calder miniature mobile that was painted steel wafers on wire rods that moved around when you touched it, there were thirty identically framed pictures of Ross Laughlin standing beside presidents, a dozen congressmen and senators, and some celebrities, including Frank Sinatra, Burt Reynolds, Liz Taylor, and John Wayne. Those impressed Peanut a lot more than slopped paint.

"Sarnov. Maxwell. Nice to see you fellows," Peanut said, standing.

"How you been, Peanut?" Max Randall asked him. "You know Serge Sarnov."

Peanut had met Sarnov once before and he knew that the Russian didn't say anything unless he had some wise-ass remark to make. Sarnov shook hands like a woman and acted like he was too good to be in the same room as you.

Max Randall was a different story. He'd been an Army Ranger parachuting into Afghanistan weeks before that invasion, along with Colonel Bryce and a few others. In Peanut's book Bryce and Randall were real men. Both men were nice enough guys, but if push came to shove, both could cut out your heart and eat it like an apple. Bryce hadn't thought twice about personally cutting the undercover agent's throat for betraying him—exactly what Peanut would have done in his shoes. Randall had white-blond hair that was short and he had a face like an action-movie star. A strong and fast fellow, Randall didn't say anything unless he had something that needed saying, and it was always something you'd want to hear.

"I can't think of anything to complain about," Peanut replied. "Wait, that sounded like a complaint!" He laughed at his joke.

Peanut would have liked to slap the smirk off Sarnov's face. First off, Peanut didn't like foreigners. He especially didn't like people from any place that had chickened their way out on Iraq, leaving George W. to do it all with just the help of the Brits and a few wormy-looking little whatnots from countries you wouldn't go to unless your plane was hijacked there.

"Gentlemen," Laughlin said as he entered the office dressed like he was going out to play golf. The lawyer shook his guests' hands with the enthusiasm of a politician greeting his prime benefactors.

"May I offer you something to drink? Serge, may I offer you a glass of twenty-seven-year-old Macallan? It was a Christmas gift from the ambassador to Scotland."

The damned ambassador to Scotland gives Mr. Ross Laughlin liquor, Peanut thought. If there was ever a more impressive or intelligent man than Ross Laughlin, Peanut sure hadn't met him. He was also the only man Peanut really trusted.

The Russian frowned. "I never drink when I am talking business."

"He might rather have vodka," Peanut said. "That's potato juice and pure grain alcohol."

"Too early for me, sir," Max Randall said, declining.

Mr. Laughlin sat down in a sleek black leather chair across from Sarnov and Max. Peanut sat heavily on the leather ottoman with the elbows of his long arms on his knees.

"So," Sarnov said, placing a gold lighter and a package of fancy cigarettes carefully on the glass coffee table. "Let's get to it, Ross."

Mr. Laughlin folded his hands on his leg. "I met with Hunter Bryce this morning. Monday evening we will conclude our outstanding business," he said. "And Colonel Bryce is ready to go on to the next load as soon as the financials are ironed out. He assures me that he can provide whatever amount of merchandise you require on a reasonable schedule and at bargain-basement prices."

Sarnov looked at Max, who nodded once and said, "Colonel Bryce can certainly do that."

Sarnov said, "Nothing I know about this judge gives me the degree of confidence you have that he will give in to pressure."

"Max's plan was a stroke of genius," Laughlin said. "It will work."

"We have his little girl and her kid," Peanut said. "And my daughter Dixie spoke to the judge personally about how to get them back safe and sound. He doesn't know he's going to be as dead as they are."

Ross Laughlin plucked a speck of lint off his pant leg. "Judge Fondren is a man who has lost his wife and son-in-law in a tragic accident. His grief is deep and he will not risk the sole remaining members of his immediate family over Bryce—someone whom he has no emotional investment in. The agent Bryce killed knew his risks, was killed in a war of sorts. Plus, I have introduced more than ample reasonable doubt to allow the judge to rule in Hunter Bryce's favor without drawing too much criticism. The judge will go for it."

"You guarantee that?" Sarnov asked.

"I guarantee it."

"My employers take guarantees as blood oaths. I sincerely hope you are correct," Sarnov said. "By refusing to divulge the location of the shipment, for which my firm paid you three million up front upon my assurances,

Colonel Bryce has in effect been extorting my employers for a year."

"The advance—a third of the purchase price your firm agreed to pay for the merchandise—went directly from me to the colonel and on to his suppliers to pay for the shipment," Mr. Laughlin pointed out.

"I understand business." Sarnov shrugged. "But the fact remains that the firm's funds have been in the hands of others, while our merchandise—which we never laid our eyes on—sits gathering dust, only Bryce knows where. We could not keep our word to the people we had promised to deliver to. It made us look like we have no control."

"You're going to make out like bandits," Peanut told the Russian. "You pay nine million and get stuff worth a minimum of three times that much."

"What *you* think," Sarnov said to Peanut, "is of no importance or of any interest to me." He turned back to Laughlin. "For all I know, the Feds have located the missing merchandise. Maybe what we have bought is long gone, or maybe they are waiting to catch us taking possession of it, or maybe they will track it and take down the people we sell it to. Perhaps the risks have risen exponentially with the passing time."

"The type of business we do is filled with maybes," Peanut said. "Bigger profits always come with bigger risks."

Sarnov continued, "My employers have decided that some changes in the terms are necessary."

Mr. Laughlin crossed his legs. "Alterations at this

point on an agreement that is in place? Your employers and I have a mutually profitable history."

"The cigarettes my people get hold of we sell to you people at less than we get from a lot of others," Peanut added.

Mr. Laughlin sat back and placed the tips of his fingers together.

The Russians bought hundreds upon hundreds of cases of hijacked cigarettes and, after affixing forged state tax stamps to the packs, sold them to store owners all over the world.

Sarnov said, "But for the other business that we do, you and your helper here would be dead already. Keeping an advance without delivering on an agreed-upon schedule isn't something we would normally allow."

"What?" Peanut said, bristling at the man's threat. He wished he could whip out his stainless .44 special and blast the Russian's heart out.

"What sort of alteration do you have in mind?" Laughlin asked.

"The up-front payment will become a rebate against the total we owe," Serge said.

"Bull dooky," Peanut scoffed.

"I could do this," Mr. Laughlin said, cool as a cucumber. "I repay the three mil out of my own pocket and you walk away from this deal. It's the long-term association that matters. I am quite certain I can line up new buyers for the Bryce merchandise."

Sarnov smiled. "In order to salvage our reputation with our buyers, we will expect to take delivery of that shipment and pass it along as planned. Naturally we will have to give the buyers a considerable discount for the inconvenience factor."

"You mean you'd like a thirty-three percent discount on the deal?" Mr. Laughlin asked, raising a brow.

"Yes. It's fair for the year you've had our money," the Russian said.

"You must be on dope!" Peanut blurted out. "Of all the screwball crap I ever heard, that takes the cake!"

Mr. Laughlin held up his hand to silence Peanut.

Peanut was running figures in his head. He was getting a twenty percent cut of Mr. Laughlin's ten points on Colonel Bryce's deals. He was getting one hundred grand for the Dockery kidnapping and disposal of the bodies. Four of his kids would get five thousand each. If Sarnov got his asked-for cuts, Peanut would lose a lot of money.

Sarnov lit a cigarette without asking permission, which bothered Peanut, but nobody else seemed to care. "We don't have any business history with Colonel Bryce."

Laughlin said, "After this is over, your people can do deals with him for years to come."

Max nodded his agreement.

Sarnov shrugged. He looked down at the ash on his cigarette, down the coffee table, and, seeing no ashtray, casually tapped ash into a cut-glass dish with peppermint candy in it.

"If we don't get the shipment, we expect you to pay us the profits we would have made *if* we had completed our end. A moment ago, Mr. Peanut set that figure at three hundred percent, which if my math is correct is twenty-seven million we would expect to receive."

"What?!" Laughlin said in disbelief.

Peanut was sure he was hallucinating. Twenty-seven million dollars for something that never happened was insanity.

Sarnov took a long pull from the cigarette and exhaled the smoke across the table. "In the interest of friendship and a valued business relationship, I'll get my employers to take nine million if the deal doesn't go through. If it works out, we pay a total of six for the shipment. After that, we do the deals like we initially agreed. A third down, two thirds upon delivery."

Peanut had watched the color drain from Mr. Laughlin's face by degrees—his lips tightening. He had never seen Mr. Laughlin physically affected by anything.

Peanut could keep quiet no longer. Mr. Laughlin didn't know Russians as well as Peanut did, having watched the History Channel. "You commies have been pulling this bluff crap since World War II," Peanut said, guffawing. He gestured with his hands in the air. "Ask for something crazy as hell, then threaten something insane like maybe a nuclear war, then y'all take the best deal going backwards you can get. You're the world's biggest bluffers." He wagged his finger and smiled. "Ballsy sons of bitches. I'll give you that. But it don't play here in America. Not any longer."

Peanut knew he had the bastard's game pegged, and he was sure Sarnov knew he knew it. The Russian had lost his ability to shock them with a sky-high demand.

Sarnov pinched the cigarette's filter between his thumb and index finger, held it up level with his face, and stared at the smoke flowing from its tip. "Negotiations are over. Ross, tell your howling monkey to shut up while you are ahead."

Peanut bristled. "You mean to sit there and poke a barky stick up our butts and say smile? Buddy, the damned Berlin Wall came a-tumbling down. In case you didn't notice, you lost."

Sarnov tilted his head, breaking off his gaze on the cigarette, and, looking at Ross, said, "I never allow hired help to sit in on business meetings. If I require their presence, I do not allow them to speak, and to insult a guest would demand severe punishment. You should explain to your *help* the fact that you are winning here. It costs you a little bit of money; we get a fair settlement and we don't have to *bury* anybody. And, for the benefit of the severely misinformed, the fact is that the Wall came down to allow us better access to business opportunities."

"I don't threaten easy," Peanut growled, rising from the ottoman, looming like a thunderstorm over the narrow Russian seated on the couch. His anger had canceled his ability to reason beyond the present. "You communist piece of—" He was already swinging his fist down at Sarnov's face, knowing that the man was as good as unconscious.

It was odd the way Peanut's perspective suddenly changed and, before the lights went out, he was somehow looking up at a fluorescent light fixture in the ceiling.

14

The North Carolina Piedmont, once a sleepy southern backwater with one hand on the plow, one on a loom, gold ore in its pocket, eyes on the Bible, and its nose to the grindstone, had become over the centuries the nation's second-largest banking center.

Winter was fond of most of the additions to Charlotte's skyline in the years since he had come to North Carolina to work in the satellite office of the United States Marshals Service, serving under Hank Trammel. The vast majority of the additions to the skyline seemed to have crossed the city's "traditional Presbyterian brick-solid" with a sense of whimsy. Towering buildings like Bank of America's headquarters and the Hearst Tower looked like inhabitable sculpture. Trammel liked to say the city was looking like the set for a Batman movie.

The Westin Hotel, one of Charlotte's newer buildings, was a sleek glass-skinned structure with the visual warmth of an ice cube.

Winter parked in the deck, grabbed his overnighter from the passenger's seat, and strode across the courtyard, going inside through one of the glass doors opened by a man in a black suit. At the front desk, he dropped his name and the clerk handed him a pair of electronic keys to room 412. No check-in required. As was his habit, he scanned the lobby for anything worth noting, allowing his mind to sort and file away its impressions.

He took the elevator up to the fourth floor, used the key and entered a room that could have been in any first-class hotel in the world. He set his bag on the bed, opened it, took out his shoulder rig and slipped it on. He unrolled a microfiber windbreaker and put it on over the weapon.

Winter had turned in his federal badge, but thanks to grateful friends in very high places, he had been issued a rare concealed-weapon permit that was valid in any state in the union. Unlike a normal civilian permit, Winter's allowed him to enter any business, any building or facility, state and federal government structures included, while armed.

As he was opening the note that had been left on one of the beds, he heard raised voices in the adjoining room. Winter opened the note and unfolded it.

Welcome, Massey. Room next door at your earliest.

He moved to the door on his side of the wall, opened it quietly, and knuckle-tapped on the second door. Alexa opened it.

"Good afternoon, Lex," Winter said. "I hope I'm not interrupting."

"No. Please come in. There's somebody you need to meet," she said, stepping aside and gesturing him into the room, which was pretty much identical to his.

The bearded man on the couch stood up reluctantly. He was medium height and looked like a man who didn't waste time exercising. His mouse-brown hair was far thinner than the graying Vandyke beard he wore. Under bushy brows, his bored eyes were light brown, and a Falcon pipe with a dull aluminum stem jutted from between his plump lips. The knit shirt was too snug around his middle, the green khakis too high over his well-broken-in chukkas.

"Winter Massey," Alexa said, "this is—"

"Clayton Able," the man said, usurping Alexa's introduction. He crossed the room with his hand extended and Winter shook it. Able's palm was warm and damp. "Pleased to meet you," he said.

"My pleasure," Winter replied, fighting the urge to wipe his palm on his pant leg.

"I've learned quite a lot about you," Clayton told him. "You are an impressive individual."

"Alexa said nice things about me?"

"Yes, of course she did. But my knowledge of you is mostly from sources other than Special FBI Agent Keen here. There's no shortage of material on *the* Deputy U.S. Marshal Winter Massey." Clayton Able had a manner reminiscent of professors Winter had known; men who were so deeply embedded in academia they believed degrees were not only badges of rank, but accurate measurements of intelligence.

"Nobody regrets that more than I do," he answered, only partly joking.

At that, Clayton's eyes reflected the sort of self-amusement that often precedes a smart-ass remark, but none was forthcoming. Instead Clayton put the pipe in his mouth and sucked hungrily on its stem.

Winter turned questioning eyes to Alexa. *Who is this prick?*

"Clayton is a colleague."

"I see," Winter said, although he didn't.

"He's giving us assistance with intelligence."

"FBI?" Winter wondered.

"Heavens, no. I am a freelance information worm," Clayton said around the pipe's stem.

"I've utilized Clayton's considerable talents in the past," Alexa explained.

"With the Bureau's blessing?" Winter asked.

"Of course not." She frowned.

"Not exactly fans of mine," Clayton snorted. "They resent my success where they have failed. They are not able to utilize the same techniques of intelligence acquisition and therefore resent what they covet."

"What sort of techniques? You're a hacker?" Winter asked.

"Guilty as charged on that score," the man said. "Also I acquire tidbits through other avenues and I swap information with select people."

"Believe me," Alexa told Winter, "we couldn't do this without him. You'll understand when you see what he's compiled. We're not starting from scratch thanks to Clayton."

Puffing up proudly, Clayton added, "I have gathered up a basket of goodies from the FBI, CIA, DEA, ATF, Interpol, Military Intelligence, and the NSA."

On its face, Able's claim sounded to Winter like that of someone suffering from delusions of grandeur, but Alexa vouched for him.

"Tell him what you just told me," Alexa told Clayton.

"Military Intelligence is aware of the Dockerys' abduction, and they know that Judge Fondren intends to let Bryce go in order to get them back."

"So why doesn't M.I. just notify the FBI? The Bureau will step in and the Attorney General will prevent that ruling. Then the FBI can get to work on the kidnapping," Winter said.

"M.I. can't tell a soul," Clayton said.

"Why?"

"Because they learned it from a wiretap they have on Hailey Fondren's telephone to gather intelligence on Bryce's trial."

"They tapped a federal judge's phone?" Winter was stunned. Not because Military Intelligence did it, but because Clayton knew about it. If it was true, Clayton was plugged into a golden source.

"They can't share their information with the Attorney General or the FBI or anyone else without admitting to the source of that intelligence. M.I. has a very big stake in this case. If you two don't find the Dockerys, people in the highest places will have to make sure Judge Fondren convicts Bryce anyway. There are two factions within M.I. Those who want Bryce freed for profit reasons and to keep him from selling them out to save his own skin, and those who want him convicted so they can get the names of his accomplices."

"This military interest in the trial judge doesn't fit," Winter objected. "Colonel Bryce wasn't a member of the military when he killed the ATF agent. What am I missing here? Does Bryce have classified information he's threatening to disclose?"

Alexa said, "This is a bit more complicated than I may have mentioned. I didn't want to go into this until you were here."

Winter ran his hand through his hair and inhaled. "Lex, you know how much I hate surprises. Let's get everything out in the open."

"The reason for kidnapping Lucy and Elijah Dockery is to free Bryce," Alexa said. "We can't sweat Bryce for the names of his accomplices because if he knows we're on this, the accomplices will too and they'll kill the Dockerys and sanitize everything."

Clayton said, "Bryce was in the process of dealing military weapons when he killed that agent and was arrested."

"What sort of weapons?" Winter asked.

Clayton said, "The good stuff. First-rate, latest military weaponry probably being sold to less-than-America-friendly people. Weapons directly from military stockpiles. No Stinger missiles yet, but just about everything else. The weapons will be shipped out of this country in containers to South America and the Far East and you can guess into what sorts of pipelines after that. We're potentially talking about drug cartels and terror groups. Bryce has connections inside the Pentagon to make this work."

"Man," Winter said. "That's insane. A soldier doing that is just crazy."

"Crazy profitable," Alexa said. "That kind of danger,

times scarcity, plus value to the recipients, translates into tens of millions."

"You can imagine that breaking Bryce's smuggling operation is more valuable to the Pentagon than any two lives. What else do you need to know?" Clayton asked.

"I don't suppose M.I. wants Bryce convicted so he'll spend the rest of his life in prison," Winter said.

"We all know it's more likely they want him facing life in prison so they can cut a deal with him," Alexa said. "What Bryce has been doing couldn't be done without brass involvement, and Military Intelligence wants those names."

"And the people involved with him want him freed," Winter mused. "Even if he walks, they're not going to be able to keep doing business with him."

"Don't bet on it. There's a power war going on above this, and both sides have a short trip to the door if they fail," Clayton said. "That is fascinating, but irrelevant. I could expound on it if you'd like."

"I couldn't care less," Winter said.

Clayton Able couldn't hide his surprise that someone didn't crave more information. "But . . ."

Winter locked eyes with Clayton. "I could care less where who is doing what to whom unless they are going to be doing it between me and the Dockerys. Anything that doesn't impact what Alexa and I have to do is drama for somebody with too much time on their hands. The only thing I want to know is where do we start."

"If we don't find them, Lucy and Elijah will be killed," Alexa said grimly. "Even if Judge Fondren did call the FBI, they'd be too late to break this open."

"But Mr. Able does," Winter said.

"I do," Clayton said, smiling. "I put it together from several different sources that, despite what the government says, do *not* share information with each other unless specific requests are made through proper slothish channels. Don't worry about M.I. They can't afford to interfere with your investigation. They will want you to succeed. Well, those of them who want Bryce to take the fall for a murder he committed will. Nobody else knows where the Dockerys are being held, or even who took them."

"M.I. is aware of what *we* are doing?" Winter asked.

Clayton removed the pipe from his mouth. "Dear boy. What I do is *trade* intelligence. I only get it as long as I give it back."

15

Seated on a sofa in the corner of the lobby of the Westin Hotel, Click Smoot played games on his laptop while he monitored the pedestrian traffic. Just about the time the power indicator on the laptop was down to a single bar, someone of interest arrived. A lone man entered carrying a black nylon bag. The man picked up a key folder from the desk clerk, got into the elevator, and went directly up to the fourth floor.

Click was sure the man was connected to the two other people on four. The stranger was close to the woman's age, was just south of six feet tall, and was built like a man who stayed active. He walked with an erect fluidity that brought to Click's mind a feral tomcat that made a living catching and eating rodents at the hunting camp. This animal wasn't afraid of anything on four legs or two, Click was sure of it.

The bastards could sit up there in a room and plot and plan solving this until hell froze over. Even if there were hundreds of FBI agents looking for the Dockery woman and her kid, they'd have to be honest-to-God psychics to connect the Smoots to the kidnapping.

16

Five-letter word for darker than dark.

P-i-t-c-h

The trailer's windows were covered with something that totally blocked outside light. The constant darkness allowed Lucy Dockery no sense of time, but since she knew the difference between the noises generated by daytime and nighttime television, she could sort of judge her place in a twenty-four-hour cycle.

Periodically a central unit would kick on, causing the trailer to vibrate violently for a few seconds. The forced air made a hissing sound as it exited the register and smelled like a vacuum whose bag was overfilled with dog hair and dust.

So far they hadn't drugged her again, so maybe they planned to let her and Elijah go as soon as her father paid a ransom. As far as Lucy was concerned, the captors could have every penny she owned. It had to be obvious that she was unaccustomed to violence, and she posed no threat physically to her larger and stronger captors. They had to know she wouldn't try anything that would risk getting Elijah harmed.

Keeping quite still, fighting back tears, she listened for her son's voice, hungry to know that he was all right. Sometimes she could hear both the television and a radio, like audio combatants. She could, when the radio and TV both lulled at the same time, hear her son jabbering. The word "no" was prominent in his recent communications. She could also hear the big angry woman barking or cooing at him, but she knew none of it contained any useful information about their circumstances.

Elijah, who walked with confidence, hadn't been afraid of strangers lately, having passed through a couple of stages where he would react badly to them. Lucy had employed several babysitters and he was long accustomed to strangers caring for him, having his mother in bed, weeping and disinterested. Grief for Walter and for her mother had been like a weight that, for weeks at a time, had made moving beyond her bedroom a Herculean challenge.

Lucy wasn't afraid for herself. The worst they could do was kill her. And dying couldn't be any more painful than living without Walter. She wouldn't have been as terrified if Eli wasn't there, but his well-being mattered like nothing in her life had ever mattered. Against the terror of Eli being harmed, no fear she had ever felt even rated a mention. She figured that was just how nature wired mothers.

The woman said they were in a trailer. *What's the difference between a mobile home and a modular home? Wheels.* It dawned on Lucy that not once in her twenty-six years on earth had she ever before set foot inside a mobile home.

Lucy had always believed that, with the possible exception of Gypsies, nobody but people without any alternative would choose to live in a flimsy aluminum-sided crate with a foundation by Goodyear. She wondered if she should regret being prejudiced against something that was merely foreign to her world. *No.* The woman who seemed at home here was a poster child for the worst examples of the trailer-park-trash stereotype. Lucy understood on a visceral level that the violent woman shared the pathology of the aristocratic-hating Madame Defarge depicted in *A Tale of Two Cities*. The woman captor hated Lucy because she *wasn't* toothless white trash.

She wished she could stop thinking like that. This wasn't about class, but about human decency—about choices. She knew deep in her heart that she couldn't depend on their captors' humanity. If this was about revenge, they were dead. If the kidnappers' motives weren't related to gain, and if the authorities had no way to find them, she couldn't just sit there and wait to see what happened. Since she had seen their faces, she had to assume they didn't think she could identify them because she'd be dead. And if she died, what would happen to Elijah?

When the woman had opened the door earlier, Lucy had seen that the bedroom she was in was cluttered and wooden crates were stacked against one wall. Might there be something there she could use to facilitate an escape? She doubted she could take on any of them, but could she use her brain to get Elijah away from this place?

Some abductees did escape their captors. The news was filled with examples of all kinds of people getting away from armed captors.

But Lucy knew she wasn't ever going to get free.

So she wept.

17

Clayton Able's top-opening valise was so jam-packed with file folders he had trouble at first prying enough of them out to free the stack. He piled the entire stack on the bed, opened one of the folders, and started flipping photographs faceup on the coverlet like playing cards.

The first picture Clayton flipped was that of a thin individual wearing an expensive suit and carrying an overnight bag. The shot had obviously been taken in an airport and, based on the angle, by a fixed security camera.

"This is from airport surveillance yesterday," Clayton told Winter and Alexa. "A little out of focus for my taste, but it's been blown up and had gone through a couple of generations before I acquired it. The face triggered some flags in the NSA mainframe. They sent the information to another computer at the Homeland Security center, and because of the location of the individual involved, my friends plucked it out of the stacks. Thank God for biometrics."

"Nice suit," Winter said.

"Serge Sarnov." Clayton tapped the photo with his finger. "He works for Intermat Ltd., an investment firm with principal offices in L.A., New York, London, Paris, Moscow, and with smaller and unlisted offices in cities not known for political stability or ethical behavior."

"Russian mob?" Winter asked, frowning.

"Mobs," Alexa answered.

"You know him?" Winter asked her.

"I've been briefed already," she intoned. "This one's for you."

"A dozen mobs united by a need to move and launder large sums of money safely. The firm, Intermat, is made up of the leadership of each group, with the president selected by them from among themselves. Just like the Pope's selection by a vote of fellow cardinals. There are at least ten major criminal organizations with links to the firm. Once they put their funds in Intermat's accounts, the money is as safe as it would be in a bank. Intermat invests the pooled currency in deals that promise a healthy profit, and all members share equally in the profits."

"And if our government is aware of this, how does this firm stay in business?" Winter asked.

Clayton took his pipe out of his mouth and smiled. "Isn't a poisonous snake in a glass case less dangerous than one running around the house loose?" he asked. "Serge Sarnov runs Intermat's department of policy enforcement. Ex-GRU, where he specialized in handling tricky state problems. This picture was taken last night at Douglas International Airport, a few miles from here."

"Where is he now?"

"In the wind," Clayton said. "You should keep an eye out for him."

"He's involved in the kidnapping?"

Clayton shrugged. "Not directly, but he has a stake in its success."

"And his connection to the Dockerys?" Winter pressed, growing low on patience.

The next picture was of a man who stood shaking Sarnov's hand in the airport's baggage area. A third shot showed the second man putting Sarnov's bags in the back of a dark Tahoe. The pictures were all taken from different security cameras.

"Here is the connection. Lt. Maxwell T. Randall, twenty-seven. Ex–Special Forces. Randall is one of Colonel Bryce's associates—served with him the last two years Bryce was active military. You don't want to mess with either of these men. The government is actively pursuing them and they are connected to continuing investigations beyond this. If you tangle with these two, the

consequences could be unpleasant no matter the out-
come of the meeting, if you get my drift."

"If they don't bother me, I won't bother them back,"
Winter said, seriously. "What's Sarnov's involvement with
Bryce?"

"Intermat was dealing for the weapons that Bryce's arrest short-circuited. Bryce is the only one who knows
where the shipment is. The only other man who may
have known is a dead undercover agent who got killed
before he could pass the intelligence to his handlers. The
firm has millions invested in the shipment Bryce has.
They won't walk away from it."

Alexa said, "Bryce had to have figured that if he told
Intermat where the container was before they sprung
him, he'd either do life, get the needle, or the firm would
kill him to keep him from talking."

"So, if Sarnov didn't do it, who grabbed the Dockerys?" Winter asked. "Randall?"

Clayton sucked loudly on his Falcon pipe. "Randall
was in Atlanta when the Dockerys were snatched. M.I.
ran the voice of the person who phoned Judge Fondren
after the snatch for a matching print. They got one the
FBI had filed as that of an unidentified female doing
business with a local syndicate."

"At the Bureau, we call them the Cornpone Mafia,"
Alexa told Winter. "They are made up of small southern
groups that are hooked up to a larger syndicate based in
Kansas City."

"That female voice has showed up several times on
taps on people doing business with this local bunch,"
Clayton said. "This one is a particularly challenging one.

Stanley Smoot, who goes by 'Peanut,' is at the top. Peanut pays the best legal firm in the region a healthy retainer, and they have managed to extricate him from every crime he's been charged with over the past twenty years. He's street-smart, a classic psychopathic personality, and he keeps his books in his head. His lawyer of record is Ross Laughlin, the senior partner at Price, Courtney, Laughlin, Vance and Associates. Of interest is that Ross Laughlin also happens to be Colonel Hunter Bryce's attorney. Laughlin's firm has fifty top attorneys in Washington, D.C., ninety-seven in Charlotte, and seventy in Miami. The old boy has some very impressive connections."

"Ross Laughlin knows everybody in Washington worth knowing, and contributes to all of the right people of both parties," Alexa said.

"Got a picture of Peanut Smoot?" Winter asked.

Clayton found one in a second file folder and put it beside the one of Randall.

Winter studied it.

"Should be easy to spot," Alexa said.

"Peanut's family has been involved in criminal enterprises as far back as records go. He's got a rap sheet goes back to his teens, but like I said, last twenty years he's been golden. He is the highest up the chain anybody's charted, and I'd say he is the top guy. Peanut's crew deals in hijacking, running untaxed cigarettes, prostitution, selling stolen firearms up North to gangbangers, extortion, car theft and chop shops, insurance fraud, loan-sharking, pawnshops, stolen credit cards, gambling, counterfeit sporting-event tickets. Not sure what the connection to Colonel Bryce is. Maybe Peanut does business with him or maybe he was just hired to do the heavy lifting on this kidnapping. But the Smoots took the Dockerys. The woman's voice is all the connection you need. The voice belongs to one of their own, and it shares definite regional accentual similarities with the rest of the clan. A female, probably mid-twenties to early thirties, who wears dentures, is all the description I have. Called the judge from a pay phone outside a convenience store on Central Boulevard. Her voice has never been caught except on pay phones and disposable cells."

"And Laughlin is the connection," Winter said.

"No proof of that," Alexa said. "Big risk for a man at his social, economic, and professional level."

Winter frowned but held back comment. Of course Laughlin was the connection between Bryce, the Smoots, and Intermat. He couldn't believe Alexa questioned it. An attorney being a crook wasn't a stretch in Winter's mind. The more powerful he was, the more above reproach he felt, the easier it would be to go bad. A man like that could see himself as smarter than anyone in law enforcement and feel bulletproof.

"How large is the Smoot crew?" he asked.

Alexa said, "Peanut's crew is made up of fifty to sixty uncles, aunts, cousins, even his own children. It's a tribe that settled in the forties in remote northern South Carolina, about an hour from here."

"Will *they* kill the Dockerys personally?" Winter asked.

Clayton nodded. "Killing a woman and child would be easy money."

"Then we have to get to the Smoots," Winter said.

"They're our starting place," Alexa agreed.

"I'll put together a field file for you with all the appropriate intel on the Smoots," Clayton said.

Winter stared at Peanut's wide-apart almond-shaped eyes, the smug arrogant smile belonging to a man who'd enjoyed a long successful run.

Winter knew that he and Peanut would meet sooner rather than later.

18

Ross Laughlin took the first-aid kit from Rudy, located and broke the cotton-sleeved vial of smelling salts, and held it under Peanut's nose. The big man came to life immediately, kicking and cursing.

"Ga-damm!" he yelled. "What happened?"

"You fell," Ross said.

"Fell hell. Fell where?"

"Were felled," Rudy offered.

Peanut sat up, put a hand to the back of his neck, and moved his head side to side. "Damn it all. My back and my neck hurts. And my chin. Was it Randall? He get behind me?"

"Sarnov," Ross said as he tossed the vial into the trash can. "Rudy, help Mr. Smoot to his feet."

"That little commie dick-smoker," Peanut growled. "I'll blow his head off."

Peanut pulled a handgun out from his belt and Ross Laughlin shuddered at the sight of it. All he needed was for this fool to start brandishing a gun, and somebody calling the cops to the building. All that mattered was getting past Monday morning.

"Calm down, Peanut," Ross soothed. Smoot had always had a temper that was very difficult to get the lid back on. "That's all, Rudy."

"Yes, sir," Rudy said instantly. He took the first-aid kit and left the room, closing the door behind him.

"Put that weapon away," Ross ordered. "You can't do anything to Sarnov."

"That little Lenin-loving queer—"

"Peanut," Ross said, infusing a hint of fatherly disapproval and concern. "Calling him names won't help us. Even if what he did was unforgivable." The lawyer fought back laughter when he remembered seeing Peanut crash-landing on the floor after going through a very expensive coffee table.

"If I'd been paying attention, he'd a got the ass kicking of his potato-drinking life. I'm lucky the glass didn't slice my damn head off."

"I guess your coat saved you," Ross said, lifting the coffee table's scratched walnut base and setting it away from the glass. Luckily, the wood hadn't been shattered by the big lummox's weight. "Unfortunately, my vintage Noguchi wasn't wearing a leather NASCAR jacket."

"A three-thousand-dollar coat." Peanut turned so he could see his backside in the mirror behind the wet bar.

"Hellfire!" He tugged off his jacket and looked at the cuts the glass had made in the smooth surface. "Damn," he bellowed. "My number three's destroyed!"

His language, more so even than his appearance, had once made Ross's skin crawl. But over the years, the hick had brought in a fortune. Of all the groups Ross had earning for him, the Smoots made more than all the others combined. And Peanut wasn't a slouch in the instincts department. He had more street smarts than any criminal Ross Laughlin had ever known. He kept complicated deals in his head, and his mental numbers were never wrong. He had, as best as Ross could figure, a genetic disposition toward criminality. Were the man normal, he could have been successful at any legitimate business venture, but Peanut Smoot couldn't think about a situation without viewing it through a filter of greed and larceny.

Gun in hand, Peanut started from the room. There was an explosive-temper aspect to the Smoots, which sometimes made problems. They got to a point and they lost it, acting rashly and worrying about the consequences later.

"Peanut!" Ross said sternly. "Listen to me. This is almost over. We need to maintain our relationship with the Russians. If you touch Sarnov, we both know what will happen. We can do profitable business with them for a long time, but if we make a stupid move, they'll take everything."

"They're going to take it all anyway if they can, and this is a test we're seeing. Those changes to the deal are to see if you'll blink, and you did. From this day on out, the Russkies are going to be chipping away, taking bigger and bigger bites. If you don't send them a message back, we're history anyway. Why didn't you tell him we're partners, that I'm not hired help?"

"Because," Ross said, his mind whirring in search of an explanation Peanut would buy. If only for a few hours, and then it wouldn't matter. "You just deal with the collateral as we discussed," Ross told him.

Ross knew that the Smoots were finished. Sarnov had stood over Peanut's unconscious form and told Ross that the Russians were in for good and that they were taking over the Smoots' territory and rackets. Laughlin hadn't argued. In fact, the prospect of Intermat taking over was appealing to him. All of Peanut's holdings were in accounts Laughlin owned with Peanut. And he had Peanut's power of attorney in his safe.

"The Dockery part has to be done right. When the time comes, I'll handle the Russians. We're partners. Trust me."

"I do trust you, Mr. Laughlin."

"Please call me Ross," Ross said, smiling warmly and placing his hand on Peanut's shoulder paternally. "We are so much more than mere business partners."

"I won't let you down, Mr. Laughlin."

19

Dixie Smoot just hoped the little bitch tried something. She'd love to see the look on her skinny face when Dixie gave her a good lesson about what happened to people who looked down their noses at other people.

The kid was finally asleep. A little cough medicine in his juice sure took his little foot off the accelerator.

Dixie wasn't exactly the mothering kind, but she kind of liked the baby. He was cute as a puppy, but kids were all more pain in your ass as not. Not like a dog you can feed and water and leave outside as much of the time as you wanted.

This old trailer was good enough to stay in during hunting seasons, but the coating of dust that covered every flat surface like rust was disgusting. The guys expected Dixie to do the cleaning, but she only did so when Peanut himself told her to do it, and as lightly as she could get by with. Soon as you swept it up, more took its place. Outside, the ground was covered with an inch of the flour-fine silt, and it fell off your shoes onto the linoleum. The TV screen was always murky on account of it, and it got in your hair, your clothes, and under your fingernails so you always felt nasty. It didn't bother the boys, but nothing bothered her brothers. Well, except Ferny Ernest, the baby. Everybody else called him Click but her. He never came out here to the trailer, because he didn't much care one way or the other about hunting. He didn't like poison ivy, chiggers, or snakes, or spiders. The others—Buck and the twins, Burt and Curt—would roll naked in chigger grass and pack their jaws full of poison ivy if they had to in order to slaughter a deer or a turkey or anything else that was made out of meat. During deer or turkey season you couldn't find a Smoot unless you were riding a buck through the woods.

The land, about 940 acres of woods, clover fields, and water holes, was for hunting. The place was thick with game, and Peanut and the boys spent a fortune on keeping it that way. And Lord help you if you was to get caught poaching on it. People who knew the family would leave a wounded deer they'd tracked there for the buzzards before they'd risk being caught by the Smoots while dragging it off their land.

Dixie worked out at Gold's Gym. She could bench-press 270 pounds. She spent part of her day in there going from one machine to the other until she was sweating to beat the band. She couldn't outwrestle her three older brothers, because they were a lot bigger, and stronger than bulls. Buck loved staying bulked up and was proud to say that nobody had ever kicked his ass. Not even when he was a Marine, which he was before he got dishonorably discharged for something he would never tell anybody about. Part of Buck's trouble was the steroids that kept his face broke out, but he'd always just been mean as hell for no good reason. You couldn't like Buck if you tried, and that was how he liked it.

Dixie had heard from Burt, who was mad at Buck, that his older brother had been feeling the skinny woman up, saying she asked him to screw her, and that he was going to do just that before it was all over. If you were a woman, you wouldn't want to spread your legs for Buck, because he couldn't get aroused unless he was hurting the girl. That was just how he was, and everybody in the family knew it.

Dixie was just as tough as her three older brothers were and smarter than all three of them put together. She didn't get as much money as the boys, but that was supposedly because they got their hands dirtier. Peanut had always said that planned killings were man's work. Dixie did whatever her daddy said to, and if he told her to cut somebody up and throw the pieces in the river, she could do it as well as her brothers could. What did testicles have to do with getting bloody?

Dixie's instructions had been straight. Peanut said she was to watch the pair until he said kill them. She was to make sure that none of her brothers messed around with the woman because it wasn't right to do it to her under such pitiful circumstances. But Peanut didn't tell Dixie she couldn't teach her a lesson or two.

Dixie looked down at the sleeping child and, despite telling them to get it done, she'd bet the damn twins were out looking for deer signs, and hadn't yet put a shovel blade into the ground.

20

Clayton Able, who had taken a break to go to his own room, returned. He opened another file. "You'll want to take a look at Smoot family members and known associates and which rocks you might have to turn over to find them."

Clayton placed the pictures down faceup, one at a time, like a salesman showing his product to prospective customers. The first picture was a mug shot of an unpleasant young man in his twenties.

"Here's what you'd get if you crossed Jay Leno and a silverback," Clayton said. "Stanley Smoot, Jr., who goes by the very original tag of Buck. Peanut's firstborn. Twenty-nine and trouble with a capital 'T.' Graduated high school at twenty due to a few teachers he couldn't scare the crap out of. Tried team sports, but Buck was prone to collecting personal fouls and generally considered a negative influence on his teammates. He could have been a poster boy for the Young Sociopath Club if there'd been one in his high school."

Buck bore a striking resemblance to his father, Peanut, but the son's scalp was accented by mogul-like waves—as if the skin on his skull was doing an impression of wavy hair. Buck's face was filled with small skin eruptions. He wore three heavy steel hoops in his left ear. His head was supported by a neck so thick that it would have looked at home on a rutting elk. He reminded Winter of a maniacal version of a long-jawed simpleton cartoon character from *Mad* magazine.

"This picture was a police-sponsored portrait to commemorate the occasion of an arrest for aggravated assault, charges dropped."

"Who'd he assault?" Winter asked.

"Exotic dancer by the name of Kitty Breeze. Kitty initially told the cops that Buck bit her nipple off, flattened her nose, broke her jaw, and shattered her eye socket. After he was arrested and placed in a lineup, she couldn't identify him and said the man who actually did it was a Mexican."

In a surveillance shot, Buck was standing beside a truck in his boxer shorts. Buck's shoulders rippled with muscles; his arms and hands were massive. Below the muscles, Buck had a swollen belly, his legs were amazingly thin, and his feet appeared to be too small and narrow to support him. It was as if he'd been put together out of the parts of two people and one of them had been a middle-aged accountant with a penchant for beer.

"Four months in the Marine Corps before they kicked his ass out. Seems the Corps didn't pay proper attention to his psychological profile. Except for thumping heads and scaring people, Buck would be jobless. He's a product of blending suspect genetic material, the brain of a Neanderthal, physical exercise, and chemical abuse. Suspect in at least a dozen killings for hire, and more than that many young ladies over the years—all of whom his family was associated with on some level. Dancers, prostitutes, employees of shady businesses."

The next set of pictures was of a very large pair of men in football regalia. Feature-wise they resembled Buck and Peanut, but each was half again Buck's size.

"These young men are the Smoot twins, Burt and Curt. This is a newer picture."

In the next photo, the twins had obviously turned their backs on the weight training that had given them their impressive high school figures, and hadn't stayed ahead of the results of consuming copious amounts of carbohydrates and beer. Winter couldn't help but wonder if the twins smiled like idiots all the time, or just when they were in the presence of a camera. They certainly got their share of the Smoot genes.

Clayton sucked on his pipe loudly. "They were linemen. Big college programs courted them, but they had problems with a lack of motivation, and their SAT scores sucked.

"These two aren't explosive, like Buck, but they aren't any less dangerous. To the best of their abilities, they do what Daddy says."

Next Clayton tossed out a picture of a woman, who looked enough like Buck in a wig to be comical.

"This breathtaking vision of southern womanhood is Dora Jeanne Smoot, known affectionately as Dixie. She is Papa's little angel. Dixie's into body sculpting."

"She's a lot like her brothers," Alexa said.

Clayton said, "She collects money, keeps Papa's painted women in line, and furnishes steroids to gyms, coaches, and her brother Buck. Dixie can do pretty much whatever the boys can. She was born with brittle teeth, so she had them all pulled and wears porcelain choppers."

"The woman with dentures on phone taps," Winter said.

"Almost certainly," Clayton agreed. "No voice pattern for Dixie on file. Our dentally challenged mystery woman always uses pay phones, and Dixie does the same. She is suspected of committing at least seven prostitution-related murders on her father's behalf. Problem pimps, a few whores. Dixie's one very nasty piece of psychotica." He turned over another picture. "And this is Ferny Ernest Smoot, called Click by his family and friends.

"Inherited the family brain trust. No arrests. Had some minor behavioral problems in school, but otherwise Click's probably as harmless as you can be, given his blood and nurturing."

"He doesn't look like a member of the same circus," Alexa said. "He's normal looking, sort of in a Civil War tintype way."

"If his hair was cut, he wouldn't look like the lead guitarist for Led Zeppelin," Clayton said.

"We still have to find them," Alexa said. "We can start by checking out their listed addresses."

Winter lifted the picture of the youngest Smoot. Something about the face tickled a memory, so he studied the eyes visible through the curtains of wavy red hair. He knew them, the skinny neck, slumping shoulders. And he knew where he had seen the young man before.

"Don't need an address for this one," Winter said. "I know where he was twenty minutes ago."

Alexa and Clayton looked at him.

"He was sitting in the lobby when I got here. Without the curly locks. Wearing khakis, a button-down shirt under a collared Polo jacket, and buckskin oxfords. Looked like a preppy student."

"How the hell can that be?" Clayton said. "You sure?"

Winter nodded.

"Of course he's sure," Alexa said. "Coincidence?"

"No," Winter said. "He was settled in. And I thought at the time he was paying me a lot of attention. When I arrived in the lobby, he was there with a computer open in his lap."

"How the hell could he be onto us?" Clayton asked.

Winter said, "I just know he was watching me when I came in."

"He must have followed Hailey Fondren here when he came here for lunch," Alexa said, obviously angry with herself.

"Why did you insist on meeting the judge in the damned restaurant?" Clayton said.

"Click doesn't know who I am," Alexa said.

"He can't know about my association with either you or Fondren," Clayton told her. "We arrived at the hotel separately. I've never spoken to Hailey Fondren period, or to you in public."

"How did he latch onto me?" Alexa said, frowning. Thinking.

"I'd bet he was following Judge Fondren. The judge came here, Click saw you, and he stuck on you to check you out. Maybe someone else is following the judge."

"What can he know about me? I'm registered under my name, but not as an FBI agent. All he knows is that I had lunch with the judge," Alexa told Clayton. "If the kid was watching the dining room, we all left separately. You and I went up in separate elevator cars."

"You know," Clayton said to Alexa, "I think he was at a table in the dining room. Had a backpack by his foot. Hailey came in after you and I were already seated at different tables. I'm not sure when the kid showed up. I was watching for the judge and you, but I'm sure he wasn't there when I came down."

"Christ. Christ. Okay, let's think this through," Alexa said. "Did I look at you? I can't remember. Did the judge? I think he might have turned to look at you."

"I was monitoring you through a reflection in the glass. I never looked directly at you."

Alexa was freaking out, which was not at all like her, Winter thought. He smiled reassuringly. "Relax, Lex. Click's just snooping."

"Relax? If they know the judge called the FBI in, Lucy and Elijah are dead."

"You're thinking that Click being onto you is a bad thing?"

"He saw you, too," Alexa reminded him. "Of course it's a bad thing. What the hell could be good about it? We don't know what he knows."

Winter smiled. "And he doesn't know that *we* know about *him*. Seems like a good thing."

21

Peanut Smoot's back was killing him, and his dislike for Sarnov was a full-blown hatred. There wasn't any repairing the #3 NASCAR jacket, but that wasn't nearly as bad as the fact that the Russian bastard had made Peanut look like a fool in front of Mr. Laughlin. No matter how much plain-sense talk Mr. Laughlin came up with about business necessities or how dangerous the Russians were, Peanut was going to deal Sarnov a hand of slow death. Damn the whole bunch of Russians. Their business would go on no matter where the buyers came from, because the merchandise was in demand and profitable to their buyers.

What was one more hole in the good earth? Who could prove it was Peanut who did anything to Sarnov? Accidents happen and people go missing all the time.

Planning the bastard's end made Peanut feel better. Wasn't going to be as simple as a twelve-gauge root canal. It was a fact that Serge Sarnov had a dirt nap in his close-up future.

There were so many possibilities for dealing punishment out that a man would have to flip a coin all day to figure which one it was going to be. For example, you might wrap a little foreign bastard in sheets soaked in blood and let a brace of dogs go to work on him for a while to get him screaming and begging. Then, while he was just scared good, you could hang him up in the skinning shed and use lopping shears and take him apart a piece at a time. No, there was no shortage of ways to pay a feller off who'd wronged you.

Peanut checked his rearview religiously as he drove. Fixes or not, you could never be too careful when it came to the cops. And that wasn't just the Feds, who were always looking for some new way to stick their noses into your business. If old Judge Fondren did go to the FBI, and they *were* looking for the woman and that baby, there just wasn't any way they could tie a Smoot in on it. Only members of Peanut's immediate family knew about the judge's daughter and her baby, and not a one of them would ever tell anybody squat. Mr. Laughlin was one secret-keeping son of a bitch. Sarnov and Randall knew some of it, but, they had more to lose if the cops solved it than anybody. So let old Judge Fondren do whatever the hell he wanted, and let him tell everybody he could find—it wouldn't do him a little bitty bit of good.

Once Bryce was cut loose, there wasn't nothing that anybody could do no matter if Fondren said he was forced or not. Double jeopardy wasn't going to happen, because there wasn't no proving that Bryce was part of anything.

Peanut was starting to feel better. His back was going to have a hell of a sore spot where the gun had been tucked in his belt, and he'd have to get a new jacket to replace his personally autographed #3, but Dale sure couldn't sign it. . . .

Peanut picked up the cell phone and dialed Click.

"Yeah?"

"Anything?"

"Naw."

"Okay, then get on out of there," Peanut told his son. "I'll call if I need you for anything else."

"Like when?"

"Like when I damn well please," Peanut snapped good-naturedly.

"To do what?"

"Wait and see, son." Peanut closed the phone. Most of the time, Peanut was fond of all his children. Click was the special one. And not just because he was the baby and all. He was as smart as any contestant on *Jeopardy,* spoiled rotten, and too good-looking for his own good. But once Peanut was out of the picture—and that wouldn't be very soon—that boy was the future of the Smoots. The others would either accept it when the time came or they'd end up like all those hairy elephants that got stuck in the ice way back when. Extinct.

Truth be told, once Peanut was dead, it wouldn't really matter if the whole bunch did piss away everything he had accumulated for them that Mr. Laughlin had legitimized. Not like any of them appreciated any of it anyhow.

Peanut slammed his *Johnny Cash at Folsom* CD into the player, turned the volume up, and sang along to the music.

Click would be all right.

And to hell with the rest of them hairy-ass elephants.

22

The second he was released from his spy duty, Click Smoot shoved his laptop into his backpack and rushed to the parking garage to get his car. He planned to spend the rest of his day burning holes in other people's credit in a few choice stores.

He got into his new Nissan Z, laid the backpack on the passenger floorboard, and drove out of the garage. The rain was falling heavily, so he flipped on both his headlights and his wipers.

Click reached under the dash and pressed a button opening a secret compartment large enough to hold two packages of credit cards each joined with a rubber band. Each package included two or three credit cards in an actual name and a driver's license also in that name but with a recent photograph of Click on it.

Click used his intellect to make money the modern way and was already expanding the family's take despite their amazing technological ignorance. Robbing, hijacking, illegal gambling clubs, whores, drugs, extortion, insurance fraud, murder for hire, and all the rest of what the family was into was the old way, and Click wanted no part of it. He wasn't interested in being killed over some whore, or drugs, or a failed hijacking because some driver belonged to the NRA and had a gun he wanted to fire at some criminal so he could get written up in their magazine.

Click was concentrating on a future that few of the people in the family's business could grasp. As far as his siblings were concerned, anything that was computerized, digitized, or involved something they couldn't fold and hold was too abstract for them. The average Smoot's capacity for grasping new technology was akin to a cat's ability to appreciate fine art.

Click wasn't like the other Smoots. Once upon a time the difference had been painful, but as he grew up he had come to appreciate how lucky he was. He had an I.Q. of 160. He had discovered early that a clean-cut young man was practically invisible.

Click didn't hate his family. He just felt sorry for and was overwhelmingly embarrassed about them. He had come to the conclusion that the only thing he had in common with them was a larcenous gene. Like all Smoots, Ferny Ernest was repelled by legitimate work, was greedy, and, like a Gypsy, got an almost orgasmic thrill when he was stealing from outsiders. Only a stolen quarter was worth spending and only a sucker depended on a steady paycheck.

Click had explained to his father that the family could make more money using keyboards than they could with an army of soldiers. And Peanut was smart enough to realize that Click had something different and had supported his son's forays into the world of computer-related crime.

When he was ready to make his big move, he would work a dozen big-dollar scams simultaneously, snatch millions, and be cashed out and long gone before anybody saw him coming. He had targeted banks and investment firms that moved millions daily. He would stand beside a flowing river of funds and, using a few keystrokes as his explosives, blow a hole in the levee. He would let the river flow into his canal a bit, then plug the hole and watch the canals he had built, each moving a tributary's worth, join together and make a river of his own.

Soon.

Peanut's latest interest in Click's computers was as an avenue for selling pornography, which he was sure he could generate, and in collecting credit card information from the horny hordes that subscribed. For example, you set up a website for bait, and you chose a subject that rich people would be looking at. They visit, you run into their computer and plant a seed in it that collects their financial information from their hard drives. You didn't even need to ask for credit card numbers, because people usually had that information on their drives.

Click had to admit that the porn thing would work, but it would attract the mob's attention since the mob controlled porn and they would demand a big slice. Dixie had all the male and female prostitutes they would ever need. Buck wanted to be a producer, but that would be like hiring a wino to work in a crystal shop and putting him up on stilts.

He parked in front of the Media Warehouse. Ferny Ernest looked at the credit cards again, decided on an

American Express card that belonged to Edmund C. Kellogg, and put the others back in the secret compartment.

"Another day, another dollar," Click said as he opened the car's door.

23

Thanks to Clayton Able's intelligence-gathering, Winter and Alexa knew who the kidnappers were. And thanks to Winter's knack for remembering faces, they had a subject to focus on.

After years of recovering federal fugitives, Winter had developed an ability to memorize primary facial features. The shape of the jaw and chin, the nose and the eyes, remain constant, where hair was the first thing people altered. The second change was of their style of dress and by utilizing distractions of one sort or another like hats, glasses, and items of clothing. In the real world, very few fugitives had the means for or the access to reconstructive facial surgery. Despite what movies wanted you to think, there were a limited number of plastic surgeons who fabricated new faces in their secret clinics or the kitchens of hideouts.

Alexa had cell phones for herself and Winter, connected by speed dial both to each other and to Clayton, who would remain in the hotel room hooked up to his sources. Alexa had acquired a GPS tracker in case they needed to follow a vehicle. Now, since there was moving-target surveillance to be conducted, and the target had seen the members of the covering team, Winter had decided to tag Click's car and see where he led them.

Alexa's tracking unit had a five-mile range. The receiver was similar to the sort of handheld GPS outdoorsmen used, the small screen showing named lines for streets.

Since they probably wouldn't be returning to the hotel for a good while, Alexa and Winter took Clayton's files on the Smoots, and the equipment they figured they might need. To avoid coming out into the lobby, they used the fire stairs, going through a side door that opened into the parking deck. Alexa unlocked her rental car and put everything inside it before she positioned herself near the mouth of the deck, which gave her a view of the entrance.

According to Clayton's files on the Smoot crew, son Click had two registered vehicles: a silver 2004 Nissan Z and a 1974 GMC panel van. Winter hoped he was driving one of them. He took one bug, a dark gray plastic wafer with a magnetized disk on one side, and found a silver Z parked on the deck's second level, its grille facing out. Winter checked the tag to make sure it was Click's, then he stuck the bug behind the license plate so that only its thin-wire antenna was visible.

Winter's cell phone began vibrating in his pocket just before he heard footsteps approaching. He moved silently to a position behind the vehicle parked beside the Z and waited. He heard an electronic chirping, and the door to the Z open and shut. The engine roared to life and the Z drove off down the ramp.

Winter sprinted to his truck and speed-dialed Alexa while he was backing out.

"I tried to let you know Click was coming up," she said.

"I planted the bug," he said. "You got a signal on him?"

"Ten and ten," she said, her voice flat and professional. "I'm pulling out behind him. Will feed location and direction."

24

Hank Trammel, Winter's law-enforcement mentor, once told Winter that law enforcement was like a twenty-four-hour, seven-day-a-week gambling casino. The bad guys ran the house, so while there were hot streaks for the cop players, over the course of any lawman's career the house odds prevailed. The best a lawman could do was to ride the hot streaks and grin and bear it when the deck went against you. Since you couldn't count on luck, you used your brain, worked hard, and called upon your skills to raise your odds of success. Life-and-death cases like this one were the high-stakes table. If Lucy and her child were still alive, they wouldn't be breathing any longer than necessary.

Winter didn't know why Click had left the hotel, but he was sure the boy hadn't run because he knew anybody was onto him.

The rain and the traffic acted as an effective veil. Winter used the cell phone's earpiece so he could talk hands-free. He stayed a quarter mile behind Alexa, who remained far enough behind Click so she could keep him in sight, but far enough back so he wouldn't notice her car.

"You think somebody spelled him at the hotel?" Alexa asked.

"Doesn't matter."

"If we'd been a couple of minutes later in realizing who he was, he'd have been long gone. We couldn't have spooked him, could we?"

"No," Winter said.

"Not like we have a lot of leads, if this doesn't pan out," Alexa said.

"The fact that he was tagging after the judge is more than enough evidence for me that the Smoots are involved in the abduction."

"Clayton's the best there is at gathering and interpreting intelligence. Far as I know, if the man says he's sure, he's right on target."

"He certainly gathered a lot of information in a very short time. Does he have his own firm?"

"He's part of a larger network, I guess you'd say."

"They know he hacks intel systems?"

"Well, if they didn't trust him, he couldn't do it. Not in these troubled times. The intel community has been under so much pressure lately."

"You've used him on official business?"

"I've used him in an advisory capacity. Brass doesn't like agents going outside, especially when it turns out they are successful where we weren't. I don't have to tell you how it works."

"Territorial imperative meets the Peter Principle," Winter said.

"All I know is that without Clayton, we wouldn't have been able to get our hands around this one. If he hadn't come in, I'd have done about as well standing on a median strip with a cardboard sign that said, 'Stop if you've seen any missing people.'"

Winter laughed. "You couldn't say which people."

"Click might not know any of the specifics about the grab or where our people are being held," Alexa said, sadly.

They were driving on Independence Boulevard in light traffic. Click wasn't trying to be evasive in the least.

"What do you hear from Precious?" Winter asked.

"Why do you ask?"

Precious was Antonia Keen's nickname. Antonia was Alexa's younger sister, but before they had found a permanent foster home, Alexa had also been a mother to the younger girl. Antonia had been a tomboy with a capital "T." Winter had never particularly cared for her, and perhaps that was because she had openly resented his relationship with her older sister. He understood the psychology, but he couldn't forgive her hostility toward him.

"Why wouldn't I ask?" he said to Alexa. "Last I heard

she was burning a path to the top of the Army. That still the case?"

"You have me in sight, Massey?"

"Sure do."

"Our boy's turning into a shopping center," Alexa said.

"I see him."

Winter noted that Alexa had just avoided answering his innocent question about her younger sister. Maybe Antonia had done something to upset Alexa, but more likely Alexa had too much on her mind at the moment to make small talk.

Winter put his mind on two people being held by scary people.

25

Lucy Dockery had lived a life of privilege. As the only child of a successful divorce attorney and a federal judge, she had attended the best schools, lived in nice homes, and enjoyed social contact with wealthy and influential people. At that moment, if she could have gone back to the worst day of her life and relived it over and over for eternity, Lucy would have done that rather than to have gone through the hours since she had been kidnapped.

Lucy's previous worst day had begun like any other, and was as mundane as any before it. Walter and her mother had left to go to an antique store to look at a grandfather clock for her father's birthday. Lucy had intended to go along with them, but she had stayed home with Elijah because he felt feverish. Around four P.M., while she was loading the washing machine, the doorbell rang. She had opened the front door to her father standing with their minister.

Her father had said simply, "Lucy, Walter and your mother are gone." The words hit her like a hammer blow that left her seeing everything through a watery filter of shock. After that, he had sat in a chair and cried like a baby. She had stood there wishing that she had been with Walter.

Battling tears, Lucy thought about that again now, recalling how her sense of life being ordered and perfect had drained away in that moment, leaving her alone in a dark, frightening place. Lucy had been cast out from a paradise into a world where everything had sharp edges and where the super-heated air wasn't breathable. Her loss had taken her like some predator striking out of nowhere and grabbing her up in its jaws. It had shaken her until she was empty of everything but fear, and an awful, unbearable blackness. And there was no doubt that she would have joined Walter had it not been for their Elijah.

But the day a drunk driver had killed her husband and her mother was a sunny stroll in the park compared to the day she was now living.

Hopeless. At that moment, Lucy wished once more, as she had often for the past year, that she could just curl up and die. What did these hideous people have in mind for her child and her? The worst that could happen would probably happen no matter what she did. So, what should she do? What could she do? She knew what Walter would tell her. *Save our son. You are the only chance Elijah has. Death will come to you just like it came to me. Live until you die, Lucy. Let our son know me through you—you who knew me better than anybody.*

The distinctive growling of what sounded like an approaching motorcycle refocused her thoughts. She had heard the sound earlier when two or three of them had roared off together.

The woman left the trailer, slamming the door.

Another metal door, very near the trailer, creaked open. Lucy had heard that door open and close before, always before someone came or right after they left.

Straining, Lucy heard angry voices.

She was sure the male voice was the vile man with scaly hands. The woman and the man were arguing about something. Lucy heard the word "twins" used several times. She also heard the names Buck and Dixie and believed those were probably their names.

The metal door slammed again.

The motorcycle started and roared off.

The woman stomped back into the trailer and slammed the door.

Elijah started crying.

The woman stormed into the bedroom, the light pouring in blinding Lucy. She put her hand up in front of her face to protect her eyes from it.

"I'm fixing to have to leave you two here by yourself for a few minutes. Don't you even think about trying to get out, because I'll know it if you do and I'll take it out on your kid. You got that?"

Lucy nodded.

"You just remember that watching one of you is easier than watching both of you."

"I understand."

"You damn well better, missy. You better. Because as the Lord above is my witness, I will twist his little head right off and pitch it out into the woods for the coyotes to clean. And stop cryin'."

"I understand."

The woman plucked Elijah out of the playpen and brought him to Lucy.

Elijah, realizing that the silent woman on the bed in the strange room was his mother, clung to her. Lucy watched as the big woman snatched a coat from the arm of the couch, and slammed the door going outside.

Lucy heard the outside metal door creak open and slam shut again. A few seconds later she heard what sounded like another motorcycle roar to life and drive away. *The other door must be to a shed . . . or a gate in a fence.*

For a precious minute she held Eli to her, caressing his head, kissing his cheeks.

"Momou. Momou. Momou," he said over and over.

"It's okay, Elijah," she told him. "I love you, baby. I love you *so* much. You are going to be safe." *Your father says so.*

She thought about the big woman's threat, and she believed the woman would make good on her word by hurting them, but she couldn't make herself believe the woman would actually kill them. If these people intended to do that, why hadn't they already done so? Everybody knew that abductees had no value once they were dead. Lucy was increasingly sure this was about money. A ransom. *But,* she thought, *the woman is obviously unstable. People in these circumstances do die, and for your sake, Walter, I can't risk that happening to Elijah.*

FREE. *A four-letter word for getting the hell out of Dodge.*

26

Peanut Smoot strolled into the brightly lit drugstore and made a beeline for the prescription counter in the rear. The store was one in a chain of fifteen regional stores owned by a pharmacist Peanut did business with. The owner had a problem that involved deviant sexual needs that respectable people didn't advertise, and Peanut had fixed it up so the man could safely get the urge met. As a result, the owner had been recruited to buy any pharmaceutical drugs Peanut's people came across as well as the other kinds of drugstore items you might find—like shampoo, tampons, and batteries—in a truck you'd hijacked.

When the owner spotted Peanut through the observation window in his office, he hurried out into the area where three lab-coated pharmacists were filling small bottles from large ones. The man seemed a little nervous, but that was probably because they usually met late at night after the employees had left.

"Mr. Smoot," he said.

"I need something for back pain, George."

"What type of pain?" The skin on George's face seemed stretched tighter than usual, his eyes darting around the store behind Peanut like he was suspicious that something odd was going on out there in the aisles.

"The back pain kind."

"By that I mean how did you injure your back?"

"I fell off a ladder."

"I have just the thing," George said, holding a finger in the air. He darted off into a back storage room. When he returned, he handed Peanut a box of over-the-counter pain medication and, after winking at Peanut, said loudly enough to be heard, "These will work as well as anything nonprescription."

Peanut handed the druggist a ten-dollar bill and waited for him to go through the cash register motions and make change for it.

"Please come again," George said with a forced cheerfulness, like he was talking to just anybody who had come in to spend money in a store he earned by marrying the owner's daughter, who herself looked like the Pillsbury Dough Boy with hair that looked like a hat made out of straw painted red.

George had made up the incapacitation liquid Peanut needed to make the Dockery woman stay put. It was a potent blend of chemicals that doctors used for operating and had the effect of making it impossible for someone to move until it wore off.

Back in the truck, Peanut opened the small pasteboard box and took out a bottle that contained, not the blue caplets the box promised, but a couple dozen capsules filled with tiny colored balls.

Peanut swallowed two of the caps and chased them with a carbonated sip of warm soda out of a can he'd had sitting in the holder a good while.

When his unregistered cell rang, he saw that it was a familiar pay phone number. Peanut knew that cellular calls were not private. Ask Pablo Escobar about using a cellular when the government wants to track you by your voice.

"What?"

"There's a little problem." It was his son Buck's voice.

"What?" Peanut felt the hollow burning in his stomach he always got when Buck said he had a problem. Buck's little problems tended to be larger than he'd admit to.

"Damn twins."

Peanut took a deep breath and shifted in his seat. "What'd they do?"

"I gave them that little digging job to do, but when I came back they'd gone off. Hadn't more than just started it."

"Go find 'em and you get it done."

"I don't know where to look."

"Hellfire, boy, they didn't go to Mars in a flying saucer. Just go to where you saw them last and track 'em down.

Y'all mess this deal up, I'm gone mess you up. You got that?"

"I hear ya. Everything's fine, except for the twins getting lost. Everything else is a hunnerd percent right like it's supposed to be."

"It damn well better be." Peanut checked his watch. "You don't find them in a hour, you call me back and I'll come out and see to it. And you make damn sure the you-know-what stays put. Don't do nothin' stupid."

Peanut closed the phone. It was obvious that Buck had ordered the twins to do what he was too lazy to do, then left them alone with just his instructions to go by. Peanut had told Buck to dig graves so he'd stay occupied. He didn't know for sure where the Dockerys would be buried, because nobody had told him that yet. Maybe they'd want the bodies found sometimes, or put under a slab, or ground into burger. He should have told Buck not to involve the twins—or leave them alone to do the digging. Some things you could tell the twins to do, some things you couldn't leave them at. Buck knew that better than anybody. Trouble was, Buck was like some kind of animal that couldn't think about food until he was nearly starving to death. You couldn't trust him to plan ahead or stick to any particular job for very long.

The psychologist that Peanut had taken Buck to because the public school made him do it had said he had behavioral issues. Peanut loved the term *issues*.

Peanut knew all there was to know about his oldest son.

Buck didn't give a damn about anybody but himself.

He didn't like people telling him what to do.

He had a hair-trigger temper.

He got a kick out of other people's pain.

He was a liar.

He imagined things.

He was a bully.

Nothing made him sick to his stomach.

He never felt guilty about anything he did.

He took what he wanted when he wanted it.

He always got his revenge.

All of the "issues" that made Buck a hellcat to teach or to get to follow orders worked in the boy's favor when it came to enjoying a successful career in his chosen field—the family business.

27

Dixie Smoot opened her mouth and snapped it closed to click her porcelain teeth loudly—something she did out of habit when she was really pissed off.

Buck said he'd left the twins to take a turn digging, and that he had just been gone for a "few" minutes to go and check on something. She couldn't imagine what he had to check on out in the plumb middle of nowhere. Now Buck was gone off to the Utzes' store down the road to use the pay phone to call Peanut about the twins. Her daddy would be fit to be tied if things weren't going smoothly. It wouldn't be the first or the last time he had needed to punch out Buck. When it came to discipline, her daddy didn't spare a rod.

Dixie figured she'd find the twins before Buck got back and joined her, because whenever he could get by with it, he'd get back too late to do any work. Buck was worse things than lazy, but what he did to others was between him and whoever he did it to. It was mostly the lazy part of Buck that complicated Dixie's life.

Dixie's four-wheeler was one of several that Peanut's people had found inadequately attended and had brought out to the house for hunting and chores. You could do a lot more with the 400cc Honda four-wheel-drive ATVs than use them for getting yourself and your gun into the woods, and bringing deer back out when you killed one. The roads on the thousand-acre property were really just trails and a challenge for the most rugged four-wheel-drive vehicles.

There was only one real road onto the land, and it was hardly more than a dirt path with some gravel scattered on it so you could get vehicles to the barn. You could get around the land on a tractor, and they had one in the shed, but the ATVs were a lot faster. The tractor had a winch on it, and if you wanted to get around on the land to work with it you spent more time pulling it up out of the steep and eroded creek banks than working.

The rain was an annoyance, stinging her face. She wished she had remembered goggles so she could open her eyes fully.

If Dixie didn't miss the turnoff and have to double back, Buck's clearing was about a mile and a half away.

As she sped along, the ATV would go airborne when she hit a mogul or a rut, and rain in her eyes or not, she couldn't help but smile. If the snotty little bitch stayed put, like Dixie warned her to, she'd be all right till Monday. Dixie doubted she'd try anything, because she was a soft little nothing. If women like that didn't put it out, there'd be a bounty on them.

Anyway, if she didn't stay put, she had her a real nice surprise coming that wouldn't be nobody's fault but her own.

By following Buck's directions, Dixie found the spot where the twins had started digging the hole. She drove the ATV around the field and soon picked up the tracks of the twins' four-wheelers. Soon she spotted their Hondas and stopped beside them.

She found them seated in an inch of rainwater with their broad backs against opposing ends of the hole. Burt and Curt Smoot looked like a pair of fat baby birds in a shoebox. They stared angrily up at Dixie, who stood in the loose dirt at the grave's edge with her hands on her hips, shaking her head.

The ground was torn up where they had tried to claw their way out of the steep-sided grave. A section of aluminum ladder lay five feet away. The hole was deeper than it needed to be by two feet, but her father had said that the hole should be deep enough to prevent anything from digging up the Dockerys, and it certainly was that.

Since Burt and Curt weighed about three hundred pounds each, and the grass was wet and covered with the dirt from digging, there was no way they could get out without the ladder, or by one holding his hands for the other to climb out and get the ladder for the other. She didn't have to be told that neither had been willing to depend on the other to get the ladder for them.

"You're dumb as sacks of barn owl poop," she said.

"It was him," Burt said, pointing at Curt.

Curt said, "You started it."

"You pulled me in!"

"You pushed me and I just grabbed hold of you and we both fell in. I *said* I didn't do it on purpose, you dumb mule."

Dixie spat into the standing water between them. "I swear, if the good Lord swapped possums' brains with yours, the friggin possums would get the short end of the stick."

"Please put the ladder down, Dixie?" Curt pleaded. "It's cold in here."

"I ought to leave you in there," she said. "Buck told me y'all was left to dig, but he came back and found you hadn't dug anything. I saw back yonder where you started the hole. How'd you end up way the hell over here? If you hadn't left the four-wheelers in plain sight, I never would have found you."

"It wasn't a good place to dig where he said to," Burt said. "Where he said to dig was rooty as hell, and we didn't have a pickax."

"We'd a needed a damned backhoe," Curt said.

"Dirt's better here," Burt said.

"Daddy's gonna be pissed," she said.

"You gonna tell him?" Curt chimed in, fear coloring his voice.

"It could have happened to anybody," Burt said.

"It happened to a pair of idiot fools." Dixie got the ladder and jammed it down in the grave between them.

"You don't have to tell Daddy," Curt said, standing.

"I sure don't."

"Thank you for not telling Daddy." Curt climbed out and stood up, offering a meaty hand to his brother.

"Don't thank me," Dixie said, walking to her Honda and climbing on. "Buck went to call him."

When the engine caught, she sped across the clover field like she was late for something.

28

Lucy Dockery had been certain for hours that she could sense rain in the air, but she had yet to hear it hitting the trailer's roof. Maybe her mind was playing tricks on her.

She wondered if this going off and leaving her was a ruse on the woman's part to see if Lucy did try to escape. She doubted the woman would stay gone long, or leave her totally unguarded. If the woman believed that Lucy was a frightened and helpless dilettante who would do as she was told, it still didn't explain why she would allow her to try to escape. Could she be that crazy or that dumb? *Well,* thought Lucy, *this might be the only break I get. People do escape from their captors.*

With Elijah clinging to her, she hurried through the trailer, looking for anything she could use.

The main room—open kitchen and den—was decorated with stuffed deer heads. A layer of red dust seemed to cover every flat surface.

It was immediately apparent that anything with an edge she could use as a tool had been removed. The spoons, knives, and forks in the kitchen were all plastic. Cast-iron pots and pans were stacked under an island with a granite top with stools on the ends and along one side. Next to the gas range a potbelly stove sat on a bed of bricks. There was not even a steel poker or shovel for the stove.

Patterns made by the soles of boots and shoes covered practically every square foot of the filthy floor. In the den area a single couch with a wool blanket draped over it was shoved against a wall. Aside from that there was a playpen, and a new TV set perched on a coffee table.

A door opened into a room on the end of the trailer with two bunk beds and a stench reminiscent of high school locker rooms. Hunting clothes, pairs of mud-encrusted boots, grimy underwear and socks were in piles over the floor. There were no guns in evidence, and that was just as well since Lucy knew she could never use one. The idea of killing horrified her to the core. She had always been anti–capital punishment, antiwar; she didn't even believe abortion was all right.

Maybe this was the sort of hunting camp Walter and his friends had sometimes stayed in. Walter had been a hunter and she'd been bored to tears when he and his hunting friends talked about it.

Lucy had never gone camping or even to the woods with her husband. Now she desperately wished she had become involved in that part of his life.

Lucy picked up a huge camouflage jacket with a hood and put it on to protect Eli and herself from the cool weather. She found an olive-colored compact flashlight that worked, which was good because it was dark outside. She put her bare feet into a pair of absurdly large leather boots and quickly wrapped the long laces around and cinched them at the ankles so they wouldn't fall off. Anything was better than going outside in her bare feet.

Cautiously Lucy opened the outside door to the trailer and discovered that it wasn't dark because it was night; it was dark because the trailer was parked inside an enormous building. It looked to be a warehouse with walls of fabricated steel. There were industrial fixtures connected to the beams, but all were unlit. Daylight illuminated narrow seams where some of the sheet metal panels joined.

The roof was supported by the kind of steel girders you would see in one of those warehouse stores.

Rain! Muted by layers of tar, rain beat down on the building's flat roof. The floor was coated with the flour-fine red dust that had found its way inside the trailer. The trailer itself, standing on piles of cinder blocks, its flattened tires gone crocodilian with dry rot, had been backed into the building. There were two matching steel-frame doors, each at least sixteen feet tall and twelve wide. The steel hinges, three per door, were each a foot tall. The doors were diagonally across from each other on two connected walls. If the trailer wasn't there, a large vehicle could drive in through one door, turn around the storage room that took up exactly one quarter of the space, and go out through the other one without stopping. The giant door facing the trailer's door had a normal-sized door built into its corner so people could come and go without having to open the giant ones. This accounted for the sound she had taken for a shed door opening and closing.

Using the light, she quickly looked around. The end of the trailer, where her cell was located, was maybe three feet from a warehouse wall. The other end, where the bunks were, was ten feet from the door that the trailer entered through.

What she figured was a storage room had corrugated walls and a large rusted steel door with crudely made hinges. A run of wood steps led up to the storage room's flat roof, where bales of hay, some ratty-looking furniture, and wooden crates were stacked. On the ground level, rolls of rusted barbed wire hung like Christmas wreaths on the walls.

The large door was before her; to her right several fifty-gallon drums—two of which had pumps in the tops with hoses ending in nozzles—lined the wall. Several plastic gas cans stood beside those drums. Between the drums and the trailer was a stack of firewood piled in a small trailer made from a truck bed.

She carried Eli down the trailer's steps, her free hand gripping the flashlight. Lucy took a few steps out into the space toward the inset door, heard a loud squeak, and spun back toward the storage room. Her heart lurched, imagining Scaly-hands or the woman about to jump out into the warehouse. She played the light beam over the door. As she watched, the hinges squeaked and what looked like a gloved hand waved at her through the slowly opening door.

Lucy ran to the outside inset door and tried to open it, but to her horror she saw a massive padlock hanging there. The lock secured two rings that held a steel bolt to the iron frame so it could be opened either from inside or outside the warehouse. The woman hadn't locked the trailer, or tied Lucy up, because she'd known Lucy could only escape from the trailer into a larger trap. And this was a trap where she and her son were not alone.

Panic rising, Lucy clutched Eli to her and backed toward the trailer. The flashlight's beam told her that what had appeared to be a hand was a blunt muzzle. The heavy door had moved due to steady pressure of powerful shoulders.

First one, then several block-bodied dogs poured into the larger space. Soundlessly, they spread out as a pack and formed a low wall before her of hungry red eyes, sculpted muscle, and bared teeth.

29

Winter Massey parked in the shopping center's lot in sight of Alexa's sedan. He saw Click Smoot spring from the sports car and run, coat over his head, through the rain into one of those coliseum-sized media stores, where both the music department and the computer department had shelves upon shelves filled with television sets. Winter couldn't imagine how any of these monster stores did enough business to keep the lights on and employ as many people as they did—which seemed to be about one for every five thousand square feet of retail space. He called Alexa on the cell phone.

"I need to grab a disguise or two," he told Alexa. "If he moves, I'll catch up."

"Grab me a hat," she said. "I'll reimburse you."

"Halloween's on me this year," he said.

Winter jumped from the pickup and sprinted into a sporting store. For himself, he selected three jackets in various designs and colors, two sweatshirts, half a dozen assorted baseball caps, and three pairs of sunglasses in different styles. For Alexa, he picked a tan jacket, a blue ball cap, and a pair of sunglasses with light yellow lenses. He paid cash for everything and drove back to Alexa's car, then got out of the truck, opened Alexa's passenger door, and climbed inside.

Eyes on the media store Click had gone into, Alexa

said, "North Carolina combat shopping champion. According to my watch, that was a shade under two minutes."

"I hope the items meet your approval. I wasn't sure which ball teams you follow."

"That's easy. None of them."

"So, aside from the job, what the hell do you do with your time, Lex?"

"Think about how to do the job better," Alexa said.

"Sounds exciting," Winter said.

"It sure can be."

"Last time we talked, you said you had run into a brick wall career-wise. Something about the Bureau putting you out to pasture teaching at the academy."

"I've made some enemies over the years, Massey, but I'm not teaching yet."

"Okay, so when the string does run out, what are you going to do with your life?"

"Watch a lot of football," she replied, putting a Panther's cap on her head. "I might open up a security firm like the one that pays you a fortune to come in for a few days every week to teach failed cops and ex–football players to protect Texaco executives. Only I'll have the kind of operation that gets back the employees they fail to protect from abductors." She smiled. "Big office in D.C. Precious and I will..." The smile started to evaporate from her face, but she salvaged it.

"Your sister," Winter mused. "She'd be a solid partner. Hard as nails. Blind ambition. She's a captain now, isn't she?"

"A major."

"That's like a step away from colonel, isn't it?"

"Antonia's doing all right," Alexa said.

"She's an MP?"

Alexa nodded.

"Both Keen girls in federal law enforcement. Mama Jack must be proud." Mama Jack had been the woman who had rescued Alexa and Antonia from the foster home shuffle.

Alexa turned her eyes to Winter and her expression softened. "Mama Jack died, Massey. Last year."

"I didn't know. I'm terribly sorry." Winter had liked Mama Jack Prior, had admired that the fearless woman had opened her loving home to something like twenty-six children over the years. All children nobody else wanted.

"She was ninety-six. Went peacefully in her sleep," Alexa said. "We all got to go out sometime."

"I'm going to take a quick look inside," Winter said.

"Go for it," Alexa said.

Winter knew that, while Click might not remember him from the Westin's lobby, the kid's subconscious mind had a record of the stranger and his brain might send a subliminal danger message that would draw his conscious scrutiny, and then he probably would recall seeing Winter. To lessen the risk, Winter had not only changed clothes but also changed his height and posture. Slumping slightly, he altered his natural stride. He sauntered into the media store like a man with a reason to be there, and went directly to the CDs. He spotted Click standing at the computer counter looking at something in the salesman's hands. The clerk was animated in his pitch about whatever the item happened to be.

Winter tilted his head down, acting like someone glancing idly through the stacks of CDs, and watched Ferny Ernest Smoot until he was sure the transaction was a normal one. Convinced, he walked out of the store and climbed into the car with Alexa.

"He meeting with anyone?"

"Seems to be buying something computer-related," Winter reported.

"He see you?"

Winter looked at her.

"I can't believe I asked you that," Alexa said, smiling. "Sorry. I'm getting senile."

"I wish we had another car and a couple of good people," Winter told her. "This kid is shopping like he doesn't have anything at all pressing to do. What about Clayton? Maybe he can come give us some assistance?"

She shrugged. "If we have to, I'll ask him, but he's not exactly a field person. Anyway, he's far more valuable in his hotel room. He's got traces running on Smoot credit cards, has nets waiting on voice-pattern matches."

"I hope he keeps furnishing the same quality intelligence," Winter said.

"I can just about guarantee that," Alexa said.

Winter yawned and sat back to wait out Ferny Ernest.

30

Click Smoot spent $828.46 on memory, DVDs, and music CDs at the media store. Actually, some mark by the name of Edmund C. Kellogg had that amount charged to his AmEx Gold card. By the time the mark got his bill, Click would have put ten times that much on it. According to the supplier of the card, the real Edmund Kellogg was on a holy-roller church-sponsored eye-surgery mission trip so some born-again doctors could restore sight to a bunch of scabby villagers way up in the mountains of Peru. Kellogg wouldn't be where he could use the card for three more weeks. Click had plans to help American Express give him about ten grand of its income.

He used the large plastic bag containing the merchandise for an umbrella, holding it over his head as he ran to his car, unlocking it with the key fob as he approached it. He didn't pay any attention to the cars around him, or anything else, because as soon as he was inside the car he was busily rifling through the CDs trying to decide which one to put into the most expensive music player on the market. The player, new speakers, and professional installation had all been a gift from a stranger named Richard D. Lewis.

He had a few places to hit, then he was going to head to the house, open a beer or three, and watch some high-definition girls acting nasty.

31

His small arms around her neck, his legs around her waist, Elijah Dockery clung to his mother like a wet sheet. He was not afraid of strangers, but dogs terrified him. Lucy had grown up with dogs. Her parents had owned a succession of dogs for pets, but these dogs were not anybody's pets. This pack was a collection of powerful, square-headed, no-nonsense canine gladiators bred to be aggressive. These were just the sort of pit bulls who had worked so relentlessly to earn the entire breed a reputation for the unprovoked violence that was focused on other mammals . . . including people.

These animals wore no collars, and but for their strong odor and the puffs of dust made by their paws as they circled the Dockerys, they might have been hallucinations. The pack's alpha seemed to be a bull-necked male—an animal whose golden hide was crisscrossed with dark scars—whose short, pyramid-shaped ears looked like ancient, rough-hewn arrowheads. A black-and-white female, the smallest and thinnest, limped and looked to be blind in one eye. Beneath her sharply defined ribs hung twin rows of prunelike nipples. She raised her head and sniffed the still air as she followed the others around Lucy and Elijah.

Lucy used the flashlight's beam to keep the dogs at

bay the same way a lion tamer uses a chair and a whip. It was dark enough so that the light hurt their eyes.

There were eight dogs—seven more than it would take to kill a helpless woman and child. The heaviest dog weighed as much as Lucy did. She wondered if they had ever attacked people. They weren't doing so at the moment. In fact, they seemed unsure, nervous.

Arms tight around Elijah, Lucy inched backward toward the trailer, anxiously watching the animals for any sign of an impending attack. Taking advantage of their hesitation, she moved faster toward the steel steps at the trailer's front door. The female stopped abruptly, positioning herself between the Dockerys and the trailer. The dog watched Lucy come on, the flashlight's beam setting a fire in her good eye. As she raised her head and sniffed, she suddenly whirled and skittered away as if her paws had touched a bare electric wire.

Lucy kept the light in the dogs' eyes and kept backing up, finally putting a boot heel on the first step, using the light like a flame to keep the dogs blinded. One of the younger animals whirled and followed the old female into the storage room.

Elijah started crying. Buoyed by the sound of fear, the dogs moved closer, but then stopped suddenly and turned their heads toward the door. Lucy knew why they had stopped. The growl of an approaching motor filled the building and harsh light shone through the cracks around the warehouse doors. Lucy opened the trailer door and saw that the dogs were slinking back into their lair. They were more afraid of whoever was coming than they were interested in harming Lucy and Elijah.

She went inside, closing the door behind her. She put Elijah in the playpen and scrabbled frantically at her boots, trying to untie the laces. Elijah was crying louder, holding out his arms, begging to be picked up. "Soon, Eli. Soon." Tears streamed down her cheeks.

The warehouse door creaked open, then was slammed closed.

One lace was knotted, and she fumbled to find a loose place in the leather straps, while Elijah cried and tried to get back in her arms. Lucy slipped out of the laced boot, leaving the knot in it. She tossed the boots into the bunkroom. Scooping Elijah up, she ran into the bedroom, set him on the bed, took off the camouflage jacket, and wedged it between two of the boxes stacked against the wall. She couldn't remember if she had turned off the flashlight, which was in the pocket of the jacket.

She sat on the bed, pulled Elijah to her, and fought to control her trembling.

Whoever was approaching the trailer was whistling a tune that was so off-key that Lucy couldn't identify it.

32

Click Smoot quit shopping around six o'clock because his car was as packed full of merchandise as it could get. He loved his Z car. It was absolutely him—sure-footed, fast as owl turds on a water slide, masculine, attractive, and hot. Really hot.

He lived in a quiet residential neighborhood ten blocks behind a vast Ford dealership on Independence Boulevard. His red-brick ranch looked pretty much like others in the area—single-family style with a couple thousand square feet of floor space on a neatly kept lot replete with shade trees, flower beds, and pruned shrubs. There was nothing to indicate that an unmarried twenty-one-year-old bachelor lived there. He parked the Z in the garage beside his old GMC panel van. The van wasn't exactly a chick magnet, but it was a flying hoot to drive, and held lots of merchandise.

He was the only Smoot with a yard that had well-kept grass. One of his father's cousins had a landscaping company that did Click's yard in exchange for a favor here and there. They had started that company as a front, but to keep up the appearance of propriety, they employed about fifty Mexicans and made sure they had good equipment and that they all worked hard. They paid them the going salary plus Chinese overtime, which was an additional five bucks cash for every hour over forty. Plus, some of them made extra money playing crash-test dummies in auto-insurance scams. While the Mexicans did the sweating, the crew chiefs cased the homes of the wealthy clients for the family burglars.

Once Click had bought something, it lost its value to him and became mere inventory, which would become twenty cents on the dollar for a great deal of trouble and the risk of getting caught at it. So that had gotten him thinking, why lose eighty cents on the dollar? Why go to all that trouble for watered-down money when you could go straight into an account and get full value on every dollar you robbed? And you could steal from anywhere on earth from anywhere you were.

Click unpacked the Z, putting the purchases he would pass to the family pawnshops on the appropriate shelves, and taking the items he had bought for himself into his house. As he entered the mudroom, he noticed that one of the bulbs in one of the three night-light fixtures was blackened and he felt a wave of anxiety as he unscrewed it and took it into the house with him.

He entered the kitchen, hung his keys on the peg.

The Felix the Cat clock over the stove cut its eyes back and forth as its pendulum tail swung side to side.

He opened a cabinet and took down a packet of night-light bulbs and pried one loose. He threw out the old one and took the new one back to the mudroom and screwed it in, cutting the lights to make sure it worked.

Hurriedly he went through the entire house, checking each night-light and the batteries in each of the dozen flashlights.

As soon as he was sure his illumination requirements were covered, Click stood still and, as he listened to the clock, a soul-crushing dark pressure settled down on him.

He felt the enormous weight of being the only warm-blooded mammal in the place, and Ferny Ernest prayed that the DVD in his hand would lessen the emptiness.

33

In his hotel room, Clayton Able sat staring at the screen of his laptop computer. He was monitoring Winter Massey and Alexa Keen. The cellular phones Keen and Massey carried were marvels of modern design, feeding Clayton their geographic locations and performing as microphones that transmitted directly to his receivers, which were being monitored by people in the adjoining room. In addition, his people had wired Alexa's car and her handbag.

The door to the room adjoining his was open, and he could see his technicians at work.

Clayton stood, turned toward the window, and yawned while stretching out his arms. Sitting at the keyboard made his back feel like someone had hit him high between the shoulders with a ball-peen hammer. It was dark out, and still raining. It had been two hours since Winter and Alexa had taken off to chase after Click.

"This Ferny Ernest thing is troubling," the woman standing in the doorway said, scattering his thoughts.

"Ferny Ernest Smoot isn't going to lead anyone to the Dockerys. I doubt the kid could even lead them to his father. Even so, Peanut wouldn't be dumb enough to go near the Dockerys."

"You didn't know Click was trailing the judge," the woman said accusatorily.

"If Massey hadn't spotted Click in the lobby, I would have given them another trail to run to keep them busy until Monday. As it turns out, it may have been a godsend blind alley."

"You didn't need to include a picture of Click with the others," the woman said.

"It was hopelessly outdated. Massey was—"

"Don't you dare say lucky," she chided.

"Click isn't supposed to be connected to this. Dixie, Buck, and those twins are doing the actual work, and they're out of circulation. Look, as long as we stay on top of Alexa and Massey, it will all work out and everybody wins."

He studied his boss, someone he admired the way he would admire something pretty and dangerous to stand too close to. Clayton knew that if he was neck deep in quicksand, and if she didn't need him alive, she'd watch him go under without altering her facial expression. She was also every bit as beautiful as she was conniving, and she was the most manipulative job of work he'd ever worked with. Clayton was glad he was on her side in this, because being on the other side was not an attractive alternative. You could ask anybody who'd ever gotten in this woman's way—if you could find them. She'd come up the ranks from an MP grunt into a position of authority within Military Intelligence like she'd been shot there from a cannon.

This Bryce business had the potential to turn very ugly. Clayton hadn't wanted Alexa to bring Winter Massey into this, but there hadn't been any way he could stop her since the FBI agent was now the key to the thing smelling right after the dust settled.

"I always said Massey would be trouble," Clayton told the woman.

"That need not concern you," she said. "I made the decision, which was mine to make."

"Massey's reputation isn't what it is because anyone can control him. You should never ever mix emotion—especially not revenge—with business. And this is very delicate business with a fortune at stake."

"I know what's at stake here," she hissed. "I know Massey a lot better than you do."

Clayton shrugged. He had no choice but to go with the flow, to follow orders. He knew that either he would make a fortune with this woman, or he would be a dead man.

He couldn't help but wonder how anyone could have ever called her "Precious." Major Antonia Keen was about as precious as an iceberg.

34

Drenched in sweat, Lucy Dockery listened.

The trailer door burst open and a familiar figure entered. Heart pounding, Lucy froze in the doorway of the bedroom, holding Elijah to her. Her heart skipped a beat and she felt a hollow burn of acid churning in her gut. It wasn't the woman.

"Wail, hail," Scaly-hands called, smiling at her across the twenty feet that separated them. "You're up and about, I see. I reckon Dixie ain't back yet." He took off his wet cotton duster and tossed it over the cold potbelly stove. His eyes were locked on her, his tongue darting in and out from the crack between rows of yellow teeth. He rubbed his hands together as he appraised her.

"You are a perty sight in that nightgown. A perty sight indeed."

Lucy stood frozen, studying the man whose greedy eyes were broadcasting that his ugly mind was cobbling together something horrible. This hideous monster, driven by a lust that smoldered in a vile and focused anger, wanted her. If she'd found a weapon, now would be when to use it, but the only thing between him and her was Elijah, who clung to his mother like a terrified monkey.

"She's coming back," Lucy told him. As frightening as the thought of the big woman was, Lucy prayed that she would come. If Dixie couldn't prevent him from doing what he wanted to do to her, probably no one could. He hadn't hurt her before and she believed that was only because Dixie had been in the trailer.

"Why don't you shuck off those panties?" he said, moving closer.

"Please," Lucy said weakly. "Not in front of my baby." She felt a wave of self-revulsion for using Elijah as a shield, and she wished she could somehow kill the man. She could kill him.

"Why not? Ain't like he'll remember it. People doing what nature wants them to ain't bad for kids. Hell, I grew up seeing people doing the dirty deed." His smile turned her blood to ice.

"Please?" she begged, trembling. "Please don't do this."

"Come out here," he ordered. "Less you want me to come in there where it's nice and dark." He stared down at her legs as she came into the kitchen. She saw that he liked the fact that she was afraid. She also saw something that looked like splattered blood on his shirt and on his hands and neck.

Reaching out suddenly, he peeled Elijah off Lucy, held the screaming child up in the air by his arm, opened the bathroom door, and plopped the child down on the floor beside the toilet. Elijah howled. Scaly-hands closed the door as the baby tried to stand.

Lucy sprang at the man's powerful shoulders and reached around to scratch out his eyes. He elbowed Lucy in the jaw, sending her sprawling, her head bouncing against the refrigerator door.

As he approached, Lucy scuttled back against the bedroom doorjamb.

"You rich gals all like it rough," he said. "You get off on big old boys treating you like two-dollar whores. You need what Buck's got, honey. And Buck's got a whole lot of what you need."

As he talked he unbuckled his belt. As he came toward her he pulled it free and wrapped it once around his fist so it would stay in place while he used it on her.

I can take it, Lucy thought. *I can take whatever he can do, and I will get on the other side of this, for Elijah's sake.*

A six-letter word for being scared witless.

T-E-R-R-O-R

She closed her eyes, drew herself into a ball, and clenched her teeth, waiting.

35

Some neighborhoods lend themselves to surveillance. Click Smoot's wasn't one of them. On Click's block, a sidewalk ran only on his side of the street, while the front lawns on the other side sloped up to the home sites from the naked curb.

Click lived at the tail end of a narrow street in a sleepy Charlotte neighborhood, so there was no through traffic to speak of. Here, except when someone had visitors, cars were parked in the garages or driveways. The houses had been built in the 1960s on land that was probably inexpensive. The homes took up no more than a quarter of their well-kept lots, and most of the homes contained young, upwardly mobile couples—with or without children—or older people who had lived there a long time. Winter had seen a thousand neighborhoods like it and knew that the residents might not be on first-name terms, but they would be aware of each other to the point where two strangers sitting in the only parked car on the street were going to be noticed. He also knew that when somebody here called the cops, they came.

If the cops showed up, Winter and Alexa were upright citizens, and there was no law against legitimate citizens sitting in a car talking, or contemplating real estate, or checking the amount of traffic the street saw, or waiting for the Rapture. There was no curfew for white-bread people in white-bread suburban neighborhoods. The problem was that Click would be as likely to notice them here as anyone else. And if the cops pulled up and asked questions, Alexa might end up showing her badge, and the cops might be friendly enough with Click's family to warn him. They couldn't take that chance.

The house two up and across the street from Click's had a steep driveway and a lot of toys in the yard. A Plymouth minivan and a Volvo sedan were shoulder to shoulder at the top of the incline. That driveway seemed the most advantageous spot from which to watch the front of Click's house.

Winter parked behind the Volvo, the vehicle nearest to the wall of shrubbery, and Alexa parked beside him. They walked to the door and he rang the bell. A tall man in his early thirties opened the door and, when he saw that the people standing on his porch were strangers, dialed down his smile. Somewhere behind him small children were making dinnertime-is-over racket.

"Yes?" he asked.

Alexa held up her badge and his smile vanished behind a cloud of confusion.

"I'm FBI Special Agent Alexa Keen."

"What's the trouble?" he asked.

"No trouble," she said.

"It isn't every day the FBI shows up at my door." His smile was making an effort to come back.

"We'd like to park in your driveway, if you wouldn't mind."

"Why?"

"I can't tell you that," Alexa answered. "But it doesn't involve you, Mr. . . . ?"

"Latham. Charles Latham."

A blond-haired woman wearing gray sweats appeared at the throat of the hallway. A small child came from the same direction to stand beside her, one hand gripping her mother's pant leg.

"Charles?" the blond woman said, raising an eyebrow. "What is it?"

"It's the FBI, Patty," he told her, then turned back to Alexa and Charles. "Please come in," he said. "You're getting wet."

Alexa stepped inside, and Winter followed her.

The woman approached them, the child shadowing her. She crossed her arms. "What can we do for you?"

"Ma'am," Alexa said. "We were just asking for permission to park two vehicles in your driveway for a little while."

"Our driveway? What for?"

"What's a while?" Charles said.

Alexa shrugged. "I'm not sure."

"And they can't tell us why," Charles told his wife.

"I'm sorry," Alexa said. "I would if I could. Really."

"I think we should tell them," Winter said.

Alexa turned her eyes on Winter and cocked her head. After a few seconds, she nodded her approval.

"We're part of a strike force," Winter told the Lathams. "We're staking out a house a few blocks away, and we have about a dozen vehicles that have to stay out of sight until it's time to converge, when we get the order. We don't know how long that will take, because we don't control what the subjects do or when they do it. We'll be long gone before you wake up in the morning." Winter turned on his warmest smile.

Patty Latham said, "I don't have a problem with it. Charles?"

"Fine by me," he said. "We can sleep soundly knowing we have the FBI watching over us."

"I'll make you two a thermos of coffee," Patty offered. "When you go, just leave the container on the side porch. There's a half bath just inside the side door. I'll leave it unlocked in case you need it. Just turn the lock before you leave."

"That would be greatly appreciated," Alexa said.

"The least we can do," Charles Latham said.

"And I expect a few ham sandwiches wouldn't hurt," Patty said, lifting the towheaded child up onto her hip.

"I can't see where it would hurt a thing," Winter agreed.

Raindrops ran down the windows of Alexa's sedan, creating diffuse golden halos around the streetlights. Winter sat in the front seat with his back against the door, so he could watch the front of Click's house through the side window. Alexa, in the back seat, exactly mirrored his posture. Winter checked his watch. It was nine o'clock.

"So, how's having a new baby?" Alexa asked.

"Sort of like déjà vu all over again. Only I'm older by fourteen years. I guess I'm paying closer attention this time. Or maybe it just seems like I am."

"I like Sean," Alexa said. "I should have known I would. She is totally different than Eleanor, except that she loves your rotten hide as much."

"You'll get to know her better, and you'll like her even more."

"I thought that, after Eleanor, I would hate whoever you ended up with. Truthfully, I was prepared to dislike Sean. I should have known that anybody you picked out would be a very special person. I can see in her eyes that she worships you . . . just like Eleanor did. What is it about you, Massey? Nobody gets two perfect matches. You know what it is, don't you?"

"No," he said. "Tell me."

"If you get two perfect mates, then somebody out there doesn't get their one. I was furious at you for marrying my roommate. Do you know how hard it was to find another one who was neat, entertaining, and responsible?" Alexa sniffed. "I brought Eleanor home to see the Delta, and she falls in love with you, my other best friend. I never had another roommate who wasn't a nightmare."

"I did apologize, and you said you forgave me."

"I miss Eleanor," she said, softly. "A day never goes by that I don't see or hear something that triggers a memory of her."

"Me too," he said truthfully.

"I guess you think you loved her more than I did."

He didn't answer for a few long seconds. "I loved her as much as it is possible for me to love anyone."

"And you love Sean that way?"

"It's not the same and it is exactly the same. Love isn't like some pie chart with a certain number of slices, Lex. There are degrees, but not that you can measure. I don't love Sean any more or any less than I loved Eleanor."

"Loved?"

"Love. I'm still in love with Eleanor."

"She's dead, Winter. Can you love a dead person the same as you can a live one? Isn't it just the memories you love now? Isn't that a different love? Sean can hold you, kiss you, laugh and cry with you. Do you feel guilty because Sean has taken Eleanor's place in your life?"

"Lex, can we talk about something else?" Winter felt uncomfortable talking about Eleanor and Sean. Alexa was prying into his heart, and if it had been anyone else he would have been angry at the intrusion. But he knew how much Alexa had loved Eleanor, and that gave her a backstage pass.

"We used to talk about everything and anything, Winter. Have you forgotten?"

"That was a very long time ago." He regretted the words as soon as they left his mouth. The silence that followed was bottomless and he couldn't make himself fill it by trying to take it back, or make it right.

36

Winter Massey closed his eyes and listened to the rain drumming on the sedan's hood.

It had been a very long time, but Winter remembered easily.

When he was asked to work on the yearbook staff his senior year, he had brought Alexa on board with him. He took her to the prom, and she was the most beautiful girl there. After graduation, while they were sitting on the eighteenth green of the local golf course drinking warm wine out of a screw-top bottle, he had kissed her. Her reaction had been instant and passionate. But a sneezing fit had ended the kiss and the mood passed, and she'd pulled back from him, joking about how close to losing their friendship they had come. A little hurt and confused, Winter had told her that he loved her and wanted her, and she had shaken her head.

"I love you, Winter," she'd said. "I love you way more than that. We'll always be able to trust each other. I know what you have done for me, and I will always love you for it. You showed me who I really was."

"But we could have it all," he had said. "Lex, we could be stars."

She'd shaken her head slowly.

"No, Massey, it isn't all right. I wish it could be."

After that, it was never the same. She was accepted to

Berkeley and left that summer to get an early start. Their good-bye had been painful for Winter. He wasn't as sorry he had tried to change the ground rules as he was that he had ever made her the promise he had the day she'd come to his house for her notebook.

They had remained friends, but the closeness they had shared as teenagers was never there again.

He had thought back on their adolescent relationship thousands of times. He had been in love. Alexa hadn't. Then he'd fallen in love with Eleanor and the direction of his life was set in stone.

He had thought about it from every angle he could look at it from.

It always came out the same way.

He and Alexa were just never meant to be.

And since the moment he'd first met Eleanor, Winter had been relieved his life had gone the way it had. Of course, he desperately regretted that Eleanor had died and that Rush had been blinded. But he didn't regret meeting and falling in love with Sean and having Olivia. He had gone on with his life, and it had flowed from one thing to the next. . . .

"Massey," Alexa said, breaking the spell. "You asleep?"

"Resting my eyes."

"Sean was married before?"

"Widowed."

"What happened to him?"

"Gunshot wound."

"Self-inflicted?"

"In a manner of speaking."

Once upon a time, he would have told her the whole

story, that Sean's first husband was a professional killer, and that he had met Sean on a witness security detail—an operation to protect Dylan Devlin so he could testify against the head of the Louisiana Mafia. Luckily, Alexa let it drop. Nobody was more curious about things than Alexa, and Winter was sure this subject would come up again later. Alexa had always interrogated people, which was why being an FBI agent had come so easy for her. If she wanted to know something, she'd ask the same question over and over in differing forms and from different angles until she had the truth. It was a natural talent born out of necessity. When you are a child that nobody wants, you learn to spot lies and you learn to hate liars. You want to know when you are about to be moved from one home to another. You learn about hidden agendas and ulterior motives, and you lose the ability to trust and accept things at face value. And, if you are trying to make sure your baby sister—the only person you have a real bond with—remains with you, it's crucial to figure out the truth of things and plan ahead. You learn to manipulate the things in your world you can change to your advantage.

"I have a question," she said.

"Yeah?"

"What kind of name is Ferny Ernest?" Alexa asked, bringing Winter back from his past. "What was his mama thinking?"

He shrugged. "No idea."

She giggled. "I guess she could have picked Beanie Weenie, or Herkel Jerkel."

Winter laughed. "We need to find Peanut or Click's

siblings," he said. "They're likely to be involved with the Dockerys. I think Click Smoot is a dry hole."

Winter had been watching the flickering TV-generated light in two of the windows in Click's house. Now he lifted the binoculars he had brought from his truck and focused them on one of the windows. "Click's not moving around."

A BMW passed slowly by the Lathams' driveway, headlights out. It drew up at the curb outside Click's house.

"Click's got company," Winter said, sitting straighter and watching the sedan.

There were two people in the car, and after a few seconds, the doors opened without the interior light coming on. Two figures stepped out and quietly closed their doors.

Winter focused on the men as they approached the first illuminated window and peered in from behind the bushes.

"Who is it?" Alexa whispered.

"The Russian, Sarnov, and Max Randall." Winter recognized them from pictures Clayton had shown them. "What the hell is this?" he asked. "They're not involved in the grab. So why are they at a Smoot house?"

"This is good," Alexa said. "Players gathering in the middle of the night. It sure doesn't look like the hole is as dry as you thought."

"Maybe this meeting isn't in Click's best interest," Winter said. "Based on the fact that they're lurking in the bushes, I don't think he's expecting them. What do you want to do?"

"Wait," she said.

"Wait? What if they came to hurt him?"

"They're professionals. If that's the case, I doubt they will require any assistance from us. We should give them a wide berth. Remember Clayton's admonition. An 'Able' admonition is not anything to ignore."

Able had also said Sarnov and Randall weren't directly involved in the kidnapping. "They've gone around the back. I'll give them time to get inside, then I'll go see if I can find out what they're up to."

"I don't know—" she said. "Okay. Just don't shoot anybody."

"If they're going to kill Click, should I just watch them do it?"

"Yes. I don't know. Play it by ear. But remember what's at stake. This isn't about Click and Sarnov. It's probably a side deal."

"Obviously they are involved. Maybe the great oracle is wrong about that."

"Clayton isn't often wrong, Massey."

"Often isn't always, Lex. Ring him up while I'm gone." Winter reached for the door handle.

"Wait for me," she whispered.

"Call Clayton. Stay with the car. If I need help, you'll know it."

Winter pulled up the hood of his rain jacket and started for the house. He tried to clear his mind of the worry that had invaded it.

The Alexa Keen he knew had never seemed unsure of herself before.

37

Click Smoot reclined in a padded leather chair in front of the twelve-thousand-dollar plasma-screen television set that someone named Dakin T. Wilson had unwittingly bought for him. It was the first time Click had gone into the Advance Capital mainframe, using a code he had purchased from a programmer at the bank. If there was a trail to Click, the programmer would make it a circular track to nowhere.

He was watching a DVD called *The Number One Stripper in America Contest,* and at that moment he was imagining that he was right there in the club and the girl was stripping just for him. Had he not been engaged in a sexual fantasy, he might have heard the strangers coming in through the back door. He opened his eyes to get another look at a blonde who was doing a series of squat twists, when he noticed the two men standing in his kitchen doorway, looking right at him.

"What the hell!?" Click yelled. The men smiled, and he knew they were smiling at what he was doing to himself under the towel in his lap. "What do you think you're doing?" he said indignantly.

"Saying hello," the smaller of the two men said in a foreign accent. "Don't let us interrupt your *beeg* show."

Click was more embarrassed than frightened or angry, but he was plenty scared and pissed off by the intrusion.

And he resented being pulled so violently from his engagement with the stripper.

"Get out," he ordered.

"Sorry we didn't have an appointment," the smaller man, who looked like a detective, said. The larger one looked like he might be a plainclothes cop too.

The strangers walked straight into his den like they'd been invited, and the small one sat on the arm of the couch, while the larger one sat in the middle of it. Click's closest handgun, a loaded Smith & Wesson .357, was under the couch cushion beside the larger guy's right thigh.

Smaller weasel-looking guy took a cigarette out of a fancy red pasteboard box and lit it with what appeared to be a Dunhill lighter. "An excessive semen supply is the curse of youth. I know that as well as anyone." He made a fist and imitated the deed in the air, leering. Larger guy smiled. "You don't mind if I smoke, Click," he said. It wasn't a question.

"You don't got a search warrant, get out."

The small man laughed. "We're not police officers. Of course, you don't know who we are. How rude of me."

Click shrugged. "Why would I know you?"

"Maybe your father mentioned me. I am with a company that does some business with your father's boss, Mr. Laughlin."

Click chortled. "You don't know jack. Mr. Laughlin isn't my father's boss. He's his lawyer."

"Max here is an associate of Hunter Bryce. You know who he is?"

"Yeah, I know who he is. He's a loser on trial for murdering a Fed. That doesn't tell me who *you* are."

"Has Peanut ever mentioned a Russian he isn't very fond of?"

"My father hates all foreigners. He hates Russians worse than all the others put together."

"My name is Serge Sarnov. My associate is Max Randall." The Russian wasn't smiling anymore.

"Cool. Now, get the hell out of my house. You know who my daddy is, then you know you don't want to piss him off."

"I am not concerned with angering your father," Sarnov said.

"You ought to be," Click said. "You sure ought to be."

Click noticed the Randall guy wasn't a talker. He was watching the girl on the screen. He had fought back a smile on the tonsil zinger.

Sarnov waved his hand in the air, lit cigarette and all. "Your father is a crude man," the Russian said. "No worldview. No grasp of current events and how things outside his realm might affect him. If he feels wronged by someone, he has to retaliate physically. He is doomed."

"He does pretty fine."

"As long as he is in his environment, so does a red-ass baboon. Does that offend you? You are not like the other people in your family. Not at all." Sarnov shook his trigger finger at Click like a teacher gently admonishing a student. "You are brilliant, my young friend. I have to wonder if you were adopted. I mean, I have seen your family. I know why you live all alone. You have all of the class they lack. According to Mr. Laughlin, you are a genius about to come into your own. *You* are the future of the Smoots."

Click had to smile to hear that Mr. Ross Laughlin talked about him. He felt himself blushing. "So what? Peanut doesn't allow outside people to mess with his folks, especially not his kids."

"I didn't come to *mess* with you, Click. On the contrary, I came to discuss exploring some mutually profitable opportunities that could make you an extremely rich young man."

"Like what?"

"Like using your burgeoning skills to make a lot of money. My organization has international reach and influence. And we have intelligence channels you wouldn't believe."

Click said, "I can do just fine with my own people, thank you."

"I know things you wouldn't think I'd know."

"About what?"

"You. You can make a little money using your credit card scams, your little computer schemes. I think if we work together, you will end up with far more than you imagine is possible. Think way above your father's level. Mr. Laughlin is a good boss for your father, but even he is well below where you can go."

Click wondered if Ross Laughlin was his father's boss—the mystery moneyman who protected them. If so, this was news. According to Peanut, Ross Laughlin was an extremely powerful lawyer with major government connections. "You know about Mr. Laughlin, then you know we've got all the connections we'll ever need."

"A lesson in structure, Click. Your father works for Ross Laughlin and Ross Laughlin works as a partner in a domestic syndicate. We are a hundred times stronger in this country than Laughlin's aging syndicate. If you are as successful as you surely imagine you will be, which you can be, how much will they let you keep?

"You know I'm telling you the truth. You know your father. You put millions of dollars on the table, and Mr. Laughlin and your father will take..." Serge crushed out the cigarette. "...ninety-five points, maybe more, because they will see you only as a worker and they are greedy and suspicious. They never even trusted you with the fact that Mr. Laughlin is your daddy's and therefore your boss. And if this Judge Fondren extortion-by-kidnap scheme doesn't work as planned, your father is going to have to accept the blame, and he might not live much longer than the woman and her child do. Even if the Fondren thing comes off, your father's days are numbered. Your only chance at long-term security lies with me, my firm. We will let you be a real partner, and for what we offer we will take but a small percentage. I can get you the things you need to make your plans work, like access codes to accounts to loot with numbers so large you wouldn't believe it."

"Like what kinds of accounts and numbers wouldn't I believe?"

"Antiquated systems controlling accounts with a combined hundred and fifty billion dollars floating around in them gathering cobwebs, with nobody keeping a very close eye on them. A man with the right ability could nibble on them for years before anybody noticed. And there are more like that all over the world."

"You're crazy as hell."

"Is that a no?"

"Damned straight it is. You're a dead man."

"Okay." Sarnov stood and aimed a silenced pistol at Click's head. "Sorry we couldn't do business."

"You said you didn't come to hurt me!"

"This won't hurt at all," Sarnov said. "At least no one has ever complained to me later that it did."

38

Lucy Dockery swam up out of the void slowly, regaining consciousness to find herself back in the gritty bed in the darkened room. She was naked, and in a lot of pain, certainly made worse because she couldn't see and had to imagine how serious the damage to her was. Her face was bruised, hair and blood was matted into stiff wafers, and she could feel lines where the skin was laid open. Her lips were split and swollen, her teeth sore but she didn't think any were broken. Her nose was swollen to twice its size and filled with dried blood. She didn't think any of her bones were broken, because she could move her arms and legs, fingers and toes, but the joints in her hands ached.

Her nightgown was gone, ripped from her body as she fought Buck from a hopeless position on the floor at his feet.

He hadn't raped her. He'd stripped her, beaten her senseless, had her flat on the kitchen island with her legs apart, and he'd stopped only because Dixie and a pair of giants came in and pulled him away. Pants bunched around his ankles, he roared as the twins dragged him out the door. Dixie had called Scaly-hands "Buck."

Lucy remembered the beating, Buck's hideous grunts of pleasure, the terrified wails of Elijah behind a door only a few feet away. She hadn't cried out because she couldn't bear to have Elijah hear her screaming. It seemed so insane, so hopeless, and she didn't have the slightest idea why these creatures were doing this to them.

Lucy knew that if she didn't escape, she and probably Eli were going to die, and if that oaf with palms like tree bark had anything to say about it, the trip to death wouldn't be fast or pretty.

Monday. Buck had said that until Monday, he could do whatever he wanted to her, because "after that she was just one more dead piece of pussy."

Why Monday? She pushed the physical pain away and thought about that. *What would be happening on Monday?* She didn't even know what day of the week this was. How long before they killed her and Eli? A day? An hour? Was it an idle threat? She didn't think so.

Why Monday? She remembered that her father had told her that after Monday they could take Elijah and go to the house in Blowing Rock for a vacation. He had been expecting to deliver his verdict on the Bryce case that day. Had these people abducted them to influence her father's ruling on that case? That made sense. But that should mean that they wouldn't kill her if her father ruled for Bryce. Was it because she had seen their faces? That was their fault. They had not tried to remain anonymous, so they must have always planned to kill her. If they were just going to kill her, that was one thing, but because they might kill Eli too, she had to do something and do it fast.

She was smarter than they were and smarter was better than stronger.

She needed a plan to get out of the steel building.

Something else occurred to her. The dogs hadn't attacked her even when Elijah had cried. She was sure they had wanted to, but something had slowed them, or had perhaps confused them. She smiled to herself as the realization washed over her. And for the first time she was sure that she and Eli might have a shot at escaping after all. A plan. All she needed was a plan, and a lot of luck. She smiled when something occurred to her, and when she did so, the pain hit her, and she remembered Buck's cruel hands on her. But smiling was worth it. She now had a spark, the beginning of a plan, a way to save her son's life.

Lucy lay in a fetal position in the dark listening to Dixie sing "Itsy Bitsy Spider" to Elijah, who, incredibly, was laughing.

39

In the drumming rain, Winter held the Sig Sauer loosely at his side and peered into Click's den. Standing back from the window, Winter was as good as invisible to the three inhabitants of the room. He couldn't hear the conversation through the glass, but he could see Serge Sarnov and Max Randall and he could read Sarnov's lips. Click's chair was positioned so Winter couldn't see the young man's face, just his white socks.

What Winter learned from reading Sarnov's lips thrilled him. The Russian made Click a job offer, which Click must have declined, because Sarnov pulled a pistol and aimed it at Click. Reflexively, Winter aimed at Sarnov's head, figuring for deflection and reflection, but he didn't fire, because—based on Randall's and Sarnov's body language—he didn't believe Sarnov intended to kill Click. He was right. The gun was just the additional incentive the boy needed to reconsider.

Winter wondered if Click was smart enough to know that what the Russian said about Laughlin's and his father's greed might be true, but he doubted Click understood that the Russians would not part with any larger share of profits than Click's own family would. "Join us or die" was not exactly a promising start to the ideal courtship.

Winter waited until Serge holstered his gun to move

away from the window. Then he walked to the edge of the yard and sprinted back to Alexa's car. She was in the driver's seat.

"What's the deal?" Alexa asked.

"The Smoots definitely have the Dockerys," he replied. "Score one for Clayton. You can tell Clayton that Ross Laughlin is not just Peanut's lawyer—he's also his boss. Laughlin is definitely our link between the Smoots, Bryce, and Sarnov, Lex. Laughlin is connected to a syndicate, but the Russians are planning to move in on them."

"You're sure?"

"Acquisition by force is a standard Russian business plan. That's what Serge said. I guess that'll be news to Clayton."

"I'm sure it will be. Did Serge happen to say where the Dockerys are?"

"Sarnov didn't say. I couldn't see Click's side of the conversation, but I don't think he mentioned a location either. Maybe Click knows, maybe he doesn't, but there's no doubt the Smoots grabbed Lucy and the baby and have them. Sarnov said they're going to kill them."

"Even if Bryce walks?"

"I got that impression. We need to find Peanut. He sure as hell knows where they are."

"They could be anywhere," Alexa said. "Do we stick with the kid or follow Sarnov?"

"I'd put a tracker on the BMW if we had another one, but I don't think Sarnov is directly involved with the Dockery abduction, based on the lip-reading I did. We have to get to Peanut, or beat it out of Click."

"You're joking?"

"No, not really. Beating it out of Click is a perfectly good idea. Lex, the longer we wait, the more likely something bad will happen to the Dockerys. They're going to be murdered unless we can get them released, and time is running out for them. You said so yourself."

"Maybe after Monday, yes."

"You aren't sure. Did they share their timetable with Clayton or yourself? If they did, fine. If they didn't . . ."

"What the hell is that supposed to mean?" she snapped. "You're going to torture the truth out of a teenager?"

"If it will save the Dockerys, yes. And he's twenty-one and a criminal coconspirator in a kidnapping and possible double murder."

"Maybe we won't have to do that. Clayton says NSA's Big Ears caught Peanut and Dentures talking. Peanut uses prepaid disposable cell phones, but as soon as Clayton can get the location for the pay phone number she called from, we'll have something tangible. They could be holding the Dockerys in one of their houses. Maybe we should be checking Peanut's house, offices, properties."

"I doubt they'd risk keeping them in an obvious place," Winter said. "But what the hell. It's worth a shot."

After she flipped through the manila folder, Alexa handed the address-printout page to Winter. He used a micro-flashlight with a red lens that he kept on his key chain to read through the stack of Smoot residences and associated business addresses. The file also contained the few known telephone numbers each of the subjects used. Not one of them had a landline, just cell phones.

There was also a list of vehicles and license plate numbers.

To Winter the files looked like a thick stack of wasted time and dead ends. Time was something they didn't have.

"Lex, I have a gut feeling that we have to get to the Dockerys tonight. As soon as we start pushing on one of the Smoots, they'll know and it'll be over for the Dockerys, if it isn't over already. We can't just sit here with our thumbs submerged."

"What do you suggest?"

"We're going to have to start some fires."

"If we make our presence known, it could cost the Dockerys their lives. You just said so."

"Damn it, Lex, Lucy and that boy are dead if we don't move. If we do it right, only the people we interview will know we're bearing down. You know I'm right."

"I don't disagree," she said. "But what'll we do after we talk to one of them—lock them in my car trunk?"

"Your trunk's too small to hold but a couple of them. We can lock them up, though."

"Kidnap people? Lock them up somewhere . . ."

"I know a safe place we can put them. We have to gather a little field intelligence. We have nothing to lose."

"Nothing to lose but my job and our freedom. You're talking about committing felonies."

"I'm not law enforcement."

"You're not a criminal either. Let's think about this."

"Alexa. We both know why I'm here. Let's get this done."

"I agree. I agree. But not yet. Look, let's run this past Clayton—"

"No," Winter cut in. "He's sitting in a hotel room sucking on his pipe. This isn't about him, or intelligence he can glean or buy. I don't need more of his information to get going. I'm not going to sit on my ass waiting for Peanut to ring up Buck."

"But I think he—"

"I signed on with you to find the Dockerys before somebody kills them. That is the only felony I'm worried about at the moment. I'll do whatever it takes. I thought you felt the same."

"I'm off the books," Alexa snapped. "That's committed. I could lose my badge and my pension for this. Going to prison isn't something I want to risk."

"Mentally you aren't off the books. I don't have a career to worry about any longer."

"You have a family that loves you. That's more to lose than a career. And you don't need a career because you have a rich wife."

"That's a low blow, Lex."

"I know. I'm sorry. But you've been off the books more than once. This is my first time on a high wire without a safety net."

"You want to play by the rules, you're in the wrong game. Go call your fellow FeeBees and they'll look up the laws for you as you go. That isn't going to help now, and you're about to get in my way."

"I think you should go home," Alexa said. "For your sake. For your family's sake. I shouldn't have come to you. No hard feelings, Massey. Clayton and I can handle this."

"Are you two going to let the Dockerys find themselves? Are you going to wait to see if Peanut Smoot makes that phone call? What if he doesn't? What if they maintain silence? What if they decide they don't need Lucy and Elijah alive until Monday? You want to rely on Clayton Able's connections, some computers and satellites being run by people who could care less if we succeed? You want to end your brilliant FBI career standing at two gravesides? You want to spend the rest of your life wondering what Eli Dockery would be doing at that moment if he was alive? I will go to prison to save a woman and her child. I don't intend to ever ask myself why I didn't do what I knew I had to do, but didn't. Those two people are more important than the lives of everybody who is even peripherally involved in abducting them."

"I agree, but…" She stared at him, uncertainly. "Bringing you in and tying your hands wasn't fair. I am an FBI agent, and I can't break the law, off the books or not."

"Then get the hell out of my way."

"I am in charge here."

"I'll tell you what, Lex. You're right: Breaking laws is putting us on their level. Why don't you go back to the hotel and put your head together with Clayton's? Meantime, I'll watch Click's house while you and Clayton work on figuring out how to figure out where the Dockerys are. You guys figure it out, call me. I see anything here, like if Peanut stops by for popcorn and soft porn, I'll call you."

Alexa shook her head. "You're going to do something crazy, aren't you?"

"Absolutely not," he said, crossing his heart. "I've made my speech, and I feel better and, bottom line, I agree with what you've said. No sense both of us sitting here in the rain."

Sarnov and Randall left the house through the front door, ran to their car in the rain, and drove off.

"Maybe I should tail Sarnov?" Alexa said.

"He or Randall would spot you before you got three blocks," Winter said.

"I guess."

"Seriously, Lex. One of us should get some rest. Two hours and, if nothing happens, we'll regroup and think this through."

Alexa thought about it for a few seconds. "You're on your own. But you keep me in the loop."

Winter went to his truck. A few minutes later, when Alexa drove off, she didn't look at Winter or wave at him.

He closed his eyes and shook his head. He had already made up his mind. No matter what Alexa said, there was no alternative to doing something crazy.

40

The last thing Peanut Smoot thought he ought to do was to drive an hour down to South Carolina to deal with his kids. It wasn't smart to be close to the kidnap victims until it was all over. It was just practical that the leader had to be protected for the good of the organization. He was tempted to go by Click's, send him down there and put him in charge. He needed to get Buck the hell out of there. Dixie was capable of dealing with the pair herself with the twins helping, but she couldn't do that and deal with Buck if he went off on a tear. However, despite Peanut's best efforts to toughen Ferny Ernest, Click didn't have the hardness the other kids had. It was better to keep Click away from violent situations because he had his mama's squeamishness. If it wasn't for his computering and other mind-necessary potential, the boy would be as useless as a milk bucket under a bull. The twins would do whatever you told them, but you had to make sure they had instructions they couldn't screw up.

Peanut's back was feeling better thanks to the pills, and the fire Sarnov had built in his gut was down to the glowing coals. He pulled over and backed into a driveway that had trees on both sides and waited there for fifteen minutes watching to see if anybody was following him. As far as he could tell, none of the people in the vehicles that passed by looked like cops in a hurry to keep up with him. He also checked the sky for helicopters. He pulled out of the driveway.

Peanut passed the Utzes' store that was a half-mile from his tubular steel gate. Just past the store he took the left fork, drove to his gate, climbed out, unlocked the padlock, and pushed the gate open. He didn't like getting mud on his best boots, but he was alone and had to get out of the truck. After he drove the truck in, he had to lock the gate back up and drive to the warehouse down the narrow road that was just a dirt path with some gravel scattered on it in places.

The four-wheelers were all parked in the open equipment shed outside the warehouse. Peanut looked into the shed and saw that Buck was roped to one of the support poles, his pants down around his ankles, his butt exposed. He reminded Peanut of a child who's lost a game of cowboys and Indians. Buck knew the sound of Peanut's truck and he didn't turn his head to look at his father. The twins came out of the woods with their shotguns across their chests. They were smart enough to wait until they were sure Peanut was alone before showing themselves.

"What the almighty hell is this?" Peanut demanded, pointing at Buck's backside.

"He was having a fit, Daddy," Burt said.

Curt added, "We had to tie him up to calm him down. And he still ain't calmed down."

"Untie me," Buck screamed. "You stupid chunks of pig vomit."

"What kind of fit?" Peanut asked.

Curt said, "He was trying to screw that woman, beating her up and all like he does, and about to kill her."

"He wanted to fight us about stopping him like Dixie said. He tried to hit Dixie, and we couldn't let him do that," Burt added.

"You should have hanged him by his goddamn neck," Peanut said, glaring at Buck.

"You want us to hang him?" Curt asked disbelievingly.

"She wanted me to give it to her," Buck yelled. "Been asking for it since she got here. It ain't my fault."

Peanut backhanded Buck, leaving a large red stain on his cheek. "Leave this mule tied up a while," he ordered, storming over to the warehouse, unlocking the padlock with his key, and going inside.

Peanut flipped the breaker that turned on the lights inside the warehouse so he could see better. He saw that the dogs' door was cracked open, and was glad somebody was thinking. Dixie opened the trailer door before her father got to the porch steps.

"Hey, Daddy!" she said excitedly. "I didn't know you were coming out here."

"The hell's going on, Dixie?" He smelled bourbon, but didn't say anything. She probably needed a belt after going up against her older brother.

"That damn Buck. He screwed her up bad," Dixie muttered. "I came back with the twins after I found them, and I caught him in here beating the cold crap out of her. Had her on the danged island deal. He'd tore her clothes off and had his pants down ready to do it. I swear, as the Lord is my savior, he'd a killed her. And he'd a killed us if he could of for stopping him. You know how he gets, Daddy."

"He said she was asking for it," Peanut said, realizing as he said it how ridiculous it was.

"A classy woman like that would as soon back up to a billy goat as Buck. Nobody wants to get beat up and screwed with her baby right there. Buck ain't right, Daddy."

"He has issues, all right," he agreed. "Where's she at?"

"Your room."

Peanut opened the door and looked in at a naked and trembling woman coiled up in his old bed. Her hair was matted with dried blood. He slid the door closed behind him, angry and thoroughly disgusted that his son couldn't keep his pants on when it was so important to business.

"I thought I told you to keep her doped up on that stuff I gave you."

"I did. But see, the bottle got left open somehow and it got knocked over in the sink. I give the kid a good dose of nighttime cold-and-fever medicine. It keeps him out for a few hours at a time. I could give her some, or I got some bourbon, I think."

"You ain't drinking on this job, are you?"

"You know I wouldn't do that," Dixie said defensively. "Just a bracer for my nerves."

Peanut reached in his pocket and took out the pills he had for his back. "Mix up these in a shot of that cough medicine. Dose her good with that and I'll run back up to the drugstore and get some more of the good stuff. She needs to be comatose. But for Christ's sakes, put some clothes on her."

"Like what?"

"Like a old T-shirt or something. She ain't a wild damn animal. And if Buck comes back through that door, you kill the son of a bitch, and that's my order. He wants the gal bad enough to defy me and he can just spend eternity with her taking a dirt nap. He sure as hell won't ever do us any good if he don't learn to control his urges."

"He's out of control sometimes, Daddy."

"Look, Dixie, all you got to do is keep her and the kid out for a few hours. We'll go on and get rid of them before sunrise. It's too dangerous keeping them alive. But I was serious about Buck. We're just gone overdose them with the good stuff. No sense in torturing the poor things without a reason."

"It wouldn't be Christian," Dixie said. "Abusing them more than we have to."

"Right." Peanut kissed Dixie on the forehead. "I'm trusting you to do this right, girl. Just lay off the liquor till afterwards."

Peanut went out into the warehouse, and as he passed the door to the storage room, he pounded on it, making a hollow drum sound, and he heard the dogs scurrying around, afraid—knowing it was him. They had been conditioned so that anybody, aside from the family, was food for them. They stayed in a steel room, ate out of ripped-open bags of dog food, lived in their own filth until one of the kids hosed it down. A vet had taken out their vocal cords when they were puppies. Peanut didn't want his dogs to bark at intruders; he wanted them silent so if somebody broke into the warehouse looking to steal from the Smoots, they wouldn't realize they were screwed until they were on the ground being torn limb from limb. Sure as dead's cold, his dogs would do it right. Wasn't like he hadn't tested them before. He had been thinking that he might just try them out on Sarnov when he got a chance.

He wasn't worried about the Dockery woman escaping, because between the dogs and the locked door, she couldn't any more get out of here than she could turn herself into a cat. But if the dogs got her, there'd likely be blood evidence left in the dirt. He watched enough forensic TV shows to know what the cops could do with just a tiny amount of blood. Since this involved a federal judge, they'd use the FBI technicians to sift each dirt crumb for blood, he was sure of it.

Peanut went out the door, padlocking it behind him. He went directly to the shed and stood beside Buck, still lashed to the post. Peanut took out his knife, snapped it open, and showed Buck the blade so it reflected the light from the shed's bare bulbs.

"I'm going to say this one time, son. If you never listened to me before, you better do it now."

"Damn it, Daddy, I already told you—"

"Shut up and listen!" Peanut growled, putting the blade against his son's throat. "By God, if you so much as go into that barn, and I mean step through that damned door right over there for any reason, I will kill you. You will stay right out here in this shed. You got that?"

Buck nodded his head, eyes downcast.

"It was her—"

"I don't care if she sticks a tittie up to that padlock hole over there, you just look at it from way over here."

The twins giggled.

Peanut cut the ropes, waited for Buck to pull up his pants, then handed him a twelve-gauge shotgun that was leaned against a four-wheeler.

"Come on, y'all," Peanut told the twins. "I'll give you a ride up to the gate."

Burt and Curt climbed into the truck's bed. Peanut looked in the rearview at Buck, who was in the shed shooting the bird at the twins for tying him up. He sure as hell wasn't mad enough to tell his daddy to go screw himself. When Peanut got to the gate, he stopped for the twins to jump down from the bed and waited until Curt opened it up.

"Don't either one of you move from right here until I get back. Anybody comes in through that gate that you don't know, you shoot them. Hide over there together," he said, pointing, "and watch the road. Anybody but me comes through the gate, blow their damned head off." Peanut wanted the twins on the same side of the gate so in case they got excited and happened to shoot they wouldn't risk killing one another.

"I mean anybody you don't know. Strangers or cops." Peanut drove through the gate, hoping they would do exactly as he told them. The twins were not retarded by a long shot, but they thought differently.

He prayed he hadn't left any "idiot" loopholes they might fall through and do something disastrous. His father had often said that you can't make anything foolproof, on account of fools are ingenious at finding new ways to mess things up. Boy, was that the truth.

41

When the man Lucy Dockery learned by eavesdropping was Dixie's father arrived, she had already gathered herself together and had explored the room using the flashlight. She put her fingers over the lens to filter and concentrate the beam into a weak slit of light. While she'd been exploring, Lucy had touched enough to leave her fingerprints in enough places that no matter how well these people cleaned, they'd never erase them all. The door in her room, which she supposed was a required emergency exit, was padlocked.

The windows in the bedroom were covered with overlapping strips of duct tape to seal out all light. The room's windows had heavy steel-screen shutters on them. She discovered that the lock hasp was being held fast by a several-inches-long, threaded machine bolt. A flat washer prevented the bolt's head from falling straight through the steel ring. Getting the screen and the window open was a breeze. Lucy wished they had used a large nail, because a nail would have given her a tool, and she'd have been able to use it to put one of Buck's eyes out, or give him a facial scar to remember her by. The window behind the mattress was very close to the warehouse's wall, but she was sure that once she got the screen open she could slip out and drop to the ground without Dixie hearing her. She'd found a spray bottle of human scent killer that she could use. Once she got out of the trailer she would have to somehow seal the dogs in their room before they came out. The noise from the TV and the thick layer of dust should help cover her footsteps. If the dogs went into a barking frenzy and alerted Dixie, Lucy would have to defend herself as best she could with whatever she could lay her hands on. She had never heard the dogs bark or even growl, so she figured they were trained not to. She had to neutralize Dixie, Buck, and maybe the twins as well. She knew that she either had to overpower Dixie and get a key to the warehouse door, or neutralize Dixie and lure whoever was outside the warehouse inside so she could get out through the open door. Then she had to make sure they couldn't get out and chase her to get a head start.

When Dixie's father arrived, Lucy hid the flashlight under the mattress and curled up on the bed to play possum when he looked into her room. She hoped she looked worse to him than she was. Buck had bruised her up good, but with scalp wounds, bleeding is often disproportional to severity. If she was going to get away, they had to believe she was incapable of escaping.

Lucy was certain her father had the authorities searching for her and Elijah, but she couldn't depend on help arriving in time, and couldn't hold out any hope for a rescue.

Seconds after the man closed the door, he and Dixie moved into the kitchen. Lucy slipped off the bed and put her ear close to the base of the door and listened to their conversation. It confirmed what Buck had said about her future prospects, but now she knew they were going to kill Elijah, too. Now she no longer had anything to lose.

She didn't have until Monday. She had a few hours at best. If Dixie's father got more of the drug they had used on her, she had to act before he returned with it. Once they dosed her with that again, she would never be able to do anything but lie there unconscious until they . . . No. That wasn't going to happen. At least not the way they planned. She wouldn't go to her grave quietly or easily.

The makeshift dose that Dixie was going to use on her was a frightening thought, but she'd deal with that when the time came.

She waited for the door to the trailer to close before she sneaked the flashlight back out from under the mattress. Then she turned it on for a moment, slid the window carefully closed, put the flashlight back beneath the mattress, and lay on the bed. She had to make a plan, go through the options one by one.

She forced herself to concentrate, running through a mental list of what she had seen out in the warehouse, and how she could make use of those items for her and Eli's flight.

She had no idea what was beyond the building's walls, so once she was outside, she'd have to play it by ear.

Eleven-letter word for exiting hell.

DELIVERANCE

42

Winter Massey felt a visceral sense of relief as he watched Alexa drive off, her lights disappearing as she took the distant curve. The FBI agent part of Alexa was a wall standing between him and any information Click possessed. Winter's gut told him that Click was the key to the Dockerys. Alexa the FBI agent saw the young man as a citizen wearing the cloak of constitutional rights, and he was protected by her allegiance to her pledge to uphold those laws. She could say she was "off the books" till the cows played cards, but she couldn't actually be that way. Alexa saw the situation in shades of gray. Weighed against the Dockerys' lives, Click's rights didn't figure into Winter's formula. When it came to life-and-death situations, Winter saw in jet black lines on bright white paper.

Winter knew what he had to do, and if he succeeded, Alexa would have to learn to live with it. His reward would come when he saw Lucy's and Elijah's living faces, and if he had to make a deal with the devil, he would do it. When he looked at Ferny Ernest, he saw a cold-blooded willing participant in a double murder of a woman and her child.

Winter had spent a lot of time talking to a psychiatrist who specialized in post-traumatic stress disorder. He had fully opened himself up to the therapy, unburdened himself as completely as he could, but despite that, he still saw every man and the one woman he had killed. They appeared with regularity in his dreams. All he had to do was close his eyes to see them. If Eleanor had lived, maybe he wouldn't have taken the forks in the road that he had. If he had never gone to Rook Island on that WIT-SEC assignment, if he had never met Sean, if he had never felt the thirst for justice and retribution, if he hadn't wandered into a world of CIA killers and mobsters to save her, things would certainly have worked out differently. He wondered if Alexa suspected that she didn't know him because the years and experiences had altered the boy he had been with her into the man he had become without her. Their closeness had been a long time ago. Alexa knew it was true.

Alexa was somebody from the past who called once in a blue moon, when she felt nostalgic or got the big blue meanies. She was a Christmas card and a birthday card on Rush's birthday.

Things change.

Life takes up all your time.

You put off making contact and that becomes emotional distance.

He and Alexa would never again be close friends. He had his heart heavily invested in a place that had no defined role for her.

Intentions not acted upon become regrets.

Intentions acted upon become regrets.

Winter checked the extra magazines, zipped his windbreaker halfway up so he could get to the SIG, put on a Gore-Tex ball cap, and climbed out of his truck.

After crossing the street, he circled the neighboring house and kept to the bushes until he arrived at Click's house.

Showtime.

43

Serge Sarnov parked the BMW beside a dark SUV, which contained three of Max's men. He knew real talent when he saw it, and Randall's guys were bright boys who didn't require rubber gloves to dive into wet work. Serge lit a cigarette and cut off the headlights. The wipers cleared the windshield at one-second intervals.

"That boy's all right," Serge said, meaning Click. In Serge's opinion the young Smoot was a koi swimming in a sewer with a school of shit-sucking catfish.

"He's going to tell his father," Max said. "Soon as he gets over seeing the barrel of your gun, he'll call Peanut. He doesn't really believe you can take his old man out of play."

Serge nodded. "You think I may have overestimated his sense of greed? I don't think so, but..." He tapped the wheel with his fingertips. "That boy has real potential."

"A lot can happen to complicate this deal. Peanut is smart, vicious, and he could complicate things. That bunch doesn't operate by any playbook but their own," Max warned him.

"The Smoots are animals," Serge said. "Click knows it. I think he will look into the future and make his decision based on that. He isn't anything like the others."

"Would you?" Max looked over at the SUV, the dark silhouettes of the killers inside. "Turn on your blood, turn down a known quantity for some money in the future he thinks he can get anyway?"

"He isn't me," Serge replied.

"Would you turn on your firm?" Max asked. "If someone came in out of the dark and said, 'You're too bright to work for Intermat for chump change. I'm going to take Intermat down. Join me or die.'"

Serge didn't answer. He was considering the value of Click weighed against the potential loss of this deal to his employers. The Smoot end of Laughlin's empire accounted for huge profits. Tens of millions over the next couple of years. He wanted the Smoots' action, needed it. Losing it now would put his life on the line, because his employers had already entered the figures into their projections. Laughlin had agreed to watch the Smoots be pushed aside, but the American probably wouldn't be sorry to see Serge fail. Maybe he should get rid of Click just in case he misjudged the boy. A bird in the hand . . .

"Let's do this," Max said. "We can keep Click under wraps until this operation is over. We can take him to the house and after Peanut and the others are done in, he'll be easy to bring over."

Serge said, "I was going to suggest the same course of action." Randall was indeed a very smart man.

"After the Dockerys are dead, we can deal with Peanut and his family and let the trail end at their corpses."

"I'm listening," Serge said.

Max laid out a plan that brought a smile to Serge's lips. He inhaled and considered it. Max Randall never disappointed. He had a strategic mind and made life-and-death decisions effortlessly. He would do fine for the firm as long as he played it straight, and Serge was sure he was intelligent enough to do just that.

"Take two men, get Click, and I will meet you all back at the house. Use whatever force you deem necessary to find out if he made any calls to his father, but keep his brain intact. That part of him we need in good working order. Use your best judgment."

"I'll handle it," Max said, slipping from the car.

Serge dropped the window long enough to flick his lit cigarette out into the wetness of the night.

44

Winter Massey saw that Click was still sitting where he'd been earlier—in the recliner, still tapping his sock feet to the music, watching naked girls on a stage gyrate to rock tunes the dancers were too young to have listened to growing up. The choice of musical accompaniment was more for its nostalgic value to the middle-aged skin-worshipping congregation that regularly attended their local branches of the First Church of the Brass Pole. People who were younger than the men who actually put donations inside the dancers' garters probably watched the DVDs and videotapes without listening to the music.

Winter wondered if Click had called his father to tell him about Sarnov's nocturnal visit and job offer, or if he was weighing that offer while the Dockerys were awaiting death. It really didn't make any difference. Winter looked in at the large TV screen, frowned, and circled the house. As he passed the rolling garbage can in the shed, he spotted the corner of a pizza box sticking out from under the lid. He pulled out the box, strode around to the front door, took out his SIG, and rang the doorbell. He pulled the bill of his cap down to shadow his eyes.

He didn't hear Click coming, but the porch light came on and the front door opened enough so that Winter could see that the young Smoot had put on a plaid bathrobe over his T-shirt and boxers. The chain on the door was a substantial model, which might not give without allowing Click a chance to fire through the wood. This kid would probably have some sort of weapon at hand, especially given the earlier Sarnov/Randall visit. With a little luck on Click's side and a decent-caliber round, Winter might find himself lying on his back bleeding out—an armed home-invading stranger. Taking the chance wasn't necessary.

"What?" Click growled through the crack.

"Pizza," Winter said. The rain striking the concrete walkway behind him helped mute his voice.

"I didn't order any pizza."

"Fourteen dollars and twenty-six cents."

"I didn't order it."

"If you're standing inside two-two-one-five you did."

"It isn't my pizza. I got one from you last night. Maybe your cheap-ass computer put me back on for one tonight."

"Fourteen twenty-six cash or check. It's getting cold."

"It was only like twelve bucks last night."

Winter shrugged. "Take it for twelve," he said.

"I didn't order it."

"Fine. Ten then," Winter said. "It'll just go in the garbage."

"What's on it?"

"How should I know? What'd you order on it?" Winter asked, trying not to laugh. Young Click wasn't going to pass up an opportunity to eat pizza just because he didn't order it.

"Ten bucks. And that's tip included."

"Sure."

"Hang there. I'll go get you the money."

When Click returned, Winter heard the sound of something heavy being set down, and knew it was a gun Click was putting on a table by the door so he could open it and pay for the pizza. Winter had been right not to try and muscle his way in.

Click opened the door with the bill in his hand, looking hungrily down at the pizza box. He didn't raise his eyes until Winter handed the box over and Click realized it was empty. When he looked up at Winter, there was mild confusion in his eyes, which changed instantly to fear when the deliveryman raised a gun and aimed it directly at Click's chest.

Click backed up, hands still clenching the empty box. Winter entered, lifted a blue-steel revolver from the narrow table cluttered with junk mail. He opened the revolver's chamber, tilted its barrel up, and let the rounds drop into a half-filled trash can before tossing the gun on a stack of newspapers in the corner.

"Wait a minute!" Click said. "You're robbing *me*?"

"No, I'm not."

"Do I know you?" Click's brain was racing, trying to sort through its memory banks to figure out where he'd seen Winter before.

"Where *would* you know me from?" Winter asked him.

"I don't know, but . . ." His eyes were darting back and forth between Winter's face and the SIG. He seemed more curious than frightened. "Have we met before?"

"Maybe you remember me from the Westin this afternoon. That's where I saw you."

Click's expression changed, a smile growing as he remembered. "Yeah, I saw you there. Why are you here?"

"Why were you there?"

"I was meeting an exotic dancer. She didn't show."

"I don't think so, Slick," Winter said. "I think you followed somebody there."

"It's Click, not Slick. No, I didn't follow anybody anywhere." Click sat on the arm of the recliner, tossed the box down, and crossed his skinny arms. "You're what, FBI?"

"Why would you think that? The FBI only deals with federal crimes. You committed any of those? Extortion, auto theft, crossing state lines in the commission, Mann Act, drug trafficking, wire fraud, insurance fraud, spying, credit card scams?"

"No." Click's smile widened.

"Who did you follow to the Westin, Click? Or should I call you Ferny Ernest?"

"You don't have a warrant, do you?"

"Why would I need a warrant?"

"To come in here."

"You opened the door to me."

"I know the law. You forced your way in by pointing a gun at me."

"Knowing your rights will come in real handy when the cops ask if you understand your rights."

"You know who my lawyer is?" Click blustered.

"It's probably Ross Laughlin. Your father's lawyer and crime boss or partner, depending on who you ask."

The smile melted. Click was trying not to look worried, and he wasn't terrible at it.

"Answer my original question," Winter said. "Who were you following? And by the way, I already know the answer."

"Who was I following?"

"Judge Fondren."

A sudden tic almost closed Click's right eye.

"I don't even know who that is."

"You know very well who he is. And you know his daughter and her baby were kidnapped, because members of your family did it at your father's direction. That's why you were following the judge, and that's why you thought I might be with the FBI."

"That's crazy. My father is a legitimate businessman."

"Kidnapping's a federal crime that carries the death penalty for everybody involved in the conspiracy . . . if the Dockerys are murdered. If they aren't, it could be probation for somebody who was only following a federal judge around and calling in that information to others. There's always phone records, positioning locators on cell towers, voice-pattern identification, surveillance cameras, and wiretaps all together pinpointing who did what to whom and where."

"Arrest me then," Click challenged, smiling again. "You got proof, take me in. I know my rights."

"Arrest you? You aren't listening to me. I am not a cop or an FBI agent. I couldn't arrest you if I wanted to. You're missing the whole point."

"What is the point?"

"I don't have a badge, so you don't have any rights. If you tell me where the Dockerys are, you'll live. If you don't, I'm going to move straight up the Smoot family tree, clipping off every diseased limb I come to until one of your kinfolk is smart enough to tell me."

"You don't scare me."

"I know you've been threatened by people with guns before."

"I sure have."

"You think Sarnov would have shot you if you hadn't gone belly-up and agreed to join up with his firm?"

This tic fully closed Click's eye.

"Not fifteen minutes ago, Serge Sarnov sat right there on the couch and said that your family abducted the Dockerys and that they are going to kill them. I have it on audio and video tape."

"Why would something some Russian I never laid eyes on before says to me mean anything? The man broke into my house."

"I'm going to ask you nicely where Lucy Dockery and her boy are, and you're going to tell me. If they are where you say, I'll turn you loose. If they aren't, I'm going to ask again, but not nicely."

Something flickered beyond Click's right shoulder. Max Randall's illuminated face seemed to be floating out in the darkness. As a gun rose to Randall's shoulder, Winter kicked out, sweeping Click's feet out from under him and falling to the floor as he did so.

There was a flash outside.

The window shattered and large fragments of glass blew into the room and showered the two prone figures.

Winter knew immediately that the weapon was an MP5-SD. There'd been a total lack of sound except for the thuds of the rounds punching through Sheetrock and the high-pitched whines of the ricocheting subsonic 9mm rounds. Grabbing Click's ankle, he dragged the skinny young man into the hallway. As he pulled the boy, a second shooter opened up and the recliner spewed chunks of cotton and foam rubber as rounds chewed into it.

One of the shooters whistled, and Winter heard their feet as they fled across the stone patio.

"Want to live, don't move a muscle," Winter ordered, and got to his feet.

Gun in hand, Winter vaulted through the empty window frame and sprinted around the house in the opposite direction the assailants had taken, figuring they might be lying in ambush around the corner.

As he rounded Click's house, Winter saw their running shapes and aimed at them, but there were too many houses behind the fast-moving men, and he didn't want the immediate attention that firing a gun in this neighborhood would bring. The two shooters jumped into an SUV parked half a block away. It roared off, leaving Winter standing on the sidewalk in front of Click's house, pelted by the rain.

He remembered Click's Smith & Wesson and the rounds in the trash can. "Christ," he mumbled and ran back toward the house, praying he wouldn't have to kill the kid, or take a round in his chest for losing track of the fact that Click was the enemy.

The front door was standing wide open, and Winter knew he hadn't left it that way. He'd been flanked.

45

"Oh my God," Click pleaded, "don't shoot me! Please, please..."

Winter turned the corner and aimed at the back of the person who stood aiming a gun down at Click's upturned face. The young man lay on the hallway floor on his back. In one hand he held the unloaded Smith, and in the open palm of the other, a pair of bullets. Click had been stopped from loading the handgun by the unblinking eye of a large-bore FBI-issued Glock.

"Shoot her!" Click yelled when he spotted Winter.

"I thought you left," Winter said, putting his SIG in its holster.

"Did you see who did this?" Alexa asked.

"One was Max Randall. The other shooter was too large to be Sarnov."

Alexa snatched Click's gun away from him, slipping her own into her shoulder bag. She looked into the den and shook her head slowly. "What the hell were they using?"

"Where did you come from?"

"I found your truck empty and I was standing at the front door when I heard glass breaking. I came in and found Ferny Ernest here loading his piece."

"A pair of MP5s firing subsonic rounds, noise suppressors. That the sort of weapons the good colonel was dealing?"

Alexa nodded.

"So, what the hell are you doing here?"

"I had an epiphany. I doubled back."

"I didn't see your car on the street."

"Parked on the next street and cut through the Lathams'."

"What was this epiphany?"

"I figured you planned to do something insane and that I should be with you so I'd know what you *didn't* do in case I'm ever asked officially. I thought about what you said about this guy's value weighed against the Dockerys' lives." She winked at Winter and smiled. "You were right. I was wrong. This is new territory for me."

"It was Max Randall?" Click asked, from the floor.

Winter nodded. "Yes, Click, I saw his face clearly."

"Why would he shoot me?"

"I'd bet he came back to cancel the job offer Sarnov extended to you earlier this evening."

"Why would he do that?" Click demanded.

"Because Sarnov as much as told you that he was planning to wipe your family out, and Max probably decided it was too much information too soon. He knows nothing you can do with a computer is unique enough to jeopardize his ass after Bryce is free."

Click said, "You saved me—so I know you aren't going to hurt me."

Alexa laughed and shook her head slowly. "Boy, for a genius, you do *not* know Shinola."

46

Winter Massey looked in his rearview mirror at Alexa's headlights, and then beside him at sulking Click's profile. Being almost killed had a sobering effect on people lucky enough to be able to remember it after the fact. Click was still wearing his red-and-blue plaid flannel robe over his T-shirt and boxers. The athletic sock on his right foot was bunched around his ankle like a badge of defeat.

"Your girlfriend was going to kill me," Click said.

"You were trying to load your gun. If you had, *I* would have killed you. What are you bitching about? You're murdering a young mother and her child."

"You have children?" Click asked.

"No," Winter lied.

"Married?"

"No."

"Girlfriend?"

He shook his head.

"Gay?"

"Don't talk to me unless you're ready to tell me where the Dockerys are."

"Why?"

"You really want to know?"

"Du-uh," Click said. "I wasn't asking so I could smell your breath."

"I don't want anything personal about this. It's business. I intend to keep your family from killing two innocent people, and I am willing to do whatever I have to do. I don't want to remember you as a real person because it might make me feel bad about what I had to do to you."

"I was just making conversation." Click looked at the road ahead, sullen. "I mean, somebody saves your life, keeps their girlfriend from killing you, and plans to torture you, you have to wonder about them."

"I didn't save you because I like you or give a damn if they kill you. I did it because I want to find out what you know. You're just a map to me. Whatever happens to you depends on how it affects my route to find the Dockerys."

"I can't help you hurt my family."

"You're not like them. They're killers, you're not."

"They might be what you say they are, but they'll be around a long time after *you're* dead. I'm no Judas."

"If they murder the Dockerys, I'll make sure you spend the next thirty years in prison without access to computers."

"Smoot blood goes back hundreds of years. Our ancestors came here from England. No Smoot has ever ratted out another one."

Winter figured the first Smoots came kicking and screaming, clapped in irons, straight from the bowels of some British penal institution.

"One way or the other, you're going to tell me where the Dockerys are. That, Click, is a dead-certain fact."

"You can't make me tell you anything."

Winter smiled.

"I bet you've never beaten anybody up or tortured them before. You don't have the eyes for it. You didn't even shoot back at Randall."

"No need to make a racket that would have brought the cops."

Click reached down, opened his robe, and pulled up the T-shirt. Even in the dimly lit cab, Click's torso looked like Jackson Pollock had created a masterpiece on the young man's canvas of skin by using a variety of blades and red-hot objects to get the desired effect.

He sneered. "Do anything you want to me. We have this family tradition that gets passed down from father to son. You can burn me with cigarettes, break bones, pull out my fingernails, or carve me up like a Thanksgiving turkey and all you'll get for your trouble is your own sweat." Click dropped his shirt and closed his robe. He said offhandedly, "Whatever you can do, I've already had. You might as well just shoot me and go on about your snooping business without wasting any more time than you already have."

Winter thought about a man who would do such a thing to his own child. He thought then about his own son and his infant daughter, and deep inside he was on fire.

He intended to find Lucy and Elijah, but after he did, he wanted to kill Peanut Smoot.

Maybe Click truly believed he wasn't going to rat out his father, but Winter knew differently.

47

The sign that had been suspended from a bar between the brick columns had been taken down. As a precaution Winter handcuffed Click's wrists behind him before he got out of the truck. He opened the padlock and swung open the steel pole that stretched, from hedgerow to hedgerow, across the asphalt driveway. The No Trespassing signs on either post glowed in the headlights. Winter watched Alexa drive through, took his truck in, then locked the gate.

The parking lot had been cut into the side of a hill studded with pine trees. The building at the base of the hill stood on a flat beyond a rock-walled stream. Its dark roof, accented by pools of rainwater, looked every bit as large as a football field.

"What is this place?" Click asked.

"Isolated," Winter said.

Winter led Click and Alexa down a long run of wide stone steps, across a wooden bridge over a rushing brook. The slopes and flower beds were buried under a carpet of rust-colored pine needles. A motion-sensitive light came on, illuminating the walkway and the front of the structure. The trio crossed an expanse of concrete, beneath a cantilevered awning, to arrive at a set of glass doors. Streaks of adhesive were evidence of logo graphics that had been removed from the inside of the glass at some point with a razor. Subtle lighting from a fixture over the reception counter, which was faced with wood veneer, allowed the arrivals a view of a lobby that had been stripped of all other furniture. Winter took his keys from his jacket and, isolating one, used it to unlock the door. As he ushered the others inside, a rhythmic beeping filled the space.

"What is this place?" Click asked again, sounding like a curious tourist.

Winter strode behind the reception counter and, using another key, opened a steel box and typed in the numbers to disarm the alarm system. He removed an odd-shaped key that hung inside the alarm box and came back around the counter.

Winter gripped Click's arm and led him roughly through a door, into utter darkness.

"No!" Click screamed, whirling in the dark. Winter pressed him against the wall with his left hand while he located and flipped a switch. The lights in the wide hallway came on.

When Click yelled, Alexa had pulled her gun, and the lights caught her crouched with her back against the wall, aiming at Winter and Click. She blinked, frowned, straightened, and put her gun back in her handbag.

Click's face had lost all its color and was twisted into a mask of horror.

They walked fifty yards to a steel door. Winter unlocked it and pushed Click into a narrower hallway, where four very solid doors ran along one wall. Each door had an eye-level, sliding peep panel. Winter unlocked the first door.

"This a jail?" Click said.

Winter hit the light switch on the wall beside the door, illuminating a bare bulb in a cage fixture high up in the ceiling.

"Get in," he said. He shoved Click and the young man hit the cell's back wall.

"What is this place?" Click asked, his eyes darting around.

"A padded cell," Winter said.

"What're you going to do to me?"

"Like you said, I can't torture you into talking. So I'm going to shelve you and move on. Sort of like a private maximum security cell block."

"You can't leave me in here!"

"Why not?"

"It's kidnapping for one thing."

"Now, that's ironic," Alexa said.

"Your family kidnapped the Dockerys. I kidnapped you. I don't know where they are. Your family doesn't know where you are. I don't find the Dockerys, they'll die. The Dockerys die, so do you."

"You won't kill me."

"You're getting the worst side of the deal, because the Dockerys will die soon, but you won't die for a long time."

"Bull," Click said. "You're not a murderer."

"You don't want to split that hair. A man can live for weeks without food before his stomach acids dissolve his vital organs. Water is a different story. Three to four days without it and you're done. But . . ." Winter reached into his coat and took out an eight-ounce bottle about half filled with water. "If you conserve it, you can ration this for a long time. It'll give you more time to think about what your family did to the Dockerys."

Click said, "It's the same as shooting me."

"Think so?" Winter scratched his head. "Doesn't seem that way to me. More like you're committing suicide."

"Screw you!" Click's voice was fierce, but his eyes reflected a deep uncertainty.

"Once I close this door, we are going to walk out of this building. If we find the Dockerys and they are still alive, I'll come back and let you out. Nobody but me will ever come back to check on you, and even if the hall out here was filled with people, they wouldn't hear you if you had a bullhorn. This room was designed so patients going through DTs couldn't harm themselves or disturb others with their screaming. After a few days in here you might decide on suicide. It won't be easy, but you might be able to get that bottle cap lodged in your throat and block the air passage, if you don't just swallow it."

"This is wrong!" Click's eyes narrowed to slits, his lips thinned. He looked around and up at the bare bulb in a steel-wire cage. "This doesn't bother me."

Winter reached over and flipped the light switch, plunging the cell into darkness.

"You turning out the lights?" Click sounded afraid.

"Tough old Ferny Ernest isn't afraid of whips, chains, knives, hot wire. But he doesn't like the dark."

"Please," the young man begged. "Just leave the slot open and the hall light on."

"Click, people pay good money to spend time in sensory-deprivation chambers. All alone with just your brilliant mind for company. You can do math problems or figure out computer programs to pass the time. Some religions believe that hell is a dark void where you spend eternity alone with only your thoughts for company. In every religion, murder is a mortal sin that guarantees hell."

Click bolted for the door. Winter body-blocked him easily and flipped him onto his back. Then Winter stepped out and closed the door, silencing Click's anguished screams. When Click pressed his face against the note-card-sized square of two-inch-thick Plexi, his eyes wild with terror, Winter slid it closed.

"How long are you going to leave him in there?" Alexa asked Winter.

"Good question."

"So, what is this place?"

"A building Sean bought to turn it into a safe house for battered women. They start work on it in a few weeks. I had the keys because we've been meeting with architects and space planners."

"Your own private Abu Ghraib. Great start, Massey. You just have one prisoner and you're torturing him."

On the way back up the hall, Winter told her about Click's scars, the conditioning to physical pain the boy had been put through for years, probably starting when he was very young.

"God, child abuse for the good of the family," Alexa said sadly.

"For the survival of the Smoots," Winter said.

"He'll bug out," Alexa warned.

"His fear of the dark is a full-blown phobia, but he

won't die from it. If I leave him in there a couple of hours, it will seem like a lot longer to him. When we come back and give him a chance to come clean, he'll do it."

"This is so wrong," Alexa said. "I can't believe you . . . that we can be so cruel."

"Without him, you'll never find the Dockerys in time, Bryce goes free, and not one of the Smoots will ever be punished for Lucy's murder. What I got from reading Sarnov's lips through a window won't hold up in court. But knowing what we know might give us leverage with the next Smoot."

Alexa grabbed Winter's arm when they entered the lobby. "I don't think I can do this."

"Damn it, Lex!" Winter yelled. "Stop thinking about this little vermin, and think about Lucy and Elijah. Click is a career criminal who is conspiring to murder two people just to throw a trial to free another murderer so Bryce can go on being a death merchant. We let him out now and it's all over."

"Turn on the light," she argued. "Keep him in there, but if he goes insane from the fear, he's no good to us either."

Winter thought it over for five seconds. "No way."

"What do we do in the meanwhile?"

"See what we can learn from somebody else."

"Peanut?"

"Don't know where he is. We could go look at each Smoot house, maybe find another Smoot or two. We can't torture them because they'll never talk. We might follow Peanut if Clayton tells us where Peanut is—or was, since this phone-trap thing isn't instant—and we could tag along behind him. If he goes to where they have the Dockerys. Too many ifs."

"Why couldn't we trade Click to Peanut for the Dockerys?" Alexa said.

"Peanut would never go for it. Click's life isn't worth a day in prison to him."

"He might if we promise we won't prosecute."

"You think he'd believe that? We both know that men like Peanut Smoot aren't the sorts you can deal with unless you have something they really, really want and can't take away from you. And I don't think Laughlin, Sarnov, and Colonel Bryce would let him do it and live. Peanut's freedom is more important to him than the lives of any member of his family."

"So how do we find Peanut?"

"We don't. You go back to the hotel and get some rest. If I don't call you by daylight, you call the cops anonymously and tell them where Click is. He doesn't know your name. If I get the location, I'll call you. I never show up, it's not your fault."

"What are you going to do?"

"The best I can," he answered. "I know you want to help, but you're in my way. If you really want the Dockerys, back off."

"Tell me."

"I'm going to go see someone who should know where they are, who might be willing to tell to save his skin."

"Who?"

"A lawyer."

"You're not serious?" Alexa said. "You're just going to tip our hand early. Laughlin isn't some kid, Winter."

"Lex, don't worry. If *he* doesn't tell me where the Dockerys are, I've got more padded cells."

48

Lucy Dockery would have one chance at survival. She had formulated a plan based on what she was sure she could lay her hands on in order to effect an escape. She had done her best to weigh what she was capable of doing against what wasn't as likely to work. For example, she had seen a bottle of antifreeze in the bathroom, probably used for winterizing the trailer's toilet. She imagined that if she could get some of it in Dixie's coffee, the woman might drink it and it would probably kill her the same way it did dogs that drank it. But as far as Lucy knew, the poison could also take a long time to work, and she wasn't going to get a chance to pour it in the coffeepot, and maybe Dixie wouldn't even drink any coffee. She was resigned to the fact that her plan was dangerous and it was likely that, if it worked, Dixie probably wouldn't survive. Well, Dixie planned to kill her and Elijah, and if she had to kill in self-defense, she was pretty sure she could do it.

In theory.

Every time she imagined striking a fatal blow to Dixie, every fiber of her being resisted the alien thought. Lucy was horrified and revolted at the very idea of taking a life.

Yes. To save Elijah, I will. If I absolutely have to, Walter, I will. I promise.

She heard Dixie making noise in the kitchen, mumbling to herself, running water into the sink, opening and closing the refrigerator. Lucy lay still, curled herself into a fetal position. When the door opened, Dixie entered carrying a glass and a plastic bowl. She had a T-shirt draped over one shoulder and a towel over the other. She sat down on the bed.

"Missy?" she said in a low voice. "Baby, you awake?"

Lucy drew herself into a tighter ball.

"You poor little thing. Dixie's going to clean you up," the big woman said. "I'm sorry for what Buck did. He got punished for it. He sometimes has trouble controlling his temper. I know you didn't mean to upset him like you did."

Dixie reached out and dabbed at Lucy's blood-matted hair with a wet end of the towel.

Lucy moaned, playing barely conscious as Dixie worked halfheartedly to clean her up. "You are one lucky gal," Dixie chirped. "This isn't near as bad as he can do. Not by a long shot it ain't. It's sort of his way of foreplaying. Buck's used to doing like he wants, and that won't never change. But he won't bother you again. Not so long as you don't give me call to turn my back and let him. Think of me as your angel standing between you and . . . Honey, you need to sit up and let Dixie put this shirt on you so you won't be naked."

Lucy allowed herself to be lifted so that Dixie could wrestle the T-shirt onto her. It was huge and reeked of stale sweat. Lucy assumed it belonged to one of the men. She remained as limp, as listless, as she could manage, returning silently to her fetal position as soon as Dixie finished dressing her.

"You know it wouldn't do you any good to try to get out of here. We know everybody around for miles and my daddy about supports half the people out here. You could say we're very instrumental in this community. A lot of the people around here are our kin.

"Honey, you need to sit up and drink this medicine Dixie got for you," Dixie said, her voice sticky with false concern. "It'll make you feel better."

Lucy had known this was coming, but she was filled with sudden terror, knowing the concoction would probably put her out, or at the least turn her into a staggering mess. If she was going to have a chance, she couldn't allow it. Dixie turned her over, raised her up, and put the coffee mug to her lips, pressing the rim against Lucy's teeth. The main odor was that of orange juice with an undercurrent of cough syrup.

"Don't make Dixie mad," the powerful woman warned. "Drink it."

Lucy wanted to scream, but instead she opened her mouth to allow the thick, sweet liquid to flow down her throat. Dixie didn't take the mug away until it was empty.

Dixie stood, letting Lucy go back into her curl. "You get some rest, missy. A nice restful sleep is just what you need. You'll wake up at home."

Dixie stood in the doorway staring in at Lucy for a long

time. All the while, Lucy was visualizing the medicine cocktail working itself into the lining of her stomach.

Keep thinking you're winning, you muscle-bound freak, Lucy thought. *Just keep thinking it.*

Eleven-letter word for Dixie.

P S Y C H O B I T C H

49

Clayton Able knew exactly where Dixie Smoot had called her father from, but he wasn't going to share that with anybody except the Major. Winter Massey was, as Clayton had insisted from the start he would, proving to be difficult to control. It appeared that if Massey was left to his own devices, he could make a very large mess of things, and generate complications they didn't need.

He turned to Antonia. "We have to stop Massey."

"Slow him down," the Major answered. "It isn't necessary to do anything so rash. Massey can't get anything done before tomorrow, and then it'll work for us. He can die as planned while shooting it out with the kidnappers. No need to change the plan."

"Randall is hot over what happened at Click's house. Says we should have warned him that Massey was there."

"Screw Randall. He didn't tell us he was going there.

This is a two-way street. Max had better not forget who's calling the tune. Where's Alexa?"

"Coming here."

"Good."

"Massey's on his way to Laughlin's."

"And Laughlin won't be home. So Massey will go back to see the Smoot kid and—"

"I've seen this happen a hundred times and I know in my gut when something is about to go up in flames," Clayton insisted nervously. "If you don't let me handle him, I'm not going to stay with this. I'm not going to spend my golden years in prison. We need to let Randall deal with Massey now."

He heard her exhale loudly. "Go ahead. But it means a change in plan. I'll work out an alternate with Alexa. Make sure Max understands that Massey's body can't be found until Monday. We'll have to play some hocus-pocus with the forensics. No biggie, since we'll be controlling the evidence-gathering process and reports."

"I'll make the call. You are paying me for my experience with these sorts of matters. It's the right thing to do," Clayton said, smiling. "The smart thing is the correct course."

"It had better be, Mr. Able. It sure as hell better be."

50

Winter Massey locked the gate to the closed-down clinic, then waited for Alexa to leave. She had the damned phone to her head before she was fifty feet away, probably calling Clayton Able for advice, no doubt begging him for some intelligence that would negate the necessity of Winter's trip to Laughlin's. Winter wasn't going to run everything he did through Clayton, or wait for him to toss Winter some eleventh-hour bone. Winter didn't care for men who sat at computers playing with human lives that were no more real to them than some teenage sorcerer in a game of Dungeons and Dragons. Clayton was working with Alexa, but the man had worked for Military Intelligence. He gave Winter the creeps, and every bone in his body told him not to trust him.

Something else was bothering him more than Clayton Able or Click's imprisonment. He couldn't shake a feeling of unease, a feeling whose source he couldn't put his finger on. Winter had never gone against his gut without being sorry he had. Right now his gut felt hollow and hot.

He hadn't wanted Alexa to come with him from Click's house because he didn't want her undermining what he was doing with Click. He had told himself that she was better off not being involved in anything that was heavy-handed or illegal due to the consequences to her career. She might want to let go and get down in the dirt with him, but she couldn't. Still it troubled him that she would bring him in to do something and then block him from doing it.

Winter picked up his own cell phone from the console and dialed Sean.

"Hello, Tiger," she answered.

"You say that to everybody?"

"Just if caller ID says they're using your phone," she replied. "How's it going?"

"It's picking up steam," Winter told her. "I borrowed one of your padded cells. Hope you don't mind."

"No," she said. "If you need it, it's fine."

"Your liability paid up on it?"

"Yes. Winter—Is everything all right?"

"Peachy keen. How's everything at the ranch?"

"There's a leak in the roof and water is running down the stone fireplace. Olivia has the sniffles. Rush saddled his horse without Faith Ann's help. Faith Ann cooked speckled trout dinner and it was excellent. Hank's complaining about everything because he wishes he was with you. This bed is so cold and lonely."

"Well, if things work out, I'll be back in it tomorrow night."

"You'd better be. This hot water bottle doesn't keep me as warm as you do."

"I'm glad you need me for something."

"Massey, I need you for everything. You know that, don't you?"

"Sure I do."

"You'd better be careful. You get injured and I'm going to be very angry with you. Is Alexa with you?"

"She's gone back to the hotel to meet with someone."

"Who's watching your back?"

"Doesn't need watching. I'm just driving around in the rain."

A horn blared. Winter, realizing he had drifted close to another vehicle, swerved back into his lane. A van sped by, the driver holding his hand out in the rain long enough to give Winter a hand signal not covered in the North Carolina driver's manual.

"What was that?" Sean asked.

"A Toyota, I think," Winter said.

"Winter, stay focused," she chastised.

"Sorry, what did you say?"

"That's not funny. You hang up and don't split your attention again for a minute."

"Okay, babe. Go back to sleep."

"Know what, Massey?"

"Yes, Sean, I certainly do."

"You'd better."

He waited until after she hung up to end the call. After this was over, he would tell Sean about the machine-gun attack at Click's. No sense in giving her something concrete to worry about. He had come within a split second of being cut to pieces. It was nice to know that retirement hadn't put cobwebs in his reflexes.

If the phone book was correct, Ross Laughlin's house was a large Tudor near Queen's College on a tree-lined street where other stately homes were surrounded by manicured lawns. The windows of the lawyer's home were all dark except for the ones on the back corner of the first floor—probably the kitchen. Laughlin's outdoors lighting was pooled for dramatic effect, designed more to show off the landscaping than to offer security. Winter assumed Laughlin had at least as good a security system as everybody else on the street. Perhaps, being a criminal as well as an attorney, his was better than anything his neighbors had. Winter didn't like the setup. There was no good place to park without letting himself be exposed as he approached the house from the front. He kept going and turned the corner and found a narrow service alley that ran behind the houses.

Winter went around the block and spotted a house that was being renovated, one end of it a yet roofless skeleton made of two-by-fours. A large container jammed with debris had been plopped down in the rutted disaster that would become a yard. The house was protected from its neighbors by a stand of bamboo. Winter cut his lights, turned in, and parked his truck behind the loaded dumpster.

He speed-dialed Alexa on the cell phone she'd furnished him.

"Yeah?" she answered.

"I'm here."

"You sure you want to go this route? Not too late to change your mind."

"I'm here, Lex. Unless you have something from Able that makes this unnecessary."

"Anything I can say to stop you?"

"I can't think of a thing."

She was silent for a few long seconds. "Don't do anything without weighing it against possible consequences. You're wide open, Massey."

Winter ended the call, reached behind his seat, and pulled out his hooded foul-weather camouflage jacket.

He set the cell phone Alexa had given him to vibrate and dropped it into his shirt pocket. He put the coat on, took the SIG out of his shoulder holster, and slipped it into the right front pocket of the coat. He opened the door and climbed out, locking the truck and pocketing the keys.

Winter decided that with current events under way, the lawyer might have special security measures in place, so Winter needed to be extremely cautious approaching the property. He had to let his eyes grow accustomed to the darkness so he could see using what little ambient light there was.

He used the stand of bamboo as a shield, waiting several minutes before he crossed the street and dodged behind a big home that backed up to the alley that ran behind the Laughlin house. Winter moved the way he stalked deer—slowly and deliberately, using the shadows and foliage and avoiding open spaces. Unlike deer, humans didn't have a sense of smell that would allow them to pick him out. The falling rain covered the sound of his footsteps. He reached the back of Laughlin's property, which was protected by a brick wall. Going over meant exposing himself and dropping into an area he didn't know anything about.

His eyes lit on a section of ladder leaning against an oak tree in the backyard of the home closest to Laughlin's. It was a godsend. He could climb up high enough into the tree to reconnoiter Laughlin's property from a safe place.

Question coincidence, his inner voice reminded him. *Anything that seems too good to be true...*

Something about this conveniently abandoned ladder that had looked so perfect now chilled him. Slowly, he backed deeper into the shadows. He put his hands in his pockets, froze completely, and concentrated on the ladder, his mind drawing lines and angles around it.

Long minutes passed while Winter closed his eyes and focused his ears until the normal sounds of the night were filtered out.

Sound betrayed them.

A muffled cough. Probably into a gloved hand.

A sniffle.

A twig snapped as someone shifted his weight.

Winter opened his eyes slowly.

Two or three invisible men trained in techniques of ambush had a kill zone set up around the bait—the ladder. A shadow beside a garden shed shifted and Winter made out the shape of a man giving hand signals.

They were communicating, which might mean nothing, or it might mean they were growing restless. Winter was positive the men hadn't been there in the neighbor's yard since dark in case someone decided to drop in on Laughlin. He was certain that they had known he was coming, and had become increasingly uneasy because he hadn't arrived yet, long after he was supposed to. How many times had he been in a similar position when an informant's tip about a location or a time had been wrong, and the fugitive recovery team had grown antsy, fearing their target had changed his mind or had made them? And when that happened, the team had communicated.

He wondered if Max Randall was waiting, finger on the trigger of a silenced MP5, its barrel still reeking of cordite from the assault at Click's house. There wasn't but a couple of ways they could have learned he was coming here.

The cell phone inside his coat vibrated.

Judas calling.

51

According to his watch, Winter Massey reached the truck an hour after he'd left it. He got in, cranked it, and drove away. As he was driving down the street away from the area, the cell phone vibrated again. With a fire burning inside him, he answered it.

"Winter?" Alexa said.

"Who else would it be?"

"Did you see him?"

"No."

"Why not?"

His mind was stringing together a lie even as he spoke. "You won't believe it."

"Won't believe what?"

"I parked and decided to take a catnap so I'd be sharp. My alarm didn't go off, or if it did, it didn't wake me."

Winter fought hard to keep the anger he felt out of his

voice. Alexa knew him pretty well, and she had a sharp ear for deceit. He yawned to flavor the lie.

"What now?" she asked him.

"Why don't I come by there and we can put all three of our heads together, try and come up with a plan?"

"Clayton's here. We'll be expecting you in, what, ten minutes?"

"About that," Winter said. "I'm going to stop by the store and pick up some things first. Need anything?"

"No."

Winter ended the call. His mind was swarming. Why hadn't Alexa parked at the house across from Click's where Winter had been parked? Why cut through yards on foot when she didn't have to? How could she have crossed over to Click's and not seen the assailants' vehicle waiting on the street? Was it possible that she didn't want to find the Dockerys? That was insane. Alexa was his friend, his closest friend—well, she had been once. What could change her like this? How could she set him up to be killed?

What could explain her behavior? Could she resent him for something he was unaware of to the point where she wished him harm? And as he went through the possibilities, he saw it. There was only one person on earth he could think of who was important enough to Alexa to explain her betrayal. There was only one person who hated him enough. . . .

Winter pulled up at a Quick Mart, got out and used the pay phone—the only way he could be sure nobody could eavesdrop on him. He dropped the coins in, dialed

Information, asked for a number. He fed the phone and called the number.

"Westin Charlotte," a voice said.

"Yeah, this is Scott Keen, can you connect me with my wife's room? Probably under A. Keen."

"Just a minute," the clerk said. Winter heard him typing on his keyboard.

"Alexa Keen?"

"Antonia."

"I'll connect you."

"Oh, never mind," Winter said. "She's calling me on my other phone." He hung up.

Precious. Antonia Keen. How had he forgotten that she began as an MP, had trained in cryptology? He suddenly remembered a conversation with Alexa years earlier: She had mentioned something about someone maybe contacting him to ask about her younger sister because of a security clearance. Nobody had called, probably because Winter hadn't been enthusiastic about the prospect of giving Antonia a reference. Clayton Able had worked with M.I., too. Winter saw now that he had just been window-dressing. There was another agenda—typical agency-style sleight of hand.

If what Alexa had told him wasn't true, what was? Was it possible they didn't want the Dockerys found until the last minute, for added dramatic effect? If that were the case, why would they try to kill him?

He remembered what Clayton had said—that Colonel Bryce couldn't operate his weapons dealing without the assistance of people in the Pentagon. Clayton had told them that some people in M.I. wanted Bryce convicted and others didn't. Able had told him the truth, but the man had swapped sides on him. *Tell enough truth so that it holds water.*

Alexa was working with Antonia, her only blood relative—probably the only person she had truly ever loved. Was it because Antonia was in danger? Alexa might do something this insane to save Antonia, and to do so, she might let Winter suffer the consequences of being in the middle. Maybe they were blackmailing her. Or maybe it was more basic. Maybe it was just about dollars and cents and security.

He couldn't be sure his vehicle wasn't bugged with a GPS device, so he called Alexa on the cell phone she'd given him. "I was thinking. You were right: I better run back and turn the lights on in Click's cell. It isn't going to help if I turn him into a babbling lunatic. If he talks, I'll call you. I'll get some sandwiches on the way back."

"Okay," Alexa said cheerily. "We'll be waiting for you."

Winter felt sick at heart. He turned at the next light and sped off into the night.

Max Randall was somehow tied into Antonia, and if Max knew where the Dockerys were, so did Clayton and the Keens. Was Clayton Able parceling out the bread crumbs he and Alexa were supposed to use to find the Dockerys' bodies?

He smiled.

If they were prepared to kill him to keep him from finding out where the Dockerys were being held, it meant that Lucy and Elijah were still alive, and he was on track to finding them.

As long as they thought Winter was ignorant of what

they were up to and were sure he was coming back so they could keep an eye on him, they wouldn't have any reason to try to stop him. By the time they figured out that he was not doing what he said, he would be ahead of them.

He only had to move fast enough to stay ahead of everybody else. There were no more good guys versus bad guys—just bad guys and him.

52

As soon as Dixie Smoot left the room, Lucy stuck a finger down her throat and vomited the foul liquid cocktail into a wadded-up blanket to muffle the sounds of her retching. Gagging, she shoved the blanket between two padlocked crates. She crawled over to the door and lay down with her ear near the bottom of it, listening.

Then she stood and, trembling, slid the door open a crack. The only light in the trailer was the flickering light from the TV. Dixie was lying on the sofa, a bottle of bourbon on the floor beside her, half-full glass in her hand.

Lucy slid the door closed, turned on the flashlight, and used the hem of the T-shirt to cover the lens to soften the light. She had figured out why the dogs hadn't attacked Eli and her earlier. The scent of the owner of the jacket had confused them. She knew that the bottle of spray she'd found beside the bed was designed to kill human scents to fool deer, and hoped it would work on dogs. She hoped they didn't decide to bark after all.

She used the spray, which smelled like rotting vegetation, on her legs, her arms, and, closing her eyes, on her face and hair. Putting on the hunting jacket, which was permeated with one of her captors' scents, Lucy went to the window, removed the bolt, and slid open the screen. She took the empty pee bucket from beside the bed. Feet first, Lucy eased her body out. Once she was hanging from the sill by her fingertips, there was no turning back.

She dropped to the dirt, landing on the balls of her feet. She prayed the sound of the television had kept the sound of her escape from alerting the dogs. She crept to the trailer's edge and looked around the corner. The dogs weren't coming out of the storage room's cracked-open door. Taking a shaky breath, Lucy moved swiftly across the expanse, made it to the door just as one of the animal's heads jutted out. She turned the flashlight, catching the dog full in the eyes. The animal's head vanished back into the shadows. Lucy eased the door closed and flipped the catch to lock it.

She crossed the dogs off her mental checklist and thought about the next step. The easy part was done. Now she had to do a couple of things out in the warehouse, go back inside, and get Elijah. If she remained calm, followed her plan, she would be outside the warehouse within ten minutes or so. That, or she would be a four-letter word for "no longer among the living."

53

Winter Massey sped to the clinic, darted from the truck, swung open the pole gate, and parked his truck on the lot. Still wearing the camo coat, he sprinted down the steps, crossed the bridge over the creek, unlocked the front door, and hurried to disarm the alarm system. He ran back to the lockup ward, opened the door, and flipped the light on in Click's cell right before unlocking and jerking it open.

Click was wedged in a corner, frozen, his blank eyes as wide open as his mouth.

He looked up at Winter and started crying. "I'm soooo sorry. I'm sorry. I'll tell you. I'll take you to find them . . ."

"Tell me where they are," Winter said, kneeling beside the sobbing boy.

Click put his hands on Winter's forearms and squeezed. "And you'll . . . you'll let me go? You . . . prom . . . prom . . . ise?"

"Tell me where Lucy and her son are, and I will take you out of here. Show me where they are. As soon as I have them, you're as free as a bird. Word of honor."

Winter lifted Click to his feet. He felt a sharp pang of remorse when he realized that the kid had urinated on himself. Winter led him out of the padded room and down the long hallway. They stopped at the counter just long enough for Click to blow his nose and tell Winter how to find the land in South Carolina where the Dockerys were almost certainly being held. Winter gave Click a sheet of clear plastic from the floor to keep him dry on their walk to the truck. Turning off the lights, he set the alarm, after which, he led Click though the door, closed and locked it. Reflexively, Winter checked out the route up the slope, holding Click by his left arm to support him and to make sure he didn't try anything. The kid might have lied to Winter about the location, figuring it would be a while before his deception was discovered. Click was extremely intelligent and crooked as a sow's tail.

"So, tell me the truth, are you a cop?" Click asked him as they walked.

"I used to be."

"Ever really killed anybody?"

"Yes."

"You'll really let me go?"

"As soon as I know for sure you've told me the truth."

Winter opened the truck door and let Click climb in, crossing the console and buckling his belt before he followed him in. He cranked the truck and started out.

"They'll kill me if they find out it was me," Click said. "Kin or not. I'm breaking the code."

"I won't tell them," Winter said.

"How many people you taking in there?"

"Just me."

"In that case, if they don't kill you outright, you'll tell them I did."

"You can tell them you knew they'd kill me so you tricked me into coming to them."

Click was silent a moment. Then he said, "You said I could go free."

"You will. But while I'm getting the Dockerys, you're going to be cuffed to my steering wheel."

Click looked down at the floor. Winter raced down the winding driveway.

"So, knowing that," he told the kid, "you maybe want to make any amendments to the directions you just gave me?"

Winter came around the final bend and saw that the heavy yellow pole was back in place. His gut twisted because he'd intentionally left it standing open.

"Duck!" he yelled, flooring the accelerator. He cut the wheel at the last second, aiming at the boxwoods between the security pole's upright steel post and the sign kiosk. He saw a head rise above the shrubs, and he ducked lower just as the automatic weapons opened up. He felt the impact as the truck exploded through the shrubbery and caught the shooter behind it, punting the man's body in a high arc. Winter's tires bounced as he ran over the assailant's body. He jerked the wheel and skidded sideways, straightening as the automatic weapons shattered the rear windshield and then the front one.

"Shee-at," Click said, straightening to peer over his shoulder.

"Down!" Winter yelled. There was a sound like a bottle of cola being dropped. The back tires went flat and what remained of the front windshield was peppered with gore as Click folded at the waist. The truck crested the hill.

They would be coming after them.

He didn't have to look at the gauges to know the truck was mortally wounded. He smelled the radiator fluid, and it was all he could do to hold the truck in the road with two flat tires that would be sliced off the rims in a matter of seconds. He turned onto a narrow county road, waited until he saw the headlights swing onto the road behind him, then he jammed the accelerator and aimed the truck at the tree line beyond the ditch.

Winter's truck went into the ditch, came up the other side, and went airborne. Tumbling, it finally stopped on its left side in the muddy field, its headlights illuminating the scraggly trees fifty yards ahead.

54

The pursuing Tahoe came to a stop, and the driver got out to look at the wreck. He spoke into his cell phone. "Massey's done. Truck's finished. We'll just make sure and we're out of here. Yeah, I know how dangerous he *was*. You get Blocker out of the street, we can handle this. Meet you back at the place in an hour."

The passenger climbed out of the Tahoe and walked in front of the headlights, carrying an MP5-SD. The driver came slowly around the SUV holding a tactical shotgun with a high-intensity flashlight mounted under the barrel.

After the killers crossed the ditch and were advancing toward the overturned truck, Winter sat up behind them. He had been lying on his back since jumping out into the mud as the truck left the ground. Silently, he put a pair of .40-caliber rounds into the back of the SUV passenger's head. As the driver pivoted at the sound of his shots, Winter put one into his right ear and a second into his neck below his jaw. He knew neither man was Randall or Sarnov because he'd seen them in the headlights.

Winter sprinted to the running Tahoe, turned it around, and drove away. He needed to catch Max Randall before he picked up the run-over corpse and left. When Winter got there, Randall was gone. Only a dark circular oil-slick-looking stain showed where the dead man had been. Winter itched to chase Randall down and kill him, but he had more important things to do. He had to find a pay phone.

55

Lucy Dockery went directly from locking the dogs' door to the gasoline drums lined up against the warehouse wall. She took the pee bucket off her arm and set it down. Taking the nozzle in one hand, she moved the lever up and down to pump gasoline into the bucket. Luckily, the pump mechanism was well greased, so the only sound was the jets of gas shooting into the container. After filling the bucket, she also filled a large-mouth gallon jar almost to the rim with gas. She carried the containers over and set them down beside the porch, where she could get to them after coming out the door with Eli.

A pickax and a pair of shovels leaning against the little porch hadn't been there earlier or she was sure she would have seen them. Her heart fell when she realized that the twins had probably brought them inside after digging the graves they intended for her and Eli. The pickax sparked an idea that added an additional facet to her plan—one that brought a painful smile to her split lips. *This could actually work.*

Lucy propped an old wooden ladder against the back wall of the trailer so she could get back into her room through the window. She took off the coat and laid it on the bottom of the window over the track edges of the aluminum frame.

All she had to do was to sneak out of the room and into the kitchen, get one of the cast-iron skillets without Dixie hearing her, then get back in her room and call out so Dixie would come stomping back there to shut her up. When she came in, Lucy would hit her in the head and knock her out cold.

Then she would get some of the matches she'd seen stuffed in a shot glass on the counter near the stove, grab her son, and go out the front door and pour the gasoline all around the outside of the trailer in the dirt and light it to draw the other Smoots from outside the building to fight the fire. When they came into the warehouse, she'd have Eli in the corner, which would be behind the door when it was open, effectively hiding them from view of the in-rushers. She'd take Eli out, close the door, and lock all the kidnappers in. She'd push a matchstick into the lock and break it off to jam it. Maybe Dixie would have a concussion, or maybe she would even die from the blow. That wasn't Lucy's concern. All she had to do to escape was to do everything . . . perfectly.

Then she felt the floor vibrate and heard the sound of Dixie's footsteps coming into the kitchen.

Lucy froze.

56

Sergeant Hank Trammel strode down a desolate stretch of south Texas highway with his olive-drab canvas duffel over his shoulder. He wore a dress uniform. His shoes were polished to a mirror finish, which allowed him to see the green beret perched on his head, the brown mustache and aviator sunglasses.

The cloudless white sky allowed the midday sun to beat down on him mercilessly and he wiped the sweat from his brow with a handkerchief. He was going to get to the ranch before Millie put little Tommy to sleep.

Since there was no traffic, he had walked the five miles from the bus stop outside the tiny community of

Los Terras, Texas, to the Flying T Ranch. Millie didn't know he was coming in for another week because he wanted to surprise her.

His mind was filled with the idea that little Tommy and Millie would be waiting for him, and how excited his wife would be when she saw him approaching the farmhouse. It wouldn't be a complete surprise, though: He couldn't get to the house without his hounds setting up a ruckus.

When the house was no more than a hundred yards away, he realized that the dogs weren't announcing his approach.

The house looked the same, but it looked different than he remembered it. He could see that the white paint was weathered off, and as he reached the porch he noticed that some of the windows were broken, and that the front door was standing open.

Hank dropped his bag in the dirt and took the steps two at a time. Slowly he entered the foyer, and although nothing had changed about the house's furnishings, he was struck by how much dust there was covering everything. And not just the dust, but spiderwebs too.

He climbed the stairs, waving the webs aside. As he approached the bedroom he heard a phone ringing, and he opened the door to see a pedestal with a shiny black telephone perched atop it.

Hank opened his eyes and the dream evaporated, leaving him momentarily confused as to where his wife and son were.

He heard Faith Ann pick up the receiver in the kitchen and say, "Hello."

He remembered that his dear Millie was dead.

His son, Tommy, a child when he went, had been dead over thirty years.

So much pain in his heart.

So fresh were the wounds.

He heard his niece coming and he reached for his glasses on the bedside table before she tapped.

"Uncle Hank, you awake?" she asked softly.

"Of course I am," he snorted. "How can a man sleep with the phone ringing off the wall?"

The door opened and Faith Ann stuck her head in. "It's Mr. Massey. I think it's real important. He sounds sort of winded."

Hank reached for the telephone and sat up, causing a bolt of pain to shoot from his ankle to the base of his spine. He took a deep breath, then said, "Hi there, Win. What's the deal?"

He listened to the request, and the brief explanation his dear friend offered.

"You called the right guy," Hank said. "Consider it done."

Hank hung up, turned on the lamp, and called out, "Faith Ann!"

She came back to the door.

"I have to go out for a while to help a friend," he said. "You lock the door and if you need anything, call Sean."

Despite the urgency of his mission, it took Hank ten minutes to dress, and the pain had him sweating profusely. He slipped on a pair of muck shoes, knowing he couldn't take the time to pull on his boots.

It had been over a year since he had truly felt needed

by anyone for anything important. He knew he was hardly more than a ward of Winter and Sean's. Officially he was Faith Ann's guardian, but the truth be told, his niece was more his caregiver than he was hers.

He reached for his crutches and, with tears in his eyes, headed for the door.

Faith Ann met him in the kitchen, arms crossed. She had put on a raincoat and her jeans bloused where they were tucked into the tops of her cowboy boots.

"You cold?" he asked her.

"Not yet. But it's chilly and wet out there."

"You're staying here," he said.

Her concerned frown told him that she didn't think he could go anywhere on his own, but he knew better. Winter needed him. Just like the old days.

"I mean it, Faith Ann. You lock up and if you need anything, call Sean."

"Where are you going?"

"On a mission."

"Important?"

"Life and death."

Hank leaned over and kissed the girl's cheek and she returned it.

"Okay," she said, nodding. "Go get it done."

Hank took the keys to his Jeep and went out the door. He was almost at the driver's door when his leg went numb and he pitched into the side of the vehicle and tumbled into the ditch, striking his head. As he lay there on his back, cold rain filled his eyes.

It was immediately obvious to him that he wasn't going to be getting up without help. He heard the back door fly open and Faith Ann's feet on the gravel as she came at a run.

"Oh, Uncle Hank!" She knelt beside him, a look of horror in her eyes.

"I'm okay, Faith Ann. My stupid leg just went stiff on me. I'll be able to get up in a minute."

"I'll help you." She grabbed his wrist and began tugging at it. He couldn't do more than sit up. He wondered if he might have broken his hip.

"Go get Sean," he told the girl.

Faith Ann wriggled out of her raincoat and put it over Hank's head to protect him from the rain. Then she turned and ran off toward the big house.

Hank was thankful she hadn't hung around to see him crying.

57

Sean Massey answered the phone on the third ring. "Hello?"

"Sean, it's Alexa Keen. I hope I didn't wake you."

"Hello, Alexa. Anything wrong?"

"No, everything's fine," Alexa assured her. "I was just wondering if you'd heard from Winter this evening."

"He called earlier when I was putting Olivia down. Maybe two hours ago. Why?"

"I'll tell you in a minute. What exactly did he say to you?"

"He told me he loved me and asked about Rush, Olivia, and Faith Ann. Said you guys had split up. Said it wasn't dangerous, which I naturally assumed was a lie designed to make me feel better. That's about it. Tell me why you're asking. I can handle anything but not knowing."

"I'm sure it's nothing. He called me earlier to say he was going to make a couple of stops, then come back here to the Westin. It's been over an hour, and I can't get him on the cell phone I gave him. He has extra charged batteries, but the one in it may have run down and he might not know it's time to replace it. I know he has a second cell phone, his own. I don't have the number."

"He forgets things," Sean said. She gave Alexa Winter's cell number. "Alexa, tell him to call me as soon as you talk to him?"

"Sean, don't worry. Winter can take care of himself."

"I know," Sean said. "I've seen that firsthand." She said good-bye, hung up, and looked across the room where Hank Trammel sat in an armchair, frowning. A wool blanket was over his shoulders.

"I haven't seen that sour-ass Trammel look since the day I met you," she told him. "God, you can be a scary fellow until a body gets to know what a pussycat you are."

"Polecat, you mean." Hank smiled. "I remember when I had you handcuffed. You looked like something out of *Oliver Twist*. Hell, I didn't know whether to turn you loose or shoot you. What did Miss Alexa Keen say?"

"Alexa says he didn't show on schedule."

Hank said, "I have a feeling she'll see him soon enough. He has a way of turning up when you least expect him to. Reckon I'd best get moving." He tried to stand.

"Hank," Sean said, putting her hand on his shoulder. "You're going to stay here."

"Bull," he said. "Help me make it up. I'll be fine once I get moving."

"Let's cut the crap," she told him. "I'll go see Judge Fondren."

"No way. Winter would have my ass. He entrusted me with this errand."

"Is it dangerous, knocking on a front door in Myers Park?"

"No, I don't expect it is."

"I walk up, ring the bell, deliver the message. Then I'll get in my car and come back home."

"I feel so dad-burned worthless."

"Don't be silly."

"I can't call Judge Fondren," he said. "Winter said the wrong people are tapping phones. He said he couldn't call anybody who could help because the bad guys could be monitoring anybody he might turn to. I'm the only person he was sure they wouldn't think he'd turn to." Saying that hurt.

"No, Hank. The only thing to do is what Winter said to do."

"It's not a good idea," Hank insisted. "He didn't call you for a reason. Winter'll freak out if you go into a dangerous situation. I'll go. I know Fondren."

"Come on, Hank. We've discussed this. You know I can take care of myself."

"I still don't like it."

"Faith Ann knows where Olivia's bottles are. If the baby wakes and won't go back to sleep, sing to her. She likes 'Do you believe in life after love,' that Cher tune."

"She'll have to settle for 'Desperados Waiting for a Train.' You be real careful. If you see anybody watching the judge's house, keep going. Call me from a pay phone and I'll call Shapiro. Agreed?"

Sean stood, slipped on a coat and a baseball cap, then kissed Hank. She knew Shapiro, the director of the U.S. Marshals, and he would do anything to help Hank or Winter.

"You be careful," Hank called after her. "I'm about as experienced taking care of infants as I intend to be."

58

The road Winter Massey had crashed his truck on wasn't heavily traveled. It was Saturday night, and only a few people lived out that way, and it dead-ended into one of the few remaining farms that hadn't been turned into a shopping center or a subdivision. The first driver down that road would spot his truck—rolled over like it was and lit up like a Christmas tree—and call the cops. Winter only hoped it wasn't discovered until he was close enough to the Dockerys that it wouldn't matter.

He was muddy and bruised from the dive he'd taken out of the truck's cab when it left the road. He didn't generally jump from moving vehicles, but he'd had little to lose by taking a chance that the ground would be soft enough to keep him from breaking his neck. Based on what the Tahoe's driver said on his phone to Randall—if the wreck wasn't found and broadcast over the police channels—Winter might have an hour before the men in black he'd killed didn't show up wherever Max Randall expected them to meet him. Add maybe another half hour before Max got word to the bunch at the Westin. He might have additional time after that before anybody got word to the Smoots to tell them that Click *might* have ratted them out.

Clayton Able, who certainly knew Randall's team was after Winter, would be monitoring local police radio channels for news of any incident. He would learn a wrecked truck had been found near the clinic, know it was Winter's, and learn pretty quickly there were three bodies. That would set up the first alarm. Winter was counting on it taking some time for the bad guys to discover that none of the dead bodies was his. When they did, Clayton and company would know that Winter was responsible for the dead men, and they'd know it long before the cops put it all together. Police interest would be piqued when they discovered that one of the men in black battle dress uniforms without any insignia was packing an illegal automatic weapon. There would be a lot of explaining to do, and hopefully he could explain it with Fondren's help and have the truth accepted over whatever cover story the military came up with.

It wouldn't be the first whirlwind that had Winter Massey at its epicenter. If he had things figured correctly, Judge Fondren might not even be aware of Winter's involvement. Once Hank Trammel got the message to the judge detailing what was really going down, maybe he could figure out some way to help Winter save his family.

59

Lucy Dockery heard Dixie close the bathroom door and sit heavily on the toilet. Through the uninsulated wall with cheap paneling nailed to both sides, Lucy could hear Dixie mumbling to herself just as clearly as if she were in the bathroom with her. Despite her father's admonition, the woman sounded intoxicated. Lucy had read that the death camp guards during World War II stayed drunk or doped to the gills to better cope with the unpleasantness of their work.

Lucy went to the kitchen and lifted a ten-inch skillet from beneath the island made of two-by-fours topped with a slab of granite. In the TV's uncertain light, she could see Elijah sprawled on his back in the playpen, motionless.

She slipped back into the bedroom and picked up the

blanket she had vomited the chemical martini into. She lumped it on the bed and put the flashlight under the blanket so that the beam shone out and illuminated the wall. Then she picked up the skillet and moved to put her back against the wall beside the door. The iron utensil felt like the heaviest thing she had ever lifted, and she was sure it would crush Dixie's skull like a bubble. How hard should she hit her? Too hard and it would kill her, too soft a blow and the musclewoman would take it away and beat her to death with it.

The toilet paper roll spun, the toilet flushed, and Lucy heard Dixie opening the door.

Lucy had never struck any living thing before, except a swipe on Walter's arm when he beat her at Trivial Pursuit, a playful pat on his naked butt when her husband passed by on his way into the shower.

Raising the skillet over her head as far as the low ceiling allowed, Lucy moaned loudly and called out, "Come here, bitch!"

Dixie flung open the door. "Jeezuscryast," she snarled, and stepped into the room, her gaze going from the lumpy blanket to the open window.

Lucy brought the frying pan down on the blond bouffant in an effort to drive the hairdo into Dixie's neck. The large woman hit the mattress and lay there shivering like she'd chewed through a lamp cord. Then she stopped moving and was still. Lucy knew that she had killed her, but she couldn't think about that until she was far away from this place.

Lucy ran into the den, grabbed up her unconscious child, clutched him to her to make sure he was breathing, then grabbed the thin blanket he had been lying on and ran. She passed the containers of gasoline as she made her way across the warehouse. Tenderly, she laid Elijah down on the blanket and tucked it around his tiny body. It was a sin to have drugged her baby, but she thanked God he was asleep. That way she could do this without worrying that he would make a racket.

Lucy ran back to the gasoline stash and realized that she had forgotten the matches. She picked up the jar and, holding it in both hands, carried it inside. Since Dixie was dead, she decided that she'd douse the living room. The trailer on fire would be a more effective lure than some flames in the dirt.

Lucy went to the shot glass filled with matches and dropped a dozen or so in the pocket of her T-shirt. She bent and started pouring the golden liquid from the pickle jar onto the floor, being careful not to get it on her bare feet. She sloshed it on the couch, then went into the bunkroom and poured the remainder on the floor there. She saw a camouflage poncho on the top bunk and she grabbed it and put it on, pulling her head up through into the hood. It would protect them outside, and hopefully make seeing her harder for the men coming in to fight the fire.

Lucy rushed from the room, feeling the cool fuel on the soles of her bare feet. She was at the door when a powerful blow caught her on the side of her head and knocked her reeling out through the door. She landed on her back on the steel porch. The hood partially obscured her vision, but she could see Dixie crawling on all fours toward her, blood covering her face like a wet curtain.

Dixie grabbed Lucy's ankle and squeezed it so hard Lucy was sure the bone would snap.

"Geahbackinhere!" Dixie was dragging her back inside.

Lucy kicked out, striking Dixie's collarbone, then the woman's mouth with her heel. Dixie sat heavily, letting go of Lucy's ankle and looking at the skinny woman who had tried to kill her with raw rage in her eyes.

"Youdead," Dixie said. Her jeans were soaked with the gasoline she was sitting in. Lucy scrambled to her feet, her ears ringing from the blow to her head.

"Whereyougoingarunto? Killyouandyourdamkid." Dixie stood and raised her hand slowly. There was a *snap* and a thick blade shot out from her hand.

Lucy brought her hand out from under the poncho.

Dixie raised the knife higher and smiled insanely.

Lucy struck the match in her hand on the steel railing and, while the phosphorus blossomed to life, she tossed it on the floor beneath Dixie.

Flames raced along the floor, consuming the fuel.

Lucy leaped over the porch railing, slamming painfully into the dirt.

Dixie stood on the porch beating at her flaming jeans with her hands. "YOULITTLEBITCH!" she roared.

Lucy grabbed the bucket at her feet and hurled its contents at the horrid woman.

When the wave of cool fuel hit Dixie, she froze, probably thinking Lucy was trying to put out the fire on her legs.

There was a fraction of a second before the flame

reacted to being fed. Then the air, filled with vapor, went bright white as the liquid caught.

Dixie's hair vanished. Her false teeth flew out of her flaming mouth, which had been open when the gasoline hit her. And she screamed.

Lucy had never heard such a howl. Lucy turned her back to the horror on the porch, ran to the gasoline drums, lifted the pickax she had placed there. Feeling like Superwoman, Lucy swung the pick like a baseball bat over and over, puncturing the drums. She stopped when she was sure there were enough holes to empty the drums.

Lucy didn't look at Dixie until streams of gasoline were arcing out of the drums. Aflame, and bellowing, a whirling Dixie fell off the porch, landing on her back. It appeared that she was attempting to roll the flames out.

Lucy ran back to Eli.

Dixie's screams echoed in Lucy's ears, the fire a roaring monster trapped for the moment in the trailer. Dixie tried to get up on her hands and knees.

Lucy watched the dark stain growing from the gas drums—flowing toward Dixie.

God, there was so much gasoline.

And it was moving too fast.

60

Peanut Smoot had driven all the way back to Charlotte to get the dope from George the druggist and was a few miles from the turnoff onto gravel road when he saw a wide section of the sky light up orange-red like the sun was rising. Peanut stared openmouthed as a fireball blossomed above the tree line.

He hoped like hell it was the underground gasoline tanks or maybe the big propane tank at the Utzes' store. But if it wasn't the store, there wasn't but one other possible source of an explosion like that one. He set his jaw and stomped the accelerator, shooting fuel to the Hemi. If this was Buck's doing, his son was a dead man.

He roared past the store, noticing that the old couple who ran it were out in the parking lot under an umbrella staring over at about where his barn was located—a half mile off. He got out at his gate to open it, and looked skyward at the column of thick black smoke boiling into the clouds, illuminated from the ground. He was startled by a series of thunderous explosions that had to be the fifty-pound crates of black powder he had stored up in the trailer, and probably the propane tank for the stove. The whole warehouse was filled with crap that shouldn't be in there if there was a fire, but that hadn't ever seemed important before.

As he rounded the first curve in the road to the metal

barn, he almost hit the twins. They were standing in the road with their backs turned—shotguns over their shoulders—watching the fire like a couple of cows.

Peanut hit his brights and smacked the horn. Burt and Curt bolted off into the weeds about a second before he would have run them both over. If he hadn't figured he would need them, he wouldn't have honked or braked.

"What happened?" he hollered out his window as it went down.

"Looks like it's a fire at the barn," Burt said.

"What the hell are you doing here?" Peanut hollered.

"You said to stay here," Curt answered.

"Get in the truck!" Peanut snarled.

The twins scrambled into the bed and squatted, one on either side of the cab. As Peanut roared off, they put their faces out in the slipstream like dogs enjoying the wind.

Peanut roared along, braking to avoid hitting a group of deer. When he made it around the final bend, he involuntarily sucked in a deep bracing breath. The place looked like one of those fireworks plants on the news that ran plumb out of luck in the unfortunate-spark department. Twisted corrugated metal was scattered everywhere. Blackened sheets of the steel had curled away from the barn's I-beam superstructure like the petals of an orchid. The steel skeleton—beams and ceiling struts—had come from a Winn-Dixie that had been damaged by Hurricane Hugo, which Peanut had bought from the insurance company for a song.

Peanut hoped the damned volunteer fire department didn't show up and come on his land, but with the explosion visible for God knew how far off, he wouldn't be at all surprised if all sorts of authorities came sniffing about, even knowing as most did that he didn't allow anybody on the place he hadn't invited. If the Dockerys' bodies were in this mess, he sure as hell didn't need anybody snooping around. Buck's or Dixie's corpse he could explain, but not the Dockerys'. He had to make some calls and head that off or get the hell out of there.

The shed was on fire. Inside, what had been the tractor, the four-wheelers, Buck's 1500, the twins' Blazer, and Dixie's 1970 GTO were all part of the burning whatnot. Peanut wondered about how much insurance he could collect on all of it. Enough to rebuild. The agent would give him whatever he could think of that was or wasn't actually in there.

"Buck! Dixie! Buck! Dixie!" the twins hollered out in a steady stream.

"Stop yelling," Peanut told them.

"You think they're dead?" Curt asked.

"Maybe Buck went off to do something like he does," Burt said.

"Don't know," Peanut said. He didn't either. Who knew what the hell Buck was liable to do when he got something in his head?

By the looks of things, Peanut figured there wouldn't be much left of anybody that had been in the structures. Buck might have caused the fire and run off, knowing he'd catch almighty hell for it. Might have done it because he was pissed off. Peanut regretted he hadn't let Buck have his fun with the Dockery woman, because at least this wouldn't have happened.

He decided it would be best not to tell anybody about Dixie and Buck being here right off. Except for the insurance policies he had on them, he couldn't see why anybody needed to know anything right off. He'd discuss how to get the policies claimed with Mr. Laughlin before he decided. Nobody he could think of would miss Buck enough to ask after him. The people from Dixie's church would wonder about her, but he could say she moved to California or some happy crap. Wasn't one in the whole congregation could out-think a rock.

Peanut saw the steel door frame was still in place, though the metal skin had been blown off. The padlock was still there. When his heel sank into something, he looked down and realized it was a blackened hand and forearm.

Peanut squatted down and lifted it up by the thumb to get a better look. Buck's Jolly Roger tattoo that he'd gotten put on his forearm before going into the Marine Corps was easy to make out. *Born 2 Kill,* read the words in the banner under it. On Buck's other arm he'd had a funny cartoon of a bulldog dry-humping a skull that read, *Devil Dog Sex.*

Peanut held the limb up to let the twins get a good look at it.

"Holy crap!" Burt said.

"Daw-gone," Curt muttered.

"Boys. It'd be best if you didn't mention this to your mother. No point upsetting her."

In the same manner a man would throw a piece of wood, Peanut slung the last of Buck off into the hottest part of the fire. For a few seconds he watched the fire and contemplated his two dead children. More than most, his kids knew how dangerous life was. It was a shame to die violent deaths, but he reckoned that it was all spoiled milk under a bridge. And the Dockerys were supposed to be killed anyhow, and it didn't pay to worry about things that didn't matter.

"Boys, y'all can remember that your brother and sister did their duty to the family. Want y'all to go on back up to the gate and tell anybody that thinks about coming in, that this is private property. Any those volunteer fire idiots show up, tell them our trailer and barn burned up and there ain't crap to do about it but let the fire finish up. The woods are too wet to burn, and we Smoots handle our own troubles out here. Tell 'em if they try and come in, you'll blow their damned heads off. Tell 'em if they don't like it, to go screw a mule."

"*Walk* all the way back there?" Burt said.

"You could have just left us there," Curt added.

Peanut just glared.

As the twins turned away to go back to the gate, Peanut opened his cell phone and made a call to Max Randall. Max would want to know about this development. He'd wait until later to tell Mr. Laughlin, because the lawyer had taken his firm's jet to Miami and wouldn't get back until just before court on Monday.

"It's a damn shame about the dogs," Curt said as he took his shotgun out of the bed of the Dodge.

61

Clayton Able had his phone to his ear. Major Antonia Keen was pacing the floor in her suite, a phone to her ear as well.

"Yeah?" Clayton said. "You're sure? Hold on." He snapped his fingers. Holding the phone away from his mouth so he could read the screen, he saw who was trying to break in and said, "Keep me posted." He brought the other caller up.

"Okay, shoot," he said.

Antonia said, "I'll get back to you when I know. You just be ready to scramble at a moment's notice to where I need your team." She closed her phone and turned to face Clayton.

Clayton listened to the second caller without interrupting. "Damn it," he said. "Damnity, damn, damn it. Anything else Massey-related pops up on the radar, call me."

"The team's on standby," Antonia told Clayton when he shut the cell phone. "What's the deal on Massey?"

"A couple of things. His truck, with about a hundred bullet holes in it, has been found wrecked in a field about a half a mile from the building where he picked Click up. Cops reported an unidentified male belted inside his truck wearing a bathrobe. We can safely assume that was Mr. Ferny Ernest Smoot."

"And Massey, too, right?"

"There were two additional unidentified corpses dressed in BDUs found just off the road, both head shots. There was no second vehicle."

"Where's Massey?"

"I presume he's driving around somewhere in a Tahoe with a frightening amount of ordnance inside it."

Antonia sat heavily on the bed and put her face in her open hands.

"I don't have to tell you that Massey was your sister's bright idea."

"He nailed two of Randall's team," Antonia answered. "And stole their vehicle."

"Three, if you count the one he ran over. He's done this exact same thing before. Taken out professionals."

"I thought his rep was exaggerated, he was over-rated. . . . Maybe he'll call Alexa."

"I think we can safely assume Massey has three very good reasons *not* to contact your sister. Like maybe he's suspicious because every time he starts off in a direction that looks promising, when he tells Alexa what he's going to do, people try to kill him."

Antonia nodded. "Been badly played."

"I don't think he fell asleep in the truck," Clayton continued. "I expect he went to Laughlin's, spotted the trap, and aborted. He told your sister he was coming back here after going by to check on Click, because he figured there was probably a bug in his truck and we'd know if he went somewhere other than where he told Alexa he was going."

"Maybe he thinks somebody else bugged him and he's not telling Alexa because he thinks their conversations are being picked up. He might come here," Antonia Keen said, hopefully.

"That's a long shot, but offers us a decent defense if he does show up with friends from high places. The more important question is, did Click tell him where the Dockerys are?"

Antonia shook her head. "Click didn't know, remember? Randall said the only people in the Smoot crew who knew the location were on-site except for him and Peanut. Maybe Massey suspects Laughlin knows—we need to keep someone there in case Massey goes back. It's the only avenue left to him and he doesn't know Laughlin is out of town."

The phone rang and Clayton pressed a button and put it to his ear. "Talk to me."

Clayton listened and sat down on the bed, putting his other hand on his cheek and shaking his head. "Keep me posted." He clicked the phone shut. "That was Randall. Peanut called him. Seems a few minutes ago the structure out in the country where the Dockerys were being held went up in flames."

"A fire?"

"Peanut described it as an explosion that could be seen for miles. Seems the fire is still burning."

"Massey," Antonio murmured. "That goddamn Massey."

"Major, Massey hasn't had time to get there. The Smoot place is out in the middle of nowhere seventy miles into South Carolina." He pointed to a box he'd drawn on a map and, after looking for a few seconds, marked the place where Winter had killed the team members.

"What about the Dockerys?"

"They were inside the structure, along with two of the Smoots."

"He's sure?"

"Smoot said a padlock was in place when the explosion happened. He's sure nobody got out."

"What exploded?"

"The place was also used to store combustibles," Clayton said, lifting his pipe and sucking on it.

"Combustibles?"

"Gasoline. Blasting powder."

"Call Randall," Antonia said sharply. "Tell him to get out there *now*. We have to make sure Massey doesn't get access to the place, or if he does, that he stays there permanently. I'll get my team on the perimeter and we'll shut down the area. National security alert or something intimidating. Nothing goes in or comes out. We sanitize everything to keep Fondren from getting wind of anything."

"The county officials are bought and paid for by Peanut. The locals are handled. Just watch out for Feds."

"We *are* the Feds. We need to know if Massey's called anybody."

"He hasn't used our cell. Signal says it's in the truck."

"Check his cell phone."

"I don't have the number."

Antonia picked up the phone and pressed a button. "Alexa. Massey's in the wind. Took out three of Randall's team and he has a loaded Tahoe.... I'll go over it in a minute. Do you have Massey's cell phone number?" She scribbled the number on a pad. "Get ready, Alexa, we're taking a trip to clean things up."

Antonia tossed the pad to Clayton. "She got it from his wife."

Clayton typed the number into his computer.

"We're going out to the location," the Major told him. "You hold down the fort and keep me posted on anything and everything."

"Don't worry about that."

"But I do worry, Clayton," she said. "I worry because my skinny black soon-to-be-wearing-a-general's-star ass is on the line. And therefore so is your fat wants-to-retire-rich-but-might-spend-eternity-in-Leavenworth ass."

62

Sean Massey used the GPS in her Lexus to find Judge Fondren's house. Most of the downstairs windows were lit up, the porch light on. Sean didn't see any cars on the street with people inside them. She had promised Hank she would make sure nobody was watching the judge's house.

Sean parked in the driveway, strolled up to the porch, and rang the doorbell.

A thin, distinguished man with white hair and reading

glasses perched on his nose opened the door and looked down at her.

"Judge Fondren?"

The man nodded reluctantly. "May I help you?"

"I hope so. I'm Sean Massey. Hank Trammel told me to use his name."

"Hank Trammel?"

"U.S. marshal. Ran the office here."

"Of course. Trammel. Do I know you?"

"No. My husband is Winter Massey. He was a U.S. deputy marshal."

"Hell-comes-to-breakfast Massey?" The judge cracked a knowing smile.

"Is that his nickname?" she asked.

"Among others. I know your husband by reputation. What's he up to these days?"

"At the present he's been working with Special FBI Agent Alexa Keen to find your daughter and grandson."

The smile vanished and Fondren's pale blue eyes scanned the street. He stepped back and opened the door wide. "You'd better come inside, Mrs. Massey."

He closed the door behind her.

"You didn't know, did you?" Sean asked. "Alexa didn't tell you about my husband?"

"Perhaps with his reputation, Agent Keen may have thought it best not to mention your husband was involved. She probably thought I'd think the chance of my family being caught in a cross-fire would cause me needless worry."

"If she doesn't have them safe by Monday, you'll let Bryce walk?"

His eyebrows rose. He considered the question, then nodded slightly.

"But Alexa isn't planning to get to them until after the sentencing," Sean said. "And, sir, Lucy and Elijah will be dead and buried an hour after you let Hunter Bryce walk. Alexa Keen is part of a conspiracy to free Bryce. Clayton Able, Alexa, and her sister, Major Antonia Keen, are not at all what they purport to be."

"And why should I believe that?"

"Because my husband said so."

"I know Alexa Keen quite well. I don't know you at all, and I don't know your husband except to say hello."

"Think about it: When did Alexa Keen last make contact with you before the abduction?"

"Two weeks ago Agent Keen was in town for a meeting. She called me up for lunch. I've known the woman for ten years."

"And before that when did you last see her?"

"Maybe two, three years. How is this important?"

"And when she met you for lunch, did she say anything like, 'If you ever need anything, call me first'? Or play up the fact that she has the number one solve rate for kidnappings? When you contacted her after Lucy and Elijah were abducted, did she suggest you *not* tell anybody else? Not to tell a single soul, because Bryce has friends in sensitive positions everywhere—even inside the FBI?"

Judge Fondren put his hand to his chin and rubbed the short whiskers.

"Winter knows who has your family, Your Honor, and he knows where. He is also pretty sure Alexa does, too."

"I've known Alexa Keen for ten years," the judge repeated.

"Winter has known her a lot longer and a lot better. And yet she's betrayed him, and people who are in on this with her have tried to kill him three times. The kidnappers are a local bunch of thugs who are getting their orders from Bryce's friends."

"Exactly who are Bryce's friends, Mrs. Massey?"

"A Russian crime group waiting for delivery of an arms shipment and members of our military intelligence who are involved in the smuggling operation. Major Antonia Keen is an Army intelligence officer. She's the connection."

"Say this is true. What do you expect me to do?"

"Winter's on his way to get your family out. He's all alone. He must have figured you'd know what to do. I was just supposed to get word to you."

"Do you know where he's going?"

Sean pulled a map of North and South Carolina out of her coat and opened it on the table. She picked up the judge's pen and pointed to the circle Hank had drawn. "Right about here. Off of Clark Road."

"I see."

"Can you get him some backup?"

"All the help he needs," the judge said, frowning. "Gentlemen, Mrs. Massey wants our help."

Sean looked up from the map as two men dressed entirely in black filled the doorway. The machine guns in their hands had large silencers on them.

"Please, Judge Fondren, there's no time—" Sean started.

He looked down at her. "I'm terribly sorry to have deceived you, Mrs. Massey. My name is Kelly Crisp. Judge Fondren is upstairs resting."

Sean felt a sour burning in her stomach. "Exactly who are you?" she managed to ask.

"We're government employees, Mrs. Massey." Kelly Crisp's smile could only be described as predatory.

63

The Tahoe SUV was full of fuel when Winter Massey stole it. He kept the speedometer around eighty, and stayed on the interstate until he was well into South Carolina. He couldn't afford to be stopped by the highway patrol, muddy, badgeless, driving a vehicle he didn't know who owned, with several ebony anvil cases in the back. He didn't have time to look through the cases to see what equipment they contained, and didn't want the cops to be the people who got first look inside them. There was also the spent brass littering the floorboard, console, and seats of the vehicle. There were discarded thirty-round H&K magazines on the passenger's floorboard, and a half dozen loaded ones on the console.

Click had said that his father had been taking people that "needed" killing to the hunting property in South Carolina for twenty years. It was a safe place because it was in a forested area owned by the Smoots and they controlled the local authorities. Click had described the layout and given Winter directions to it—directions Winter had committed to memory.

Winter had called Hank's private line from a pay phone, and had entrusted him to deliver a message to Judge Fondren, hoping he would get some firepower on the scene before it was too late.

He topped a hill to the sight of three patrol cars, blues flashing, pulled off on the shoulder. He slowed, joining the traffic that crept by so the drivers could rubberneck. A passenger van had been pulled over, its contents unloaded in the grass. Several luckless Mexican men stood in the rain in wet clothes looking like flood victims while cops in raingear casually tore their vehicle apart.

After passing over the next hill, Winter floored the SUV. All the cops in the area, he figured, had their hands full for the moment.

64

Because it was dark and Click Smoot hadn't given Winter exact distances between turns, he had to read the signs at every crossroad and intersection he came to. Some of the road signs were impossible to read without slowing. After he spotted a blood-red glow on the horizon, Winter was sure he would find the place just by steering a general course for the flames. It could have just been a coincidental house or a barn fire, but his instincts told him that the source of the blaze was the Smoot place and that it had something to do with the Dockerys.

Perhaps, knowing Winter was on his way there, Clayton Able had called the Smoots to sanitize the scene— and few things destroyed evidence like nice big fires. If that was the case, it was all over and the consequences of his actions during the past several hours could be very unpleasant. It would be best for the Keens and Able if Winter never got a chance to present his side of the story. Winter could only hope that Hank had gotten his message to Judge Fondren, to explain what was really going on. He wasn't at all sure that the jurist could do anything in time to make any difference. The Dockerys were probably dead.

One last right turn off of Clark Road onto State 332 and two miles down that gravel road and a left fork just past a country store and he'd be at his destination, a red gate. As he rounded a curve, he saw the unmistakable blue strobes of a police cruiser, and again he slowed. The rain had stopped, and he flipped off his wipers. Red lights behind him signaled an approaching fire truck.

A pair of sheriff's department cruisers blocked a gravel road off Clark Road and deputies were turning away traffic. One of the deputies was having a discussion with the driver of a pickup truck with a flashing red light sitting on its dash. The fire truck flew around Winter's Tahoe and stopped at the intersection behind the pickup, but the sheriff's department cruisers remained in position, blocking the fire truck's path.

Winter kept going, slow and steady, not flicking on his turn signal. He noted the firmness in the deputies' rebuff of the firemen. Winter didn't know if there was another way in, so he was going to have to hide the SUV and go in on foot.

A quarter mile farther down, he spotted a private road and, turning off his lights, pulled onto it. At the tree line a gate made up of strands of barbed wire stretched across the dirt road. He aimed for the No Trespassing sign that hung from the topmost strand, and snapped the wires as he roared through.

Only when the road made a sharp left turn did he stop the Tahoe. Climbing out, he went to the tailgate, lifted the rear door, and started undoing the casket hinges on the cases. He was looking at the tidbits every proper assassin needed to have close at hand.

Sometimes God smiles.

65

After Max Randall's second heated phone call, Peanut leaned against his truck, thinking. Max was on his way, and the Russian, Sarnov, was tagging along. Peanut couldn't see why they were wasting their gas. He figured he was going to be the only loser in this deal. One, he probably was going to have trouble collecting the kidnap-and-killing fee on the Dockerys that Bryce was supposed to pay Laughlin, even though the woman and kid had been kidnapped and killed successfully, which was the point and it shouldn't matter so much—check the damn small print—how or when. And second, he had lost prime buildings and two Smoot-blood employees who would be a sight more difficult to replace than structures. Third thing was, none of this mess was his fault. The fire was obviously an act of God—an accident. Of course Sarnov would do his communist best to keep him from collecting one red cent. Peanut doubted Randall, who was pretty danged upset, would go to bat to get Peanut his money. And Peanut wasn't getting points in the arms deals in the future, which didn't sit right, considering that Laughlin was getting plenty.

The county sheriff, a first cousin of Peanut's wife by marriage, was going to earn his five-grand pay envelope this month. Although, at the moment, he was busy over at the Grissom place because Mr. Grissom, twice his wife's age, had murdered her and disappeared. Sheriff Sparkes was making sure the fire department stayed away from Peanut's place, ordering his deputies to tell the volunteers there was no need for them out here, because everything was under control, and being investigated and monitored by the sheriff, who would call the fire boys if he needed their help.

The deputies would let Max Randall and his pals through, but nobody else. Maybe Peanut would ask for more money since he was using his valuable contacts to

keep the scene off-limits. Randall had said to make sure
the scene was sanitized, which Peanut assumed meant
cleaning up the body parts after the fire cooled off. Hell,
a fire like this one didn't leave body parts.

The sound of hollering drew his attention. He turned
to see one of the twins pelting up the road, waving his
flashlight around like he was being chased by a swarm of
hornets. Peanut took a deep breath and scratched his
head. The twins hadn't had time to get to the gate, so
why in the hell was one of them disobeying his orders so
soon?

It was Burt, and he was so winded, he had to sag
against the truck to catch his breath before he could say
anything that Peanut could understand.

"Traaaack ... woooon't beeee ... lieve it ..."

"What the Sam Hill are you doing back here, boy?"
Peanut slapped the back of his son's head so hard Burt's
forehead hit the side of the truck.

"It's her ..." Burt wheezed, putting a huge hand to his
reddening cheek. "She's not ... dead. She left footprints a
ways up in the mud."

"Dixie?" Peanut felt a wave of relief. "My baby's *alive?*"

"Naw. Dixie's feet are big as mine. It's a bunch of little
bitty gal tracks, headed out toward the gate. Curt's following them and I came back here to get you."

"Get in the truck," Peanut growled. He jumped into
the cab, made a U-turn in the grass, and roared off. He
grabbed the phone and pressed Redial as he drove.

One thing he never imagined was possible was that
that little gal could escape from Dixie and Buck. The
damned barn door padlock was still in place and locked.

He had seen that for himself. How in the hell could she have got out of there without turning into a ghost and walking through the walls? She'd tell him how she did it before he filled her sorry ass with holes.

66

After Lucy understood that the gasoline cans were going to go up and the explosion would kill her and Elijah, she had run back to the corner beside the door to scoop up Elijah, intending to hold him against her until the end. Hearing yelling, she'd looked up to see Buck's illuminated face framed in the padlock hole.

"DIXXXAAY!" he hollered. "GAWD, I'M COMIN', DIXAY!"

He'd undone the padlock, hurled the door open, and raced into the barn, going straight for the garden hose not ten feet from where Lucy and Elijah hid. She slipped around the door and into the rain. She started looking around frantically for the padlock.

Yelling something incomprehensible, Buck had grabbed the coiled garden hose. The water ran from it in a trickle because it had become pinched in several places as he tugged it toward his flaming sister.

Lucy spotted the padlock on the dirt and reached for it, holding Elijah tight.

Buck turned, saw Lucy, dropped the hose, and bolted for her.

Lucy put the unconscious child down on the gravel, shoved her weight against the door, and managed to get the lock's ring through the hasp. Fumbling, she tried to snap the lock closed.

Buck slammed his weight against the door a split second too late. He had somehow gotten the padlock in his fist before Lucy could break off a match in the mechanism, as she had originally planned. He had a key in the other hand—now he was fighting to shove it into the lock, roaring curses at her as he did so.

Looking down, Lucy had spotted a U-shaped piece of rusted baling wire on the ground. She pushed it through the hasp an instant before Buck pried open the padlock and flipped it off. The lock landed between Lucy's feet. Despite the fact that he was clawing blindly at her, despite the fact that the sharp steel was cutting her hands, Lucy had somehow managed to twist the wire in place.

As he had worked to unwind the wire, Buck cursed her through the hole—promising her more of what he had already given her.

She had known he was going to undo it.

Desperation enveloped her. Lucy scooped up the open padlock, removed the key, shoved it through the hasp beside the twisted wire, and locked it. Trembling, she tossed Buck's key off into the wet weeds. His left arm shot out of the padlock hole and gripped the hem of Lucy's poncho.

He jerked and pulled her toward him violently. When he released the poncho, he grabbed her hand, but she jerked it and her fingers slipped from his grip. She leapt back away, safe for the moment.

It looked like he was trying to get a grip on the edge of the steel sheeting to peel it off the frame, but it was sturdy and had been riveted in place. He sounded to Lucy like a Tasmanian devil. He cursed at her as if he thought he could terrify her into opening the door for him.

Lucy wondered if the others would figure out a way to get the door open and she knew Buck would come after her again the moment he was freed. All she could do was run for it. Lifting Elijah, who babbled at her and burst into tears, she went into the shed, where they would be shielded from the driving rain. Maybe one of the vehicles in there had keys in it.

"Let me out!" Buck screeched. "Them gas drums are going to blow any second! There's blasting powder in here! Let me out, damn it!"

Lucy knew there was no time to get a vehicle from the shed. She kissed Elijah's slack face, which was wet with rain, tucked him under her poncho, and ran.

"Help me!" Buck screamed through the hole. "You rotten bitch!"

Maybe it was the adrenaline coursing through her, but Elijah seemed weightless. He squirmed restlessly against her. She gripped him tighter, scared she'd drop him, and kept running. As she ran, the gravel sliced the soft soles of her naked feet, but that didn't slow her.

She had gotten no more than a hundred yards away when the fumes inside the gasoline drums caught a spark. She turned in time to see the warehouse roof rip open and unleash a fireball that appeared to draw a black tornado into the sky.

Lucy gasped. She realized that she had just killed two human beings. She told herself that she would never erase the memory, the absolute horror of it, from her mind. She told herself, too, that, necessary for her and Elijah's survival or not, she would feel guilty about her actions for the rest of her life. But she would deal with guilt later. Right now, she had to find help.

And the plain truth was that Lucy Dockery had never felt stronger or more alive in her life.

Elijah jerked and cried out. He was coming around.

Luckily, Lucy had seen the headlights coming in plenty of time to get off the road and lie down in the wet high grass. As the black truck thundered by, she saw the massive forms of the twins in the bed, hunkered down against the cab. When the truck suddenly stopped, she was terrified that they had seen her, but then she saw several deer illuminated by the truck's headlights as the frightened animals ran for the trees. She pressed her lips against Elijah's cheek, murmuring his name, and to her relief, her son remained quiet until after the truck drove on, and the sound of rain on dead leaves again filled the night.

67

After what felt like an eternity, Lucy and Elijah arrived at a padlocked gate. Although she was hopelessly lost, she didn't panic. Nothing that lay ahead of her could be nearly as bad as what was behind her. She had no earthly idea whether the direction to their safety was to her left or right. The main gravel road in front of her was wide, with steep shoulders, ditches on either side, and beyond that, tall weeds and the woods. Looking at the soaked ground, she could make out that vehicles turning right off the gravel road had made the majority of the tire impressions. So she'd go that way. She put down her hood and climbed over the gate, keeping Elijah in her arms as she did so. Then she struck out, keeping near the right ditch. If any vehicles came, they might be carrying more of the bad guys. She remembered that Dixie had boasted that her family *owned* that part of the county.

Elijah was fully awake now, and he was fussing steadily. Her left side was growing numb under his weight. His diaper was wet, and he was cold and hungry. There would be no quieting him now. The rain had stopped, but still dripped loudly from the trees.

Lucy walked as fast as she could. She was thirsty, and growing very hungry herself. After she had gone what seemed like miles, the road curved and she smiled because she could see a lighted sign in the distance. Buoyed by the sight of civilization, Lucy switched Elijah to her rested hip and, despite the pain of the gravel on her bleeding feet, she picked up her pace.

As she drew closer, she saw the building was a wood-frame country store with a low-peaked roof that extended out to cover a raised porch. The porch light was off and the store's front windows—mostly covered with product logos and advertisements—were dark. There was a pay phone, but she didn't have the coins to operate it. The store appeared to be closed, but an old pickup truck and a large sedan filled a rickety-looking garage that was just behind and off to the side of the main building.

As she went around the building, Lucy slowed in the way of a wary animal.

Her ears picked up the sounds being generated by a television set. Lucy tried to imagine some viable alternative to approaching the rear of the store. If the people inside weren't friends or relatives of the kidnappers, weren't aware of who she was, maybe she could get to a phone and call her daddy.

Suddenly Lucy Dockery felt a new stab of panic. Dixie and Buck's father and twin brothers were close by, and although she couldn't imagine how they might discover she wasn't dead inside the warehouse, they might have a way and come looking for her.

Somebody would certainly report the explosions, and firemen and policemen would come. But what if they were under the influence of that family? It was hard to believe, but who knew what people were like in this rural place? She could be in some redneck backwater where everybody was related and everybody was suspicious of outsiders.

Maybe the store owner was one of them. She might be able to steal one of the vehicles, or sneak in and use a phone without their knowing it. Maybe she could play to their greed and offer them money to help her and Elijah.

The only windows on the side of the long structure were in the last twenty feet of the store building, and they were lit up brightly. Obviously the owner, or manager, lived there. The place couldn't be properly insulated, because she could hear the television set as though it was in the yard.

She crept forward and peered into the first window. In a cozy living room cluttered with porcelain knickknacks and family pictures, an elderly couple sat in matching recliners, watching television. One of the pictures Lucy could see clearly was of a young marine, and there was a black ribbon on one corner of the frame. She studied the couple's faces. The woman looked like Mrs. Santa Claus. Her cap of white hair framed a face that looked to be accustomed to smiling. She was short and plump. The man was short, too, but thin. His white hair and mustache were neatly trimmed, his face stern. He reminded Lucy of pictures she'd seen of William Faulkner. Elijah started crying and the startled couple looked away from the TV and straight at her.

Lucy froze and stepped back out of the light.

The porch light came on.

The back door opened.

The man and woman came outside onto the small porch and stared out at Lucy, standing in the shadows with Elijah clasped in her arms. The woman grabbed her husband's arm, looking frightened.

"What do you want?" the man demanded, frowning.

"You gave us a start," the woman said. "Who are you, dear? What in the world's happened to you?"

"Please," Lucy began. She held Elijah tightly, and to her astonishment she started crying. "Pl . . . pl . . . please?"

"You in a wreck?" the woman asked, not moving.

"We were abducted," Lucy sobbed. "Escaped."

"What in the world?" the woman said. "Kidnapped?"

Lucy nodded. "Please . . . help us?"

The elderly woman looked questioningly at her husband. Then she stepped off the porch and went to Lucy and Elijah.

68

"Who kidnapped you, child?" the woman asked, her brow creased with concern.

"I didn't know them. Buck and Dixie. These two big twins. A large man who drives a black truck. Near here."

"Those got-damned Smoots," the man said bitterly.

"Ed, language. You poor things. Come in, dear," the woman said, putting her arm around Lucy's shoulders.

"Are they important people in these parts?" Lucy asked.

"They're crooks and worse. Some like them. More's

just scared of them. That Buck is a monster," the man said.

"You'll be safe here," the woman told Lucy.

The old man stepped off the porch and stood for several seconds, gazing out at the road.

Lucy went into the kitchen with the woman. The old man came in behind them, closed the door, and turned off the porch light. She saw a long gun leaning against the wall beside the door.

"Sit down here," the woman told her. "Let's get y'all cleaned up. Your little boy looks starved. Ed, go get some diapers from stock. I'll make these poor people something to eat."

"Tell me what happened," Ed said, not moving to obey his wife. His eyes looked worried.

"Where are we?" Lucy asked.

"Tuttle's Ford," the woman said. "About nine miles from Skeene."

"My father is Judge Hailey Fondren in Charlotte. Please call him. He'll give you whatever you want to get us back."

"That's not necessary," Ed said.

"Those horrible people!" the old woman said. "Those horrible, horrible people. Evil. Just pure-dee evil."

"It's not a good idea to call anybody about the Smoots," Ed said. "They got kinfolks all around here and some are on our party line. I expect Smoot would pay a lot to keep you from telling anybody what he did. Money is hard to come by out here."

"You still have party lines?" Lucy said.

"Might be the only one left on earth," the woman said, smiling. "We want privacy, we write letters."

"We'll get you cleaned up and fed and I'll take you out to a phone that's safe, or drive you to Charlotte. I'm Ed Utz and my wife's Edna. We had three children ourselves, but they're grown and living all over."

"Seven grandchildren," Edna added proudly. "Three greats. We lost a grandson in Iraq this past July. Roadside bomb. There's a lot of evil in the world, honey, and you don't have to go all the way around the world to find it either."

Lucy looked at the mirror on the kitchen wall and was stunned by the sight of the pitiful creature whose ruined, grime-streaked face stared back at her. Elijah, as filthy as his mother, sat in her lap silently, watching the elderly couple through wide-open eyes.

"You want to take off that rain slicker?" Edna asked.

"Sorry. I don't have any clothes. I'm wearing an old T-shirt under this."

"You're closer to Ed's size than mine," Edna decided. "If you don't mind wearing his pants, we'll get you in something warm and dry."

Five minutes later Lucy had put a diaper on Eli and washed both her own and her son's faces and hands using a warm washcloth Edna furnished. Feeding her son a bowl of cereal and milk, Lucy told the couple the story. They listened quietly to her as they shook their heads in disbelief.

"We never liked the Smoots," Edna Utz said when Lucy had finished. "They shop here from time to time, but we never cared at all for any of them. Wanted to sell us stock at a discount that they probably steal. Ed told them absolutely not."

Ed said, "I can call your daddy from the pay phone out front. Peanut Smoot had it put there, but it might be safe enough. Never could imagine why the Smoots couldn't get a phone put in at their place instead of having one out on my porch that nobody but them ever uses."

"It's handy for people you don't want using your phone," Edna said. "At least the Smoots don't have to come inside to make calls."

"Give me your daddy's number," Ed said. "I'll go call him."

Lucy scribbled the number on a church bulletin Edna handed her.

Taking the shotgun with him, Ed Utz went out through a door that led into the darkened store.

"So it was you started that big fire," Edna said.

Lucy nodded.

"Very appropriate," Edna said, nodding. "Didn't the good Lord use the very same instrument to destroy Sodom and Gomorrah?"

69

Serge Sarnov lit a cigarette, more to pass the time than because he wanted one. He enjoyed pushing his smoking on people that didn't appreciate it, because he was powerful enough to get away with it. He did it for the same reason a dog pissed on a tree that some other dog had already peed on.

Max Randall cracked the window behind Sarnov. Opening the one behind him channeled the smoke away from Randall without making the statement that he found the smoke annoying.

The two military-trained men in the back seat were napping like children without a care in the world. Combat-seasoned men like them learned quickly to cat-nap in the spaces between actions. When the time came, both would open their eyes and be good to go.

"How much further?" Sarnov asked.

"Twenty minutes," Randall told him.

"The woman and child can't get far in woods they aren't familiar with, running from people who are. And if by some miracle she gets to a phone and calls her father, we're covered, right?"

"Our people have the judge's incoming calls blocked. Anybody dials his number, we'll have their location inside five minutes."

"You think this U.S. marshal is headed here?"

Randall shrugged. "If Click didn't know, Massey doesn't know either. If he does, it would save us the trouble of tracking him down."

"He's got some of your toys that he could use to make a big problem."

Max frowned. "He's competent."

"Competent?" Serge laughed. "Yes, he seems to be somewhat *competent*. It's too bad Peanut's little family hasn't been."

"I should have handled it. But Laughlin was insistent on letting them do it."

"We'll deal with Peanut tonight."

"The Major wants her sister the agent calling the shots on the Dockery deal. It has to be done a certain way."

"And you agree?"

"Without the Major, we don't have the connections into the Pentagon. She's setting up the agent's future, and I think having the agent's credibility and insights is worth allowing her to clean up the kidnapping. That's the sister's expertise. She can make this into a kidnapping based on financial gain, not Bryce's trial."

"Needlessly complicated if you ask me," Serge remarked, eyes on the wet road ahead of them. "Especially now with this Massey running amok. It seems a pointless bit of drama now."

"Mine is not to question why," Max said.

Sarnov was going to enjoy working with Max Randall.

Randall's cell phone rang and he opened it. "Okay," he said. "Directions?"

Serge watched as Max listened, his eyes on the windshield.

"We're ten minutes out."

Max snapped the phone closed.

"The Dockerys are in a store up the road from the Smoot place," he said. "Time to wake up, boys."

"They're sure?"

"Smoot found her tracks."

Max's phone trilled again. "Yeah, Major. We're on it." He listened. "That's confirmation on what Mr. P. told me ten seconds ago." He closed the phone. "Somebody just placed a call to the judge's phone from the store's pay phone. The Dockerys are definitely at the store."

Serge smiled. Behind him there were metallic clicks as the two men double-checked their weapons.

"It's turned into a beautiful evening for a hunt," Serge said.

70

Alexa Keen concentrated on the road ahead, the traffic. Antonia had been giving her driving instructions since they left the Westin thirty minutes earlier. There had been only silence between the sisters since they had gotten on the I-77 going south, only Antonia knew where.

"That ga-damned Massey," Antonia said, sighing. "You swore to me that you could keep him in check. You've made me look like shit, Lex. You know what's at stake here."

"Precious, why do you talk like that?" Alexa blurted. "It's . . . it's unbecoming an officer."

Antonia burst into laughter. "Christ on a cross, Lex. How in God's name you can give me crap about what comes out of my mouth given the present circumstances is something only you could do."

"I don't like foul language. You know that."

"We're about to murder two people, no, make it five people in the next little while—six, if we're lucky and find your old pal. And you're offended by my language?"

"I am not murdering anybody," Alexa insisted. "I'm just cleaning up a mess. And doing my best not to let it get any bigger. I can fix it unless your people get sloppier."

"For which you're being paid more money for cleaning up than any maid in history. That's for sure."

Alexa frowned. "This isn't just about the money, Precious."

"It isn't?"

"The money's nice. But I wouldn't be here if I wasn't being pushed aside at the Bureau."

"Put out to pasture before your time. Now you'll retire rich and you'll stay that way, working for people who write very large checks for a consultant who knows how things really work."

"I was leaving a real mark, a legacy. But those boy-club bastards are giving me the bum's rush because they're jealous of me. My abilities. I was the best. I *am* the best. JERKS!"

"Men," Antonia said bitterly. "If they didn't have erections, they'd be useless."

Alexa laughed despite herself. "Like Max Randall."

"Max," the Major said, laughing. "That man fu... screws you and you have been very well nailed, believe me."

"You cuss like a man," Alexa said. "Worse than a man."

"Massey never cared about you beyond getting in your pants."

"He never got in my pants," Alexa said.

"He got in your head. He stole your girlfriend and married her."

"Eleanor was *not* my girlfriend. She was just my roommate."

"Yeah, right. This is me, Alexa. I know how you felt about her. I know how bad her dying screwed you up."

"You don't know squat."

Antonia reached over and wiped the tear from Alexa's cheek.

"You don't cry for plain roommates," she said.

"*You* don't cry for anybody," Alexa shot back.

"We're going to kill Massey for you, big sister. We're going to even things out once and for all."

"I don't like talking about it," Alexa said. "He's not going to be in the way now."

"He's too unpredictable. He has friends and he can make big problems."

Alexa nodded thoughtfully. "Maybe. But he isn't easy to kill."

"But you agree he has to go?"

"What is necessary is inevitable. I agree he has to go."

"Can you get him to come to you, so Max can make sure he goes down for good?"

"Yes, I can."

"How?"

"He will come anywhere to save his wife."

"Okay. Admit one thing. He isn't as washed up as you said he was."

"Second wind."

"Second wind. You hear that, Clayton? Massey's just caught a second wind."

Alexa turned to her sister, her face reflecting both disbelief and indignation. "You have my car bugged?"

"No. Clayton does. Your cell phone and Massey's had GPS and transmitters in them. This car, Massey's truck."

"You don't trust me?"

"Nothing personal, Lex. Trust is in very short supply when so much is on the line for so many people. We had to make sure you stayed on task."

"You think I could betray you?"

"Of course not. If I did, you wouldn't have been brought in."

Alexa understood that Antonia had been talking about Alexa's involvement not only in the kidnapping but in the killings coming up. She had Clayton recording their conversation for leverage, for an edge. Antonia was always playing an angle, grabbing power any way she could, power over everybody; even taking out insurance against her own sister. Alexa had to smile. Antonia Keen was some nasty piece of work. And they shared blood.

"How long have you, Randall, and Clayton known where the Smoots are holding the Dockerys?"

"I know everything, Lex. Having the intelligence is how I stay in control. And we both know how important control is. Don't we? Didn't you teach me control is the most important thing there is?"

"Yes," Alexa said sadly. "That's true. I guess that's *all* I taught you." She sighed. "I'm not interested in opening any more of my life up to Mr. Able. So let's just drive without talking. Able gives me the creeps."

"Close your wax-encrusted, hairy-assed ears, Clayton!" Antonia yelled. "That's an order, you sheep-diddling schmuck!"

Antonia's rich baritone laughter filled the car. Alexa couldn't help but join in.

71

Edna Utz watched as Lucy fed Elijah his cereal and talked to him. "That's a good little man," the old woman said.

"Guuud," Elijah agreed, grinning.

"Thank you," Lucy told her. "I don't know what we'd do without your help."

"Don't be silly," Edna replied. "We're happy to help." She waited until Lucy had put another spoonful of cereal in Elijah's mouth before adding, "But it would be best if you didn't tell anybody we helped you, dear."

"Why?"

"Because we'd be burned out, dear. It isn't much of a store, but it's all ours, Ed's and mine. We're a bit too old to start over."

Ed came back into the apartment from the store, closing the door behind him, then bolting it. "I called the number," he told Lucy. "I got one of those 'All circuits are busy please try your call again later' messages."

"That happens sometimes," Edna said.

Ed shrugged. "I'd best drive these kids home," he told his wife. "Her daddy must be worried sick."

But Edna was thinking. "It's funny," she said. "Well, not as funny as it is odd. Ed called the fire department number over an hour ago when it started. You'd think they'd have been here by now."

Lucy felt a growing unease. "How far is the fire station from here?"

"Six or seven miles," Ed said. "But some fire out in the woods when it's this wet might not have got their total attention, especially if there was a house burning somewhere else."

Lucy caught the nervousness in Edna's eyes.

"It's a volunteer department," Ed explained. "But they get the job done."

"Call them again," Edna told her husband. "Ask them what the heck's holding them up."

Ed lifted the receiver and put it to his ear. He pressed the button down several times, then replaced it in the cradle.

"Somebody on it?" Edna asked.

"Of course," Ed said.

There was an explosion outside and the lights went out.

Elijah started to wail. In the sudden darkness, Lucy put her arms around him.

A vehicle roared around the building and bright headlights blazed in the windows, filtering through the closed blinds.

A loud voice hollered out, "Utz, sounds like you got a baby in there!"

Ed yelled out, "That you, Smoot?"

"You know it is. Send out the gal and her baby and we'll get out of your hair."

"Well, Smoot. Why don't you just come in here and get 'em?" Lucy saw Ed move, and knew he was reaching for his shotgun.

"Hell, Utz. Senile as you are, you might shoot me."

"I might."

"My boys are out here with me," Peanut yelled. "One out front and the other right here. Make this easy on yourself. This ain't about you. That gal murdered my Buck and Dixie in cold blood."

"He'll kill you both," Lucy whispered to Edna.

"Well, he'd have to do that anyhow since we know." She patted Lucy's leg reassuringly. "You just let my Ed handle this. He was in Korea."

Ed taunted, "You won't be the first murdering heathen I've sent to hell in my life, Smoot. You don't scare me."

"No hurry," Peanut yelled back. "We've got plenty of time to nee-go-see-ate. Plenty of it."

"I'm a patient man myself, Smoot. Lead don't rust."

"Terrible people," Edna whispered to Lucy. "Just awful."

Lucy clutched Elijah to her and prayed.

"Goodness, I should get out another gun or two." Edna said it as if she'd forgotten to bring salad forks to the dinner table.

72

From the equipment cases in the rear of the Tahoe, Winter Massey took what he thought he might need and put those few items into a black nylon knapsack. He took off his coat and holster rig, put on a ballistic vest, and put his figure-eight rig and camouflage coat back on. Using face paint he found, he blacked his face and put on black gloves. Selecting an H&K Tactical twelve-gauge with a high-intensity flashlight mounted under the barrel, he loaded it with alternating 00 buckshot and Hydroshock slugs. He put on a pair of night-vision goggles, slung on the backpack, grabbed the shotgun, and jogged off into an eerie world of vibrant green.

He set an angle for himself that should intersect the gravel road well behind the roadblock. The carpet of wet leaves gave him a surface almost as silent as wool, the only sound the occasional snapping of a twig. The goggles allowed him to run as fast as the undulating terrain permitted. He ran along a ridge for a long while, spooking three deer and a fox before he came to the road.

He slowed, took a bottle of water from his pocket, and sipped a few ounces. He wasn't hungry, but knowing he needed to feed his muscles, he opened a packet of jerky and chewed the stiff dried meat as he ran. When he arrived where he was going, he wanted to have his full mental and physical faculties to call upon.

Reaching the gravel state road, he decided to run on it to save time, planning to veer off into the woods if vehicles came along. He knew from Able's file that Peanut drove a black Dodge truck, and what the other siblings drove. If he saw any of those automobiles, he would have no choice but to stop them just in case the Dockerys were being transported in it. The roadblock was keeping everybody out; that had Winter convinced that dead or alive, the Dockerys must be ahead of him, and if they were, so were the Smoots.

Winter saw headlights before he heard the approaching vehicle, and leapt off the road to get behind a tree. He raised his goggles so he wouldn't be temporarily blinded. The SUV that roared past was identical to the one he had stolen. Winter couldn't make out how many people were inside, but he hoped Max Randall was in there. If he was, he was probably accompanied by whatever backup he could call upon. More could be coming along.

Before Winter had made another hundred yards, he had to leave the road again. This time he recognized the car that passed by, and he knew instantly who the two people he glimpsed inside it were. Alexa Keen and her sister the Major. Now Winter was even more certain that the Dockerys were ahead of him.

Winter felt energized. He didn't wait until the tail-lights were out of sight before he started running behind the car driven by his dear enemy.

73

If it was up to him, Peanut Smoot would have set the store on fire and shot anything alive that came out through a door or window. The Utzes were outsiders who had inherited the store from a relative of theirs. They were smug bastards, who figured they were too good to do business in a way that would make their little cracker-box store a profitable enterprise.

Since Mr. Laughlin had asked him to do what Max said, he'd wait for Max to get there before he went in to get the Dockerys. Getting those two out without destroying the store meant that Peanut might buy it from the Utzes' estate for chump change already stocked. He doubted any of the Utz kids would come out to the middle of nowhere and run a store that didn't sell enough goods to pay them minimum wage. If they did, he'd make it plain that they had no alternative but to sell it to him.

He had already figured he would have to stage an accident that would explain the deaths of Ed and Edna

"Busybody" Utz. The sheriff would investigate it, hold a midnight inquest, and the funeral home would cremate the bodies by accident, and that would be it.

Peanut smiled, pleased by the perfection of his plan.

Terrible tragedy was a part of life. You live, you lose people you love, you make money, you die and you go to heaven—if you'd accepted the Lord Jesus as your savior, which Peanut had on many occasions.

He could hear the kid bawling through the walls of the store.

Peanut hollered out, "Ed, I got an idea! Why don't you and Edna just go take a drive and when you come back all this will be like it never happened."

"I already phoned her daddy," Ed called out.

"I bet you never talked to him, though," Peanut said.

"Yes, I did. He'll be sending people you don't own out here to straighten you out."

"Naw, Eddie. See, my people got something called *sophistication*. They've got the judge's phone blocked and wired. Point is, nobody is coming out here but people I'm partnered with. They'll come, and they'll kill you all with poison gas or something that won't leave bullet holes in you."

"Hey, Peanut?" Utz called out. "I got an idea."

"Yeah?"

"Kiss my *sophisticated* butt."

Utz's barky laugh was exactly the kind that could piss a man off.

74

Serge Sarnov saw the store ahead and unzipped his jacket to make sure he could get to his gun quickly.

The cell phone in Max's lap rang and he picked it up. "Yeah?"

Serge stretched his arms out.

"We're coming up on the store now," Max said. "Okay. That's good. We'll call them in if we need them."

He closed the phone. "The Major and the FBI agent are coming in through the roadblock. Two cars with Major Keen's people are there and they'll hold back unless we need them."

"Fewer hands involved, the better," Serge agreed.

Max turned into the lot, illuminating one of the twins, who was dressed completely in hunter camouflage and holding a shotgun across his chest like a soldier. Max pulled in beside him, threw open his door, and stepped out. The men in the back seat did the same. Serge slowly opened his door and got out last.

The twin put a walkie-talkie to his ear. "There's that Tahoe full of men here." He listened for a second. "Are one of y'all Max Randall?"

"I'm Randall."

"Yeah, Daddy. One's him."

"What's the situation, pal?" Randall asked the twin.

"The old people that own the store won't give us our hostages."

Max said, "Where is Peanut?"

The twin raised his arm and pointed at the store. "Back there with my brother Curt. We got them boxed up. They live in the back part."

"And the Dockery woman and child?" Serge asked.

"Inside."

"The occupants, these Utzes, are they armed?" Serge asked.

"Everybody around here has guns," Burt said. "I'm supposed to shoot anybody that comes out the front door, but the woman that killed Buck and Dixie is Daddy's. My daddy said you can go around there." The twin smiled.

"Who cut the power line?" Sarnov asked.

"I shot it in half."

"What marksmanship," Serge said.

"We shoot good on account of all the hunting we do."

"What's your name?" Serge asked.

"Burt."

"You just stand here, Burt, and don't do any more shooting. We will do any shooting that needs to be done."

"Even if the Utzes comes out?" Burt asked.

"Yes, even then," Serge said.

Burt exhaled loudly and shook his head as he thought it over. His breath was like something that might be expelled by a bloated corpse being opened up. "Okay. But if you need me to, I will."

Max and Serge were about to walk around the building when Alexa Keen's sedan came into view and pulled off the road.

Alexa and Antonia Keen climbed out of the car.

Serge had never met the two women, but he could see a resemblance between them. One was two or three inches shorter and lighter skinned. The Major held herself more stiffly than her sister. The agent was the more attractive.

"Major, this is Serge Sarnov. He's—"

"I know who he is," Antonia Keen interrupted, offering her hand.

"Why'd you bring her?" Serge asked Major Keen, meaning Alexa.

"What is your problem?" the agent asked. "As far as I can tell, this has nothing to do with you. So why are *you* here?"

"My understanding was that your sister wasn't supposed to have a location until Monday." The Russian ignored Alexa, spoke to Antonia.

"I didn't expect her here now," Max agreed.

"I didn't expect it would be necessary to bring her in now either, but it is," Antonia Keen told him. "Do you want to delve into *why* it is necessary now? I trust her. She's had twelve years' experience with volatile situations such as this one has become due to a series of screwups."

In Serge's book, the FBI agent was an unknown, unproven quantity. The woman could be a valuable asset, but he had a well-founded distrust of cops. With the crooked ones, loyalty was just a commodity. And most of them carried a lifelong dislike for their old enemies.

"I insisted on coming here," the FBI agent said. "So far, this is strictly amateur hour. The woman and child were supposed to be captives. How hard is that? They sure as hell aren't captives any longer. Not only did this young lady, whose background in combat is limited to the bridge table, escape, but she managed to kill two people with extensive experience in criminal violence in the process. This clearly has to be handled by someone who has the expertise to make sure it is done right from here out. I am the only one who can do that. I will make sure the deed is done in the manner of kidnappers, make sure the right evidence is left for me to find."

"She'll clean up this mess," Major Keen said. "Any more questions?"

Serge told the Major, "I trust you because you're up to your ears in *our* deal."

"She's my sister and she's in this up to her ears, too," Antonia said.

"She brought in Massey," Serge reminded her sourly.

"She had her own reasons. She cut him loose when he started making progress," the Major informed him curtly.

"If I wasn't in on this, he'd have already crawled up your asses," Alexa said. "Now, thanks to you people jumping the gun and trying to take him out prematurely, I don't have him to lend credibility to my story. Am I wrong?" she demanded.

Serge thought about it as he stared into the agent's hard eyes. He had a talent for detecting lies and she was not lying. This was a woman who was tired of being taken for granted, a woman who wanted to make the kind of money the firm could pay her. Just like her younger sister, this one had a sociopathic, selfish bent. Alexa Keen was one hard-core bitch. She'd go along with killing the Dockerys. And with killing the Smoots, who had been set up to take the blame.

"Okay," he said. "Fine. Show us how to do this right."

"First off," the FBI agent said, "you can't just take machine guns and shoot up the place, because the evidence recovery team won't buy it. Bodies and buildings riddled with holes won't work. No redneck kidnapper would do that. The subjects have to be put down with a knife, or a bullet in each skull. And preferably not before Monday in case Fondren needs proof of life."

"We altered the timeline," Max said. "This can't wait. We do them now, especially with Massey somewhere out there. We'll stash them dead and you can find them on Monday. I never saw why they had to be found at all."

"Because," Alexa said, sternly, "unless I find them, I won't get the publicity. I won't be able to control the evidence, so I won't get my payoff, my reputation won't be enhanced so I can't open my security firm, and you won't have a name to put on the large checks you are going to write me over the next ten or fifteen years. That's why. Do it my way or I'm out of this."

"If you're out, you're dead," Serge said.

"You touch a hair on her head," the Major said, "and you'll have to shoot me, too. I die, the chain breaks. Without the contacts I have, Bryce will get the needle."

"Okay," Max said. "Hell with it. But first thing that goes queer on this deal, and sis's dead and we'll sanitize everything down to bare dirt."

"Fine," Major Keen said. "If Alexa's not on the level, you can kill her as many times as you like."

"So," Serge said. "How do we do this?"

"What are we facing?" Alexa asked.

"An old couple inside. Man's armed. They won't give up the Dockerys without a fight."

"So, any ideas?" Serge asked the agent.

"The oldest one in the book," the agent told him. "How's your Greek history?"

75

Winter Massey used the woods as cover to reconnoiter the store. Two men in black BDUs in front of the place, one of the Smoot twins off by himself. Sarnov, Randall, Alexa, and Antonia Keen having a discussion out of earshot of the others.

He picked his way around to the back where Peanut Smoot and the other twin were guarding the rear, using the black truck for cover and lighting. The twin stood beside the truck, aiming his shotgun at the store. Peanut was behind the open driver's door, holding a handgun casually.

It was a siege. Someone was inside the building holding the Smoots at bay. Winter's ear caught the unmistakable sound of a child crying. It had to be Elijah Dockery. He had no idea where Dixie and Buck Smoot were, but he doubted they were inside the store. Was it possible that Lucy had somehow escaped and made it here?

Winter figured his odds with a frontal assault were all against him. The men in assault suits wore ballistic vests, and his flashes would instantly give away his position. The Hydroshock slugs might not penetrate the vests, but they would break or at the least shatter ribs, take the men off their feet for a while. Inside twenty-five yards, the 00 buckshot pellets would remain within a twelve-inch cluster. He was more accurate with a handgun, but as soon as he started shooting, all of the targets would be firing at him, and he'd never get a chance to use his pistol. Even with tree cover, his chances of surviving the first few seconds were not good.

The twins had shotguns—probably three-inch Magnums loaded with buckshot—Peanut was brandishing a large revolver, the three men in black had MP5s, and Sarnov probably had a pistol. Alexa was carrying a Glock .40. As far as Winter could tell, only Antonia had no weapon.

Winter couldn't imagine shooting Alexa, but he well might have to, and he knew he could. Her killing a woman and child was more incomprehensible. He was amazed that she could have hidden her true self so effectively for so many years.

"Ed and Edna!" Peanut hollered. "Send the woman and kid on out. I'll let both you live. You got my word on it. Ain't like they're your kin. She killed my Dixie and Buck. I can't allow that to go unanswered."

"If you've seen the condition this young lady's in, you know that whatever happened to your kids was a site less than your kin deserved!"

Winter knew he had to act before the people out front

spread out. These people were all accustomed to violence.

His only advantage at that moment was that nobody knew he was there. Surprise only took you so far, and sometimes the surprise was yours.

76

With Elijah clutched to her, Lucy Dockery huddled beside the refrigerator where Ed had put them. Edna sat beside her, back to the wall, holding a pistol in her lap. Ed had dead-bolted the door into the store. He had reinforced it so that in the event someone broke in, they'd make a racket trying to get into the back where the Utzes lived. The Smoots might come in that way, but they'd be ready for them.

"What will prevent them from setting the place on fire?" Lucy asked.

"Nothing," Ed had answered.

It was obvious to everyone in the store that Peanut Smoot had somehow kept the fire department and the cops away. The warehouse fire was probably out by now. Lucy didn't hold out much hope of help arriving. But she had tried her best, and had done more than she'd ever believed she could. She was heartbroken that Eli was going to die, and she regretted that she had gotten the Utzes involved.

"I hear a car." Ed peeked out through the window blinds. "There's lights . . ."

Lucy heard a thunderous sound, and a vehicle roared around the building. Several more shots rang out.

A woman yelled, "FBI! Put down your weapons!"

"I'll be," Ed said excitedly. "The danged cavalry's here!"

"Don't shoot!" Peanut called. "We give up!"

Ed nodded. "Looks like old Peanut's done in." He set his shotgun against the wall and straightened up.

"You, in the store!" the female voice called out. "Hold your fire. I'm Special FBI Agent Alexa Keen. Are Lucy and Eli Dockery in there?"

"They sure are!" Ed answered.

"Unlock the door. I'm coming in."

"I know who she is," Lucy said, softly. "My father talks about her."

"Come on in," Ed called out.

Ed unlocked and opened the door and a woman dressed in a business suit came into the kitchen, backlit by the big truck's headlights. She had a gun in her right hand, a badge in her left. She closed the door behind her, put her badge away, and, at the sight of Lucy and Eli, smiled.

"Are you all right?" she asked Lucy.

"I'm fine now that you're here," Lucy told her.

"No, you aren't," a man's voice said.

A man with a black face stood aiming a shotgun directly at the federal agent's head. "She's with them," he said. "Drop your weapon, Alexa. Sir, stay away from that gun. Ma'am, you keep that pistol where it is. Sir, bolt that door or the next person who comes through it will be Peanut Smoot."

77

Serge Sarnov watched the FBI agent go into the building. She had said she should have the old man disarmed in short order, just needed a couple of minutes to reassure the people inside that they were safe, and then she would let Randall and him enter and take the Dockerys.

He checked his watch. The agent had been inside for thirty seconds.

The lights should be on in there, but that idiot twin had fixed that. He'd let Smoot kill the old couple and then they'd take the Dockerys to a warehouse that Smoot owned outside Charlotte. Max would make sure the killing was done to Keen's forensic specifications and then they'd use two weapons to stage a fatal shoot-out between Massey and Agent Keen, and Peanut and his twin oxen.

One minute and twenty seconds. "What the hell is taking your sister so long?" Serge asked the Major.

"She knows what she's doing," the Major answered. "Relax and let her do her job."

"We should go in," Serge said.

"She'll tell you when," Major Keen said. She reached

into the car and flipped the high beams on and off several times.

"Call her cell phone," Max said. "Ask her."

The Major sighed loudly, took her phone out of her pocket, and dialed. Serge heard the agent's phone ringing inside the building. "What's going on?" Major Keen said into her phone. As she listened, her mouth opened and her eyes widened.

"What?" Max asked.

"She's gone wrong," Serge said. "I guess now we can kill her as many times as we like."

The Major held her phone out to Serge. "Massey wants to speak to you, Serge."

Serge put the phone to his ear.

"Sarnov," the voice said. "You have two minutes from now to withdraw or I will kill Alexa Keen."

"Just a minute," Serge said. "I'll consult with the others." He put his hand over the phone so Massey couldn't hear him. There was no time to waste.

"Massey is inside the store."

"How'd he manage it?" Randall said.

"It had to have been before Peanut arrived and set up on the place. Peanut," Serge murmured, "the man in there killed your son."

"Buck?" Peanut asked, confused.

"Click. Blew his brains out because your boy wouldn't give you up."

"Oh, my dear God," Peanut said, genuinely shaken. "Killed my baby . . ."

"Have your son there smash down that door, and you guys go in and kill everything in the place."

"Just a minute," Randall objected. "We should think this through."

"There's no time," Serge argued. "That's Winter Massey in there." He looked at the Major.

"Do what you have to do," she said, nodding.

Peanut went over to his son and gave him instructions.

"Maybe my guys should handle it. This Massey's no slouch," Max said.

Serge spoke in a low voice. "Let the Smoots storm the beach and test the sand for us. Tell your men around front they're to go in as soon as the shooting starts. We wait until Peanut and his son go in and we flash-bang and we go in and finish this."

Serge put the phone back to his ear. "Okay," he said. "You win, Massey. We're leaving." He pointed his trigger finger at Peanut, who had taken up a position against the wall beside the kitchen door.

Letting out a howl, the Smoot twin ran up and shouldered the door. The sound of the wood frame splintering filled the night air as the door collapsed into the room. The twin raised his shotgun. There was an explosion that lit up the kitchen, and Curt's head came apart, his corpse falling into the kitchen.

Peanut looked down at his dead son and screamed, "You're dead, YOU—MOTHER—"

Three shotgun blasts sounded within the space of two seconds. The first slug punched a quarter-size hole in the wall between Peanut's right shoulder and the door frame. The second round—double-aught buckshot—made a fist-size hole through Peanut's chest between his nipples, and the third blew most of his left shoulder away. He died with two thirds of his final curse spoken.

Without hesitation, Max tossed a flash-bang grenade into the kitchen, waited until it went off, and sprinted into the kitchen with his MP5 before him, spraying the room from left to right.

"Kitchen's clear!" he yelled.

Major Keen ran into the building with Serge behind her, gun out.

The kitchen was thick with swirling cordite. Serge saw a tactical shotgun lying on the floor just inside the den. The team that had broken down the front door rushed in from the store, their MP5s aimed at the bedroom door.

"Open up, or we'll drill the walls, Massey!" Max Randall hollered.

Serge, standing beside the Major, heard the Dodge truck out back roar to life. He whirled and ran to the back door, and fired at the truck.

"Stop them!" he screamed at the Smoot twin out front as he sprinted after Peanut's Dodge, emptying his Walther .380 at its wide tail.

He heard the last living Smoot's shotgun go off three times, followed immediately by a dull wet thud.

78

When Winter Massey told Alexa to drop her gun, what Winter saw in her eyes was the last thing he had expected—relief and excitement. "Massey?" Then she smiled, and said, "Thank God! I didn't know how I was going to keep them alive by myself."

"I said put the gun down," Winter again ordered. "I know what you're doing, Lex. How could you?"

"Massey," she repeated. "I'm sorry I couldn't level with you. The two of us have a chance, but you have to trust me. I'll explain it later, but we only have a few seconds before they storm this place. If I put this gun down, you'll be alone."

"You set me up twice." Winter's voice was curt.

"I had no choice. I didn't bring you in to get you hurt. I brought you in to do what I couldn't do on my own and I knew you would. I'm sorry Randall came after you. I tried to help you at Click's house. I couldn't at Laughlin's or the clinic. I was playing a man-in-the-middle defense—I knew they were listening to everything I said and probably seeing what I was doing. Winter, if you ever trusted me—if you ever believed in me—do it now."

"How in hell can I trust you?" Winter said.

"Because I gave you Eleanor," Alexa told him.

Winter felt like he had put his hand on a live wire.

Those five words, spoken in hardly more than a whisper, were deafening.

The headlights of the sedan flickered angrily against the cotton curtains. The killers were growing impatient.

Because I gave you Eleanor. And although he had suspected it at the time, he hadn't truly believed what it had cost Alexa, hadn't accepted it as a sacrifice. Now he knew it was true and, for the first time, he knew his friend's heart.

"How did you get in here?" Ed asked Winter.

"The same way you're all going out," he said.

"You can get us all out past them?" Alexa asked.

"If we move fast," Winter said. "I came in by the root cellar. I lucked into the trapdoor while I was trying to find a way under the building. The last two ladder steps are rotted off and there's a foot of standing water down there."

"I'd plum forgot about that. Hadn't been down there in years," Ed said. "Thought I'd sealed it off good."

Winter looked at Alexa. "Lucy, you and Elijah and this nice couple need to go with Special Agent Keen and stay with her. I'm going to keep them busy. You take everybody to the root cellar through the bedroom closet, and wait at the outside door for me, or the sound of them inside the store." He took the light off the shotgun and handed it to her. "Don't use this until you're in the closet. I'll do what I can. The truck out back may be your best bet."

"I reckon I'll stay here and give you a hand," Ed said.

The baby started crying and Lucy hugged him tightly to her. "It's all right, Elijah," she crooned.

"Sir, Alexa here and these people need you worse. I'll be right behind you and I'll be moving fast."

That was when the phone in Alexa's pocket rang. After Winter took the phone to talk to Serge, he motioned for Alexa to take the others out.

Seconds later, when the twin shouldered the door in, Winter was kneeling just inside the den, using the common wall and the heavy stove for protective cover while aiming the shotgun at the kitchen door. He pointed at the giant's head and squeezed the trigger.

Winter readied for a second shot. When he heard Peanut's booming voice, Winter aimed at the wall just left of the door and pulled the trigger once, quickly moved the barrel farther to the left, and fired again... and quickly again.

79

As soon as he had fired the last shotgun round, Winter dropped the weapon and ran for the bedroom. When the flash-bang went off, he was locking the bedroom door. Hastily he shoved a chair under the knob and, slamming the closet door behind him, scrambled down into the root cellar.

When the heavy footsteps from above echoed down

into the cellar, Winter had joined the others, huddled like refuges, at the door leading outside.

Silently, with Alexa watching their backs, they followed Winter to the corner, then ran to Smoot's Dodge. Winter checked for the keys, and got everybody in through the jump door behind the driver's door, filling the rear seat. Lucy and her son sat in the middle between the Utzes. Alexa scrambled into the cab's passenger seat. Without closing the door, Winter slid in, cranked the engine and throttled the Hemi. The truck roared like a wounded beast, as its tires spun in the wet grass and fishtailed.

"Get down!" he yelled. He'd said the same words to Click Smoot just before he was killed for not listening.

The pistol shots somebody fired at the escaping truck were no surprise, but the remaining twin, centered between Alexa's sedan and the second Tahoe, was. The twin stood still and aimed his shotgun at the truck hurtling toward him.

Winter ducked.

The twin fired three quick shots before the truck punted him high into the air.

Winter sat up and spun the truck onto the gravel road. The shotgun had not just blown a hole the size of a saucer in the windshield, but had also hit the grille. Winter couldn't smell the coolant that was probably streaming out of the radiator, but he knew he'd be lucky to make it a mile before the Hemi seized. If he was going to save his passengers, he'd have to move fast.

"Everybody okay?" he asked. "I'm going to get you

down the road as far as I can. Ed, you know the layout of the woods, the roads?"

"Sure do."

"There's a roadblock up at Clark Road. I parked an SUV on the land just north of it on the access road about a hundred yards in—keys in the ignition. Ed, you'll lead everybody there. I'll hold them back as long as I can."

"Winter, Antonia has six or seven of her people at the roadblock. You'll never get through. She'll have radioed ahead—they'll be waiting."

"I'm going to stop, and I want everybody out and in the woods and hidden when the Tahoe comes after me. Soon as it passes, you go fast as you can for the SUV. Just around the next curve. Get ready."

Winter turned the bend—and found himself faced with something he hadn't expected. The headlights of two vehicles in the road ahead blinked on, blinding him and forming a rolling roadblock coming straight at the Dodge, shoulder to shoulder.

"Alexa, as soon as I stop moving, move."

Winter slammed the brakes. The truck slid sideways, blocking the road. The approaching vehicles stopped thirty feet short, their brights blasting the Dodge. He could see that the two vehicles were full of men. He knew he would never walk away from this one, but maybe if he could do enough damage, the others would have a chance.

"Run!" Winter hollered as he jumped out, aiming his SIG at the cars.

"Drop your weapon!" an amplified male voice ordered.

Winter turned his gun on the car on the left.

"No!" Alexa gripped his shoulder. "Massey, you've

trusted me. Trust me again. Drop your gun right now, and put your hands up."

Doors opened, but Winter's vision was totally impaired by the headlights.

Without hesitation, he opened his hand and released his weapon.

80

Major Antonia Keen was on her phone to Clayton Able as she ran toward Randall's SUV.

"Get them in here *now, Clayton!*" she shouted into the receiver. "Tell them to block the damn road. Tell them to use extreme prejudice. You got me?" She slammed the phone shut.

Randall drove. Serge was in the passenger seat; Antonia and one of Max's men were in the second seat. The other man was on the Tahoe's roof, lying on the luggage rack, aiming his MP5 at the road ahead.

"Your sister disappointed me, Major," Serge said. "I'll have to insist we deal with her. If she survives the next minute or so."

"If she turned—and I do not believe it for a second— I'll frigging shoot her myself," Major Keen hissed. "If Massey didn't kill her and leave her behind, he has her at gunpoint. Did you see her in the truck?"

"No," Sarnov said. "I glimpsed some heads before they all ducked."

"Let's wait and see. I know her better than you do. Massey was in there when she went in and he knew she set him up. He killed her, I'm sure of it."

"They escaped," Serge said. "She didn't yell, she didn't fight."

"She didn't turn, damn it! If she's in that truck, she's playing along with him. She can manipulate him."

"You can't get between her and those men coming in," Randall said. "That Dodge and anything inside it is toast."

When Max made a curve, Serge saw men illuminated by bright headlights aiming automatic weapons and shotguns at the black truck.

Max slid the SUV to a stop, and everybody jumped out. The man on the roof stood up, his gun ready.

The men who'd been aiming at the truck turned toward the Tahoe.

A voice from the men surrounding the truck yelled out, "Put your guns down!"

"You idiot!" Major Keen hollered. "Hold your fire, soldier! I'm Major Keen!"

"So you say. I said *put your weapons down!*"

"Okay, don't freak out," Max called. "We'll comply."

Serge shrugged. He set his gun gently on the hood of the SUV. Max and the man next to him put their weapons on the ground. After a moment, the man on the Tahoe's roof squatted to place his gun on the roof by his feet. One of the men who had been firing at the Dodge stepped forward. He gathered up the weapons and stacked them in the road in front of the SUV.

The apparent team leader, a white-haired man in a black jumpsuit, came onto the road from the trees. His men kept their aimed shotguns at the people from the SUV.

"What's the matter with you people?" Antonia snapped. "What is your name, soldier?"

Alexa Keen came around the Dodge, striding toward her sister.

"Antonia," she said, "allow me to introduce to you Special FBI Agent in Charge Kelly Crisp. The others are members of the FBI's Immediate Response Team. I'm placing all of you under arrest for kidnapping, murder, conspiracy to kidnap, conspiracy to commit murder, crossing state lines to commit those crimes, and . . . well, I'll make sure you get a comprehensive list of the charges at FBI HQ. Agent Crisp will read you your rights."

Serge was being cuffed when he saw that one of the men who'd been firing at the Dodge was wearing a camouflage coat and had his face blackened. When the man caught Serge staring at him, he smiled. *Massey!*

Antonia Keen said nothing, standing stiffly, glaring at her sister.

Agent Crisp said, "If you're wondering about the people who were at the roadblock, they're all in custody. Clayton Able and his crew are being taken into custody about now."

As Alexa snapped cuffs on her sister's wrists, Antonia said, "You better help me out. I have you on tape."

"And I have you on tape, too, Major," Alexa replied.

"I've been recording every discussion we've had for months."

"You're my sister."

A tear rolled down Alexa's cheek. "I wish to God I wasn't."

"I can explain all of this," Antonia said, raising her voice. "My authority supercedes yours, Agents. This is a matter of national security. My men and I are part of a joint military and Department of Homeland Security operation."

"I'm sure you can explain how all of this murder and mayhem was perfectly justifiable," Agent Crisp answered sarcastically. "But we'll just hold you temporarily at HQ until it's all straightened out, okay, Major?"

81

Winter was more than a little surprised when he arrived back at the roadblock on Clark Road and found his wife waiting there for him, drinking hot coffee and joking with highway patrolmen and firefighters. Judge Fondren was also there, and his grandson Elijah in his arms. EMS personnel were examining Lucy, but her worst damage wasn't physical.

"Hey, stranger," Sean said as Winter climbed out of the FBI car.

"What the hell are you doing here?" he asked her.

"Where else would I be?"

"I don't know. At home?"

"Jeez, Massey." She looked him over, set her styrene coffee cup on the hood of the highway patrol cruiser behind her, and embraced him. "You kept your word."

"My word?"

"You didn't get yourself shot up or beat up too badly. I'll have to see what's under the minstrel mask later."

"I'm at a total loss. How did you get here?"

"Well, you know how Hank was supposed to go see Judge Fondren and deliver your message?"

"Yes."

"Well, he wanted to. He really did, but he wasn't up to it."

"So you went instead."

"Got it in one, mister."

Winter felt anger rising in him. "Sean, didn't it occur to you that I called Hank because going to Fondren might be dangerous? It was quite possible that he was being watched over by some nasty people. Hank has experience, and nobody looking at a man on crutches would think he was a messenger."

"And I don't? Get real, Massey. As it turned out, the judge *was* being watched, but by Agent Crisp, Alexa's partner. He had a dozen armed men along with him. I'm sure you met him. He explained to me that Alexa wasn't trying to hurt you. It still doesn't begin to excuse her. She could have gotten you killed."

"I'm not real happy about it myself," Winter said truthfully.

A large helicopter appeared from the north and circled until a highway patrolman popped a flare in a hollow space between the highway patrol cruisers, fire trucks, and EMS ambulances clustered on the shoulders of Clark Road. The copter touched down thirty yards from where Winter was standing, then cut back its power, leaving its blades turning.

Alexa and Kelly Crisp were supervising the loading of their prisoners into a long van staffed by members of the U.S. Marshals Service. Winter didn't know the four deputy marshals, so they probably weren't from the region.

FBI agents and highway patrolmen were going in to secure the store and the Smoot warehouse crime scenes. Evidence technicians would process them over the coming hours.

Ed and Edna Utz were going to be taken to Charlotte, where they would be guests of the federal government at the Westin Hotel until their store had been put right and the techs released it.

While Winter and Sean were talking, Judge Fondren, Lucy, and Elijah were escorted to the waiting helicopter. The judge turned and strode over to Winter and Sean. "Mr. Massey," he said, shaking his hand. "I wanted to thank you for saving Lucy and Elijah. I hope you will allow us to show our gratitude properly at a later date."

"I've been amply rewarded, sir."

"Well, at least I hope you and your lovely wife will join us for dinner sometime so Lucy can thank you properly. At the moment, my daughter is unable to adequately convey her feelings on the matter. You should know that you and Alexa have saved *my* life along with theirs. I don't think I could have faced life without them. And from what I am told, I wouldn't have lived out the day if I'd set Colonel Bryce free." He smiled and winked at Sean. Then he turned, trotted to the helicopter, and climbed in.

Alexa stood with Winter and Sean as the chopper built rotor speed. Lucy's face appeared in a window. As they watched, she held her son up. Taking his little hand in hers, she waved at the trio.

"You are going to explain all of this to me, right?" Winter asked Alexa.

"Sure," she replied. "We've got a lot of report writing to do. Debriefing. Official explaining to construct."

"Can it wait until tomorrow? I'm too tuckered to talk."

Winter looked at his wife, who was now leaning against the cruiser with her coffee cup back in her hand.

"You going to be all right?" Winter asked Alexa. He was referring to the fact that Alexa had arrested her own sister.

She knew what he was talking about. "My heart's been broken before."

He smiled at her, put his hand under her chin, and kissed her forehead.

"Massey, I put you in harm's way without telling you the truth. I had to do it the way I did it, to save the Dockerys. You were the only person who could do it. Antonia and the others had to believe I was on their side."

"I forgive you."

"I don't," Sean said, still fuming. "It's a miracle you didn't get him killed. I thought you cared about him."

"Sean, I wouldn't forgive me either."

"Why was everybody working so hard to put my husband in front of a bullet?"

"Sean," Winter said. "It worked out." He turned back to Alexa. "But you could have trusted me with the truth, Lex."

"I knew the more the odds were against you, the more likely you were to succeed."

Sean didn't smile.

"We'll talk tomorrow," Winter said, yawning.

He embraced Alexa. When he turned back to Sean, he noticed that she responded to Alexa's good-bye with an almost imperceptible nod.

"You ready to go home?" he asked his wife.

Sean nodded.

"You shouldn't be mad at Alexa," Winter told her, smiling.

"What makes you think I'm mad?"

82

On Monday morning at eight A.M. sharp, Ross Laughlin, who had arrived an hour earlier on his law firm's jet after spending two days in Miami with a senator to build an alibi, took a seat at the defense table in a federal courtroom. He opened his briefcase to retrieve his crocodile notebook and his shiny amber pen, and pulled the shirt cuffs out so his cuff links were visible. He was going to look his best when he appeared before the mob of press gathered on the courthouse steps expecting to announce Colonel Hunter Bryce's conviction.

The U.S. marshals escorted a stern-faced Colonel Hunter Bryce to the table and removed his handcuffs. Before he sat down, the colonel straightened his tie and tugged at the hem of his blazer. Laughlin had to admit that he wished his own suits fit him like Bryce's fit their owner, but you can't buy a body like that.

In a low voice Bryce asked, "How does everything look?"

Ross opened his notebook, and on the first sheet he had printed, *Free at last, free at last.*

"How long will it take to do the paperwork?" Bryce asked.

"An hour, if you get someone from the clerk's office who's literate. The press will be going apeshit. You'll have to avoid making any statements."

"I'm great on TV."

"Gloating would be ill advised, Colonel. There'll be a shit storm when Fondren turns you loose. The media is discussing whether you'll get life or the needle."

"I was messing with you, Ross. Loosen up. Where's Randall going to be?"

"I haven't spoken to him. I assume he's been busy cleaning things up."

Colonel Bryce turned to look at the faces in the seats behind the defense table. Aside from the journalists who had been covering the trial, he didn't see anyone he recognized.

Just as he was about to turn back, two women entered the courtroom. "Oh, man," Bryce said to Laughlin. "Looks like somebody's babe's been in a car wreck."

Ross Laughlin snapped the cap off of his pen, then turned to look at the woman Bryce was referring to. She was pretty despite the bruises and lacerations. Something about her seemed familiar, but Ross couldn't quite place her. The attractive woman with her was dressed in a gray suit and carried a leather handbag.

He assumed the second woman was an attorney who had come to see him lose one. Like a lot of people, she was in for a surprise. He glanced at the prosecutor, a self-assured ass.

"Mr. Laughlin?" the woman in the suit said.

"Yes?" he said, putting on his dignified political smile.

"I don't believe you've met Lucy Dockery. Lucy, this is Ross Laughlin, Mr. Smoot's business partner."

The pretty woman with the bruised and scratched-up face studied Ross with an expression that could have driven dull nails into solid oak. "My pleasure," she said through tight lips.

Laughlin was aware that Hunter Bryce was squeezing his arm, and that the bailiff was calling the court to order. Stunned, Ross sat through a very long pronouncement of guilt delivered by Judge Fondren, who never once took his cold blue eyes off Hunter Bryce. The judge set a date for sentencing, then vacated the bench.

As Hunter Bryce was being led from the room in handcuffs by U.S. marshals, Special FBI Agent Alexa Keen introduced herself to Ross Laughlin, read him his rights, and handcuffed him.

Lucy Dockery made her way to the door leading to the judge's chambers, where her son was waiting with his favorite sitter.

Alexa Keen and Special FBI Agent Crisp escorted the stunned attorney from the courtroom past a phalanx of reporters, photographers, and camera crews.

83

All day Sunday Winter had been at FBI HQ being debriefed. It had rained off and on all that day, which had suited Sean's dark mood. Monday turned out to be warm and the sun worked hard to dry up the ground left spongy by the rain. Winter told Sean that morning that he had invited Alexa for lunch, which meant Sean was scrambling to get it prepared. Winter and Hank had taken Rush, Faith Ann, and Olivia to the grocery store in Concord for some things Sean needed to finish the meal. She was busy in the kitchen when she heard a vehicle pulling up out front.

Sean went to the door and saw Alexa approaching the porch. "You're early. Winter isn't back yet," she said, trying not to sound curt. She seriously doubted that Alexa's appearance while she was alone was accidental. "I've got some wine in the fridge."

"I wanted to talk to you alone," Alexa said.

Sean led Alexa to the kitchen and stood until Alexa sat at the table.

"I wanted you to know that I am truly sorry I put Winter in harm's way."

"He's forgiven you, I guess I can, too," Sean told her as she sat across from Alexa. "It turned out all right. The Dockerys are safe. Bryce is where he belongs for the time being."

"He is."

"But Winter is sure he won't be for long. I mean, we all know how the weasels deal."

"All's well that ends well," Alexa said softly.

Sean got up, went to the refrigerator, took out a bottle of wine, and removed the cork. She took a pair of wine-glasses from the counter and poured them full of white wine. She handed Alexa one and, taking hers, sat.

"I guess your sister is up a creek."

"That's her own doing. She approached me a while back assuming I was like she is. They needed me to get to Judge Fondren in order to keep the FBI from getting involved. I thought it was going to be an extortion of some sort until the kidnapping. I never would have let that happen. Then I had to figure out a way to get the Dockerys free, but I knew my sister's men were going to be watching me every minute. They have miniature cameras, all sorts of devices. I knew Winter was my only hope. I insisted on bringing him in because I told Antonia I couldn't do it alone since not having a capable partner would invite too much official skepticism. My people thought it was a good idea and I convinced Antonia that Winter wasn't the man whose reputation he carried. I told her he was burned out, fat and happy, suffering from an old wound, and gun-shy. I said he would back up my story to enhance his own reputation. Precio—my sister agreed and convinced the others. Only I knew it was a lie."

"Why did your sister think you'd go along?" Sean said.

"She's heard me complain for years about the Bureau. I bitched and complained around her, even though it wasn't how I felt. I guess I vented to make her feel like she'd done better than I had, made better choices. After she approached me with this, and I realized that she was dead serious, I went straight to my director. Antonia was vague, keeping me on a strict need-to-know on everything. I went undercover as a coconspirator, joining Antonia's plot."

"Still, she is your sister."

"I'll always love her because she is my only blood relative, but she's twisted," Alexa said evenly. "All hell's breaking loose at the Pentagon this morning with people trying to cover their butts, or running for cover. Antonia claims she hooked her star to the side trying to catch the men involved in the arms dealing, playing both sides against the middle. Maybe she is telling the truth, and was getting Bryce out as part of some sting, maybe not. Not my problem. Max Randall claims that the agent Bryce murdered wasn't the only undercover plant. He says he was, too, working deep cover with Homeland Security. But no matter what the truth is, Antonia and Randall planned the kidnapping, and they were going to sacrifice the Dockerys—either to get Bryce off, or to make a far bigger case against the Russian Mafia who were going to buy the weapons."

"What do you think?" Sean asked.

"Who was really doing what on which agenda doesn't make any difference to me. Based on Antonia's ability to survive, she may just play the right angles and get off light. But even if by some miracle she avoids prison, her military career is over."

"So what do you do now?"

"I'll stay with the Bureau. It's my only family now," Alexa said. She took a swallow of the wine and nodded her appreciation of the vintage.

Sean felt a pang of sorrow for Alexa. The idea of being married to a job, of having only fellow agents for relatives, was sad.

"That isn't why I came early, Sean, what I wanted to say to you. It's hard for me..."

"You wanted to tell me you're in love with my husband," Sean said, getting it out in the open. She had known it the night before, when she'd watched Alexa's face as she hugged Winter.

"He doesn't know, does he?" Alexa asked.

"He's never said so. Most men are fairly dim when it comes to that sort of thing. Why didn't you ever tell him?"

Alexa set her glass down and folded her hands. "I was confused. I had a rough childhood."

"Winter told me about it. Some. Enough, anyway. That you were sexually and physically abused."

Alexa studied Sean's eyes, nodding. "Okay. Well, in my mind, love and sex were direct opposites. Sex was a weapon that had been used against me, and it did all the destructive things to me we all know about from television shows. After I left home for college, I spent a lot of time in therapy. I finally decided that if I could get past that, I could get there with Winter. I believed that he could help me heal." Alexa blushed. "You know, he kissed me once, and I freaked out. I was going to talk to Winter when I was home one summer. I even brought Eleanor with me for moral support. She didn't know that, of course. Sean, I could tell Winter anything, but saying that I loved him that way was different. . . ."

"I understand," Sean said honestly. "Winter told me what you said in the store that night. He said that Eleanor had figured out what you did. That you were as in love with Winter as anybody could be. She believed that you knew that she would be a perfect woman for Winter. She was sure you had stepped aside because you loved him that much. But sacrificing him must have broken your heart."

"In a good way, Sean." Tears glittered in Alexa's eyes. "Seeing them so happy was a wonderful thing. I loved them both. I still do."

"I wish I had met Eleanor," Sean said.

"You would have liked her and she would have liked you. Sean, it's important that you know I'm not a threat to you. Winter could never love me the way he loves you or he loved Eleanor. And I could never be the lover and partner for him that Eleanor was or that you are."

Sean nodded. She understood. "I appreciate your honesty, and I can see why you're so special to Winter. How could I resent anybody who knows and loves Massey?

Alexa, I hope you and I can be friends, and I hope you will always be in our lives. And you should think of us as your family."

Sean hugged Alexa. When they broke the embrace, Alexa started crying again and had to wipe her eyes. Then she laughed and held her glass up.

"To the Masseys," she said.

Sean touched her glass to Alexa's.

Winter pulled up out front and he honked twice.

There were loud footsteps on the porch, the front door swung open, and the old farmhouse filled up with the rich sounds of a family coming home.

About the Author

JOHN RAMSEY MILLER'S career has included stints as a visual artist, advertising copywriter, and journalist. He is the author of the nationally best-selling *The Last Family* and of three Winter Massey thrillers: *Inside Out*, *Upside Down*, and *Side by Side*, and is at work on a stand-alone crime novel, *Too Far Gone*, which Dell will publish in 2006.

A native son of Mississippi, he now lives in North Carolina with his wife and writes full-time.

If you enjoyed
John Ramsey Miller's electrifying
Side by Side, you won't want
to miss any of his crime novels.
Look for **Inside Out** and
Upside Down, both featuring
U.S. Marshal Winter Massey, and
for **The Last Family** at your
favorite bookseller's.

And read on for an exciting early
look at the next thriller from
John Ramsey Miller, **Too Far Gone,**
coming soon from Dell.

TOO FAR GONE

by
John Ramsey Miller

TOO FAR GONE

An Alexa Keen Novel by
John Ramsey Miller

1 | New Orleans, Louisiana, 1976

Crashing thunder woke the four-year-old.

She lay still, taking deep breaths, huddling with the teddy bear as the storm's fury assaulted her ears. Running bolts of lightning slashed the black sky.

Wind blasted the rain hard against the window's panes.

The massive oak tree outside flailed its branches—like furious arms reaching out for the lace curtains.

She clenched shut her eyes.

"There's nothing to fear," her mother had said on other stormy nights. *"You're perfectly safe in your bed, Casey."*

Each dazzling flash made the familiar objects in her room both strange and malevolent. The stuffed animals perched on the window box instantly became monstrous shadows against the shadowy wall.

She listened for some sound to let her know if her parents were awake and perhaps moving around somewhere in the house. *They will come tell me it's all right.*

The bedroom door was cracked open, the hallway a dark and endless tunnel.

"BAM!" A shutter on a nearby window, suddenly un-hooked, slapped at the side of the house like an angry fist against a door. "BAM! BAM! BAM!"

She pushed back the covers, slid off the mattress, and shot to the door, thinking of the safe, warm nest between her parents in their bed.

Throwing open her door, she ran across the hallway to her parents' bedroom, clutching the bear to her chest. *They won't be mad.* She turned the knob and slowly crept into the bedroom, where lightning illuminated the crumpled bedding.

They are not here!

The bathroom was dark.

They have to be downstairs.

Casey hurried to find them. On the stairs, between the peals of thunder, she could hear loud noises below, like dogs barking, or seals at the zoo.

One hand on the banister, the other clutching the soft animal to her, the child slid down the wide staircase one step at a time. The noises stopped before she reached the first floor and the sudden silence scared her more than the sounds.

In the den, flashes formed into trapezoidal slivers by the windows lit the room eerily. The chair her father always sat in when he was in the room—it was vacant. *Not in here.*

She padded off down the hallway toward the rear of the house. *Mommy? Daddy?*

Casey saw a yellow band of light at the far end of the hallway under the swinging door to the kitchen and she ducked her head and ran for it. She imagined that something large was rushing at her in the darkness, something that would pounce at any second and sweep her up in its jaws like the lion on the television always did to the deer.

"Mommy!" she yelled out. "Mommy!"

Reaching, she pushed at it. Because it didn't swing open but a tiny bit, her chest and her forehead struck it hard, and she whimpered at the pain. She fought to push it open, but it wouldn't budge. In her panic she dropped the bear and slammed her hands against the wood, beating, beating, beating and hollering for her mother.

Little by little, as whatever was making it stay shut moved a little at a time, it opened just a bit. The kitchen lights poured out into the hallway through the growing crack.

Casey heard an odd sucking sound and a loud grunting.

Something warm and wet touched her toes, and she looked down to see a pool spreading from under the door to her feet. Her bear was lying there on the floor, his black eyes staring up hard at her as the puddle swallowed his head and his arms.

Casey pushed hard again.

The door swung in suddenly and Casey pitched head-long into the brilliantly lit kitchen.

She was lying facedown in the warm red liquid that was everywhere.

She looked around and found herself staring into her mother's face. It was not at all the right face. So many boo-boos. She knew her father was there too, but she wouldn't look at him. She closed her eyes tightly and screamed and screamed.

"STOP IT!" a voice boomed. "STOP IT RIGHT THIS MINUTE!"

Casey quit screaming. Turning, she saw two bare feet

inches from her face and let her eyes follow the legs to the hem of a dress. Casey sat bolt upright and looked up into the eyes of a witch wearing a wet dress. The witch's blond and crimson hair stuck out from her head like twisted garden vines. The unfamiliar face, smeared with red, smiled down at her. Two of her front teeth were missing. She knelt and put the cook's meat-chopping thing down on the floor.

Casey couldn't move. She stared at the bloody hands that reached out for her and she squeezed her eyes shut tight as the witch embraced her, pressing Casey's cheek, now wet with tears she didn't even know she was shedding, against her heaving chest.

"What a good baby girl you are to come find me," the husky voice told her. "I was just getting ready to come get you."

2 | Thirty years later

Using her Mag-Lite to prevent tripping over fallen tree limbs in the dark, Special FBI Agent Alexa Keen followed the long string of crime-scene tape that had been placed by responding officers to form a trail to a Day-Glo–bordered trapezoid. At the end of the tape she entered the crime scene. The corpse appeared to be wrapped tightly in a rust-colored blanket—a covering Alexa realized was composed of tens of thousands of fire ants. As she squatted for a better look, the dead man's lids suddenly opened and he stared out at her through eyes of wet obsidian. His mouth formed a silent, screaming circle.

Alexa jerked awake in the darkness and lay still, piecing the shards of reality together. *The hotel. New Orleans. Law enforcement seminar. Friday.* A real siren outside had clawed its way through the gossamer walls of her dream about a dead man she had seen only in photographs until his naked corpse had been discovered in the Tennessee woods two days after his family had paid a half-million-dollar ransom. Charles Tarlton had been one of her first cases—the first involving the murder of an abducted individual—and it played in the theater of her dreams with some frequency. As Alexa's nightmares went, this one was hardly a two—a ten was being awakened by labored wheezing and lying frozen in terror as a pair of clammy hands explored her prepubescent body.

The bedside clock had the time at five past twelve. Alexa slid her hand beneath the pillow beside her to feel the pommel grip of her Delta Dart, an eight-inch-long triangular-bladed weapon made of glass-reinforced nylon. It was always there in case she was ever again surprised by anyone climbing into her bed. The inexpensive dart's edges were as dull as the point was sharp, and was strictly a stabbing weapon. Used correctly, it penetrated like a high-powered-rifle bullet. And Alexa Keen knew how to use it.

Except for her removing her shoes, Alexa was still dressed in the clothes she'd worn to dinner with two other special agents she'd never met before they checked into the Marriott. She always slept in her clothes when she was away from her own bed. She lay awake for several more minutes with her eyes closed—her mind shifting gears and speeding through a world of troubling thoughts. The most disturbing were of her sister, who was sitting in a military safe house, waiting to testify at a string of court-martial proceedings.

Beyond that stack of mind manure, Alexa's mind started going through the cases she'd worked that had ended badly, wondering what she missed, how she should have done things differently. Everybody made mistakes, but when Alexa Keen made one, the consequences could be devastating and deadly.

Alexa's life was one long stress test. She thrived on edge living—consuming gallons of coffee and running headlong through nights and days without meaningful sleep. She loved the atmospheric highs that success brought and she slogged her way out of the pit that failures brought. The job was her life. She read inside politics expertly, for doing so was a necessary evil: it often meant the difference between being relevant and sitting behind a desk in Fargo. She walked the walk—navigating the spiderweb red-tape bureaucracy—and talked Bureau-speak. This was the life she had freely chosen, and the other badges were almost the only family she had left. Alexa's was a family headed by inflexible, often paranoid, and generally disapproving parent figures who were slow to reward and eager to punish—and a family where sibling rivalry was unrelenting and pitiless.

Alexa rose from the bed and crossed to the window. Opening the heavy curtains, she peered down through the rain-streaked glass at a wide-awake city. Twenty floors below, an ambulance attendant slammed the door of the vehicle whose siren had awakened her and she listened to its scream as it made its way toward Charity Hospital, which had the closest and best emergency room in the city. And New Orleans did its dead-level best to make sure it remained the busiest room in town.

Alexa Keen hadn't yet found any place that felt like a comfort zone. She sometimes wondered if there was a nurturing place for her. She knew that home wasn't a location, but most people sure seemed to be anchored to some geographic cradle. All through her life she had settled in superficially, learning the relevant streets in the cities she lived in, and developing preferences in stores and restaurants. In each city, there were people whose company she enjoyed. Her apartments were attractively decorated, but they might have been sets in a furniture showroom designed to give clients an idea of how a properly decorated place was supposed to look if you kept people out of it. The same framed art hung on the walls, the same sleek modern furniture always filled the space enclosed by the walls. No extraneous clutter. No plants to be watered. No pets to anchor her. Alexa's telephone seldom rang and her mailbox collected only junk mail and bills. Her television set played strictly for information. Her sound system reflected her mood in shades of Billie Holiday, the Gypsy Kings, R.E.M., Green Day, the Beatles, or Elmore James.

The pedestrians down on the sidewalk—most of them tourists, she was sure—were hardly more than marks. Their wallets held the blood that powered the city's real heart—the French Quarter, and now the casinos. Alexa had visited the Crescent City only on FBI business. It wasn't her nature to spend her vacation time in places like New Orleans, San Francisco, Las Vegas, or Miami. When she had time to fritter away—her forced vacations—she hiked obscure trails, floated down rivers, camped where few other people wanted to be. She liked the beach, but only in the winter. She loved best being alone on the side of a mountain under a giant blue sky, sipping creek-chilled wine while sitting in the cool grass reading. Alexa didn't like New Orleans. Once, some years earlier, while fighting her way down Bourbon Street on Fat Tuesday, chasing after a man who had just shot a pair of deputy U.S. marshals, she had caught a glimpse of what Hell must look and feel like.

During Mardi Gras, the Quarter was jam-packed with drunken hedonistic fools dancing to a tune of no-holds-barred wretched excess.

She also didn't find New Orleans particularly inviting in the space between Fat Tuesdays. She didn't find the blend of grinding poverty, wholesale crime, decaying structures, the crumbling infrastructure, the third-world corruption, or the decadence at all attractive.

Despite the fact that she was wide awake, the ringing telephone startled her. The red numerals on the clock said 12:22.

"Yes," she said.

"Special Agent Keen?" a male voice asked.

"Speaking," she responded.

"This is Detective Michael Manseur," he said. "I'm with N.O.P.D. Homicide."

"Winter Massey's friend," she said, smiling. Six months earlier, she and ex–Deputy U.S. Marshal Winter Massey, a close friend of hers from childhood, had worked together on a kidnapping case in North Carolina. In one of several conversations about an incident involving the murder of a friend's niece, and Winter's efforts to find her missing daughter before some hired killers and corrupt cops did, he had spoken very highly of Michael Manseur.

"Well, I expect *friend* might be a stretch," Manseur responded. "Acquaintance is closer to it. I have nothing but respect for Winter, that's for sure. He is a remarkable and memorable individual."

"I spoke to him last week and he told me I should call you. I really did mean to."

"He called me three days ago to say I should call you while you were here at your seminar. He said we should get together. I intended to ask you to join my family for dinner while you're in town, but I've been up to my belt loops in alligators."

"I'm leaving first thing in the morning," she told him truthfully.

"I'm sorry to hear it," the policeman replied.

What Alexa couldn't imagine was why Manseur was calling her well after midnight. Maybe he'd been working in a windowless room and lost track of time. It had happened to her enough times.

"Maybe the next time I'm in town . . ." she suggested.

"David Landry, our missing persons detective, sat in on your talk today," Manseur said. She liked his voice. He stretched his vowels out like taffy. The deep timbre and heavy accent were warm and comforting.

"There were a lot of officers there. It was a big room."

"In his late twenties. Six two, one forty or thereabouts, blond, wears horn-rimmed glasses. Landry looks more like a professor than a cop."

She remembered the man whom Detective Manseur was describing but didn't acknowledge that. "Well, maybe we can get together next time. It was nice talking to you, Detective Manseur."

"That isn't why I called you, Agent Keen. I'm thoughtless to a fault, but I sure wouldn't bother you at this hour just to chitchat. I *was* wondering if I could impose on you a little bit."

"Please do." Perhaps he had a pressing question on a case he thought she might have an answer to.

"We've got ourselves a potential situation. I was hoping you could spare me a couple of hours."

"My flight leaves at seven-twenty this morning."

"I mean right now. This deal is what you do, and Winter says you're one of the best at it."

"An abduction?" she said, straightening and letting the curtains drop shut, closing out the rainy night.

"Might be. Going missing in New Orleans is hardly unusual. Ninety-nine times out of ten, the case solves itself pretty quick. I hope you might be able to help us assess the situation. Tell us what you think we've got. It's a pretty delicate deal."

"You're the commander of Homicide, aren't you?"

"That's pretty much a temporary assignment."

"How does this situation concern Homicide?"

"Missing Persons is technically a department under Homicide, since identifying the deceased folks we run across is a big part of our deal. I hoped I could get your opinion on this since you're here and carry the reputation you do. That's all."

"I see." She was flattered.

"And then we can tell Massey that we got together. Are you free to go to a location with me?"

It isn't just a question or two over the phone. "How soon?"

"I'm in the lobby," he told her. "Standing by the elevators. I'm wearing a green raincoat. You have one, you might want to bring it."

Michael Manseur's voice had thoroughly misrepresented him. The voice was something along the lines of Tommy Lee Jones. The man waiting at the elevator bank looked more like a chronically unsuccessful door-to-door vacuum cleaner hawk than a detective. Even with the thickness of the soles of his scuffed brown wingtips, Manseur was no more than five seven and, except for the laurel of short pale hair anchored by small ears, he was bald. His round face was covered with skin a shade darker than porcelain and featured intelligent but sad eyes with dark bags beneath them, a razor-thin nose, and a smile like that of a child with a huge secret. The green trench coat had oily stains on the hem. The knot on his predominantly yellow tie had been loosened hours ago, and the left side of his stiff shirt collar was bent up like a hand waving.

"Agent Keen?" he said.

"Alexa," she said, smiling. "Please call me Alexa."

"Certainly. Call me Michael," he replied, nodding. He swept his arm to indicate the direction she should travel to get to his car, which turned out to be a white sedan waiting at the curb.

Manseur opened the passenger door for Alexa, closed it gently, then hurried around to take his place behind the wheel. He checked the rearview, pulled out, and headed away from the Mississippi River, turning on the blue light centered on the dash to cut a path through the traffic as the sedan gathered speed.

"Where are we going?" she asked him.

"Uptown a little way," he replied, as if that answered her question.

Alexa sat back and watched New Orleans pass by.

3

Manseur drummed his fingers on the steering wheel as he sped along streets Alexa wasn't familiar with. Policemen, firemen, and ambulance drivers were required to learn the streets of their cities and towns until they were human GPS devices. If cabbies and delivery people didn't do the same, they were less effective at their jobs, but people didn't usually die on account of it.

Alexa's understanding of the layout of New Orleans was at best sketchy. She knew that the streetcar ran from uptown, through the Garden District, and made a loop at Canal Street. She knew the Mississippi River curved around the city, which was why it was called the Crescent City. She knew that Lake Pontchartrain was north and that the twin-span bridge across it was the longest bridge in the world. She knew where the French Quarter, the Central Business District, the Federal court building, and FBI headquarters were located.

She knew a lot of cities in the same general way, which was as much as she cared to know about any of them. Normally, she was with a team, and usually they had local agents or policemen to get them efficiently from place to place. And these days there were GPS devices in most Bureau cars and rentals.

"You ever hear of the LePointes?" Manseur asked her.

"Can't say I have," Alexa replied.

"They're about the most influential family there is around here. Truth be told, I don't know if they even know what all they own. Any questions so far?"

He stopped talking to navigate a turn.

"LePointes are wealthy people and everybody around here knows it," Alexa echoed. "So the missing person is one of these LePointes?"

"Gary West, who married Casey LePointe."

"So I may presume Gary West would be a valuable target for a kidnapper?"

Manseur nodded.

"What were the circumstances of his disappearance?"

"He didn't come home for dinner."

"Missed dinner? Obviously a kidnapping."

"Oh, you're being sarcastic. I'm sorry if I'm not doing this briefing right. I just want you to know who we're dealing with."

Alexa laughed. "Being a smartass is part of my FBI training. Go ahead."

"I don't mind." Manseur had slowed the car down and Alexa figured they must be getting close to wherever they were heading. "Dr. William LePointe is presently the last male LePointe. His brother, Curry, has been dead for about thirty years. Curry LePointe was murdered, along with his wife—Rebecca, I think her name was—by a lunatic with an ax. Dr. LePointe's niece Casey has the husband Gary, was there at the time. From what I remember of it, a pair of patrol officers answered the burglar alarm and saved the child. Gary and Casey West have a daughter who'd be I'd guess three, maybe four years old."

"The family's influence explains why an out-of-place LePointe rates the commander of Homicide." *And an FBI agent.*

"Dave Landry, our missing persons detective who was at your lecture, will be meeting us there. Maybe you can watch how he handles it, possibly suggest things to me or whatever. The LePointes don't want a big fuss made about this until it's been established that there's a need for it. They're the kind of people who like to keep everything low-key."

"Like keeping it a secret when one of them is missing?"

"Well, for instance, they don't take credit for what all they do, good things for a whole lot of people. You don't see what a LePointe is doing in the newspaper except on the society page. William LePointe was Rex when he was about thirty.

"Rex?"

Manseur smiled. "You're not familiar with Rex?"

"I know it's the number-one name for German shepherds."

"It's King of Carnival. It's about the biggest deal in New Orleans society. Well, being Momus is probably bigger, but Momus is always masked, so nobody but a few people in the secret society know who he is. Momus bids adieu to Mardi Gras."

"How did I miss that?" Alexa said. Manseur talked about Rex and Momus like a Catholic might speak of saints, or the pope.

"Just so you know, I didn't mention to anybody that I was asking you to come along."

"You didn't?"

"We have a new superintendent of police. Jackson Evans. Evans told me to do whatever I needed to make sure this was done right. You understand, nobody wants to involve the FBI in this unless it turns out to be an FBI matter—"

"Of course not."

"Which nobody thinks it is. I'm just . . ." Manseur hesitated, as if he were looking for the right word.

"Covering your bases."

"Covering my something. The LePointes give millions every year to all sorts of things like schools, libraries, the zoo, museums, scholarships, after-school programs, homeless and battered women's shelters, summer camps—all manner of civic-betterment deals. They've donated fire-fighting equipment and ballistic vests and service weapons to the police. They are very generous to New Orleans."

"Their generosity extends to political campaigns?" Alexa asked.

"Local, state . . . and national."

"Say no more," Alexa said.

Carnival Pride℠
April 2 - 9, 2006.

7 Day Exotic Mexican Riviera Itinerary

DAY	PORT	ARRIVE	DEPART
Sun	Los Angeles/Long Beach, CA		4:00 P.M.
Mon	"Book Lover's" Day at Sea		
Tue	"Book Lover's" Day at Sea		
Wed	Puerto Vallarta, Mexico	8:00 A.M.	10:00 P.M.
Thu	Mazatlan, Mexico	9:00 A.M.	6:00 P.M.
Fri	Cabo San Lucas, Mexico	7:00 A.M.	4:00 P.M.
Sat	"Book Lover's" Day at Sea		
Sun	Los Angeles/Long Beach, CA	9:00 A.M.	

ports of call subject to weather conditions

TERMS AND CONDITIONS

PAYMENT SCHEDULE:
50% due upon booking
Full and final payment due by February 10, 2006

Acceptable forms of payment are Visa, MasterCard, American Express, Discover and checks. The cardholder must be one of the passengers traveling. A fee of $25 will apply for all returned checks. Check payments must be made payable to **Advantage International, LLC** and sent to: **Advantage International, LLC, 195 North Harbor Drive, Suite 4206, Chicago, IL 60601**

CHANGE/CANCELLATION:
Notice of change/cancellation must be made in writing to Advantage International, LLC.

Change:
Changes in cabin category may be requested and can result in increased rate and penalties. A name change is permitted 60 days or more prior to departure and will incur a penalty of $50 per name change. Deviation from the group schedule and package is a cancellation.

Cancellation:

181 days or more prior to departure	$250 per person
121 - 180 days or more prior to departure	50% of the package price
120 - 61 days prior to departure	75% of the package price
60 days or less prior to departure	100% of the package price (nonrefundable)

US and Canadian citizens are required to present a valid passport or the original birth certificate and state issued photo ID (drivers license). All other nationalities must contact the consulate of the various ports that are visited for verification of documentation.

We strongly recommend trip cancellation insurance!

For complete details call 1-877-ADV-NTGE or visit www.AuthorsAtSea.com

- -

For booking form and complete information
go to <u>www.AuthorsAtSea.com</u> or call 1-877-ADV-NTGE

Complete coupon and booking form and mail both to:
**Advantage International, LLC,
195 North Harbor Drive, Suite 4206, Chicago, IL 60601**